CALIGULA BOOK I

BEAUTY IS THE BEAST

D. JAMES MCGEE

FROM THE TINY ACORN . . .
GROWS THE MIGHTY OAK

Caligula, Book 1: Beauty Is The Beast
Copyright © 2020 D. James McGee. All rights reserved.
Printed in the United States of America. For information, address
Acorn Publishing, LLC, 3943 Irvine Blvd. Ste. 218, Irvine, CA 92602

www.acornpublishingllc.com

Cover design by Damonza
Interior design and formatting by Debra Cranfield Kennedy

ISBN-13: 978-1-947392-88-5 (hardcover)

ISBN-13: 978-1-947392-87-8 (paperback)

To Anne-Marie, Joanna, Cara, and my mum Eileen.
Thanks for all the food, shelter, love, laughs and for being
my zones of sanctuary when I needed you most.

To Mike Eckard, the quintessential "Grey Man"
thanks for proving to me that the deadliest among us
are usually also the most amiable and polite.

To Az, without your encouragement and steadfast friendship
I would be lost.

To Dave Buckley, my ever-vigilant mistake finder,
your dedication to this little project has been invaluable.

And to Missy and Cara once again, thanks for providing
the inspiration for the skills and attitude of the protagonist.

Prologue

Tuesday, August 6, 1811
Brighton, England

BARON EDWIN DELACY ARRIVED BY CARRIAGE AT THE Steyne, a fashionable promenade in Brighton, just in time for his scheduled visit. It was hot and muggy and had been for the entire three-day journey from West Yorkshire. Edwin and his valet, Mr. Jacob Richards, had stopped just twice for a short respite, once in Birmingham and once in Oxford. Richards doubled as driver of the coach. He knew just how much the horses could take and had pushed them to their very limit, to ensure that the regent was not kept waiting. After all, he was, without doubt, the most powerful man in the known world.

It had been six months since Parliament had transferred power from King George III to his son George, Prince of Wales, making him the Prince Regent, and now Edwin had received a royal summons.

Edwin felt uneasy about the meeting. King George III was the first of the Hanoverian monarchs born and raised in England, with English as his first language, a fact of which he was proud. He was both the last king of America and the first king of Australia. The American revolutionaries blamed him for their tax increases, and yet it was the legislative branch who had insisted on the increase, to the king's chagrin. Nevertheless, he was quite unfairly vilified by the Americans.

He created the Union Flag and coined the name of the United Kingdom. He bought the Queen's House in London and added to it, creating Buckingham House as the official residence of the monarchy.

He was an astronomer who plotted the transit of Venus, watched it from his own observatory with his beloved wife Charlotte, and correctly calculated its return in 2004. He was a writer, his own personal secretary, and tried to be an everyman, mingling with the lowliest of his subjects at every opportunity. He was the single best-informed chief executive in the history of Great Britain. In his youth, by all accounts, he was a magnificent king.

When he aged, things took a turn for the worse. He was driven mad by porphyria, a blood pigment disease. So mad that those close to him were convinced he was suffering from vampirism. His physician ordered that he needed to be strapped to his bed during the night, followed by intense sessions of cupping and bleeding in the mornings. He would eat nothing but meats and soups. His beef and venison would be prepared rare, so rare that his plate would be bloody before his feast and his chin would drip with blood afterwards.

His rages were the stuff of nightmares. Footmen, servants, and slaves alike would run and cower as he'd chase them with a steak knife, intent on taking their lives at the slightest mistake in formality or perceived slight.

His Majesty, however, tolerated Edwin's moral stances. When the Chancellor of the Exchequer reported to His Majesty that Edwin's taxes had decreased due to his stance against the slave trade, His Majesty ignored the report and left Edwin alone to conduct his business.

The regent, however, was a different animal altogether: a playboy, whose lifestyle was so opulent that every penny in the Crown's coffers mattered in the extreme.

Edwin exited the carriage and brushed down his clothing. He knew by reputation that the regent wouldn't take too kindly to a man who dressed better than he did, so Edwin had chosen a plain, navy blue cutaway topcoat with brass buttons, a beige waistcoat, pantaloons, and knee-high black riding boots for the meeting. He looked like a humble country gentleman.

Edwin was nervous, so nervous that his hands trembled. He held them out in front of him and willed them to stop.

Brighton House stood before him. It was a grandiose farmhouse, with a pavilion facing south towards the sea and a grand rotunda perched on the land before it. No fewer than a dozen footmen in blue coats and powdered wigs hurried around the pavilion carrying silver trays and jugs. A grey-haired man, walking with a cane, his sleeves rolled to his elbows, directed them. He wore nothing but a waistcoat to cover his shirt. As Edwin approached, the man turned, nodded, and walked with a pronounced limp towards him. "Baron DeLacy," he announced, with the right side of his mouth curling into a smile, "allow me to introduce myself. I'm His Royal Highness's private secretary, John McMahon." McMahon held out his hand and Edwin gave it a firm handshake.

"Sir John, your reputation precedes you," said Edwin, his voice cracking under the stress of the visit. Sir John turned and gestured towards the pavilion.

"Come now, his Royal Highness has had me prepare lunch for you," Sir John remarked jovially.

"Thank you, Sir John, but I still have no idea what this meeting is about," replied Edwin, shaking his head in anxiety.

"I saw the worry on your face, m'lord, and your hands are trembling like a freezing spaniel," said Sir John as he placed his arm around Edwin's shoulders. "Don't worry. If things were amiss, there wouldn't be such a splendid feast awaiting you."

Edwin had been caught up in the musings of Sir John and hadn't noticed the figure standing before him by the rotunda. "Edwin, welcome to my humble summer home, Brighton House," said the regent in the same cordial manner. Edwin snapped to attention and, in a panic, bowed as deeply as he could, making sure that his eyes focused firmly on the stone footpath. "Oh, stop that," demanded his host, waving his lace handkerchief and rolling his eyes in the process, "we're nothing but friends here."

Edwin was taken aback by the regent's clothing. He was wearing a beige, silk banyan tied at the front—similar to a dressing gown—and ruby red slippers.

"I'm told that you no longer deal in the trade of slavery," the regent said matter-of-factly.

"No, Your Royal Highness, my . . . my . . . my conscience forbids me," replied Edwin, with a pronounced stutter.

"Quite right, Edwin! If your conscience forbids you, who is anyone, even a king, to tell you otherwise?" The regent placed his right hand on Edwin's left shoulder.

"Thank you for your wise and gracious understanding, Your Royal Highness," Edwin replied with a sigh of relief.

"Do you know why I summoned you, Edwin?"

"No, Your Royal Highness."

"I have a new favourite dessert. Mr. Simcott's custard tart." The regent took the lid off a silver serving tray, revealing four perfectly round and browned tarts. "Please, try one." The regent gestured towards the desserts with his eyes.

Edwin reached down and picked up one of the four tarts, instantly bit into it, and began to chew. The regent watched Edwin with what looked to be an intense curiosity. When Edwin smiled and nodded, the two instantly burst into laughter.

"What did you taste, Edwin?"

"An overwhelming taste of West Indian nutmeg," replied Edwin in delight.

"Yes, Edwin, my dear friend. We were both named after our fathers, and they were cruel masters, but now I hold the keys to the empire, and you hold the keys to this culinary magnum opus. Your refusal to trade in human suffering is admirable, dear friend. Your father's fortune was built upon slaves and spices. From now on, spices such as these will be your only offering, and, as such, you will delight the masses with such wonderful tastes. I summoned you here, Edwin, to tell you that from this moment onward, you shall be known as The Lord Edwin DeLacy, First Earl of Britewood." Edwin stood aghast.

"Now tell me, my friend, how is that daughter of yours, Victoria?" The regent asked sincerely.

"Since the death of her mother, Your Royal Highness, and, given that she's my only child, she's been my right hand. In fact, sir, now that you've brought her into the conversation, and given the fact that you've been so generous, having bestowed on me such a prestigious title, may I ask of you one small favour?"

The regent turned his head to the side and raised an eyebrow. "Go on, Edwin," he said, "I'm listening."

One

Friday, November 22, 1985
Leeds Central Train Station

IT WAS LATE IN THE AFTERNOON, FOUR-ZERO-EIGHT TO
be exact. Leeds Central Train Station was a hub of activity.
Commuters rushed on and off carriages, shoving others in
the process. Loudspeakers chimed and calmly announced
arrival and departure times. The odour of fumes, the chugging
of engines—a cacophony of sounds and smells crowded the
senses. The excitement of the weekend filled the air.

She carefully stepped off the train onto the platform.
She wasn't used to the cheap, shiny, black, knee-high boots
she'd chosen for the evening. She hurried with the crowd to
the exit of the station, tugging on her clothes as she walked.
Nothing she wore was comfortable. Her black fishnet
stockings chafed the skin behind her knees, and her tight
black-leather miniskirt prevented her legs from walking
with her regular stride.

The sun was about to set, and as she stepped outside
into the frigid air, she realized that the white, torn T-shirt—
covered by the blue Levi's denim jacket she was wearing—
was a poor choice. Her only saving grace from the cold was
the heavy blonde wig that she'd purchased, like everything

else she was wearing, from everyone's favourite thrift shop, Oxfam. She pulled her jacket closed and held it together with her right hand, as she slung the grotesque, pink worn handbag over her left shoulder. She rolled her shoulders forwards and shivered, pulled the large, circular sunglasses from her face, and stuffed them into her bag. Hopefully no one would recognize her; after all, she was famous for her thick, dark eyebrows and exquisite, sapphire eyes. She hoped that the heavy purple eye shadow and exaggerated pink blush would do the trick.

She rushed to the nearest taxi and slammed the door as she slid into the back seat. "Drop me at the Northern School of Contemporary Dance, love," she said, hoping her thick Yorkshire accent would be accepted as legitimate.

"Not a chance, darling," the driver replied, shaking his head slowly as he looked back at her. She held out a crisp twenty-pound note. He snatched it from her without a second thought. "It's your funeral, love!" he said.

In an instant, they were on their way.

She stood facing the building and turned back to slam the door of the taxi. Without hesitation, the car screeched away from the curb and disappeared. The Northern School of Contemporary Dance had been a synagogue until the previous year. A large, red brick building worthy of any religious organization, it'd been redesigned and fitted with a giant steel and glass extension, before being opened by the Lady Laura Lacy and the British Lord of Dance, Bruce Forsyth. It was the crowning glory of Chapeltown. The one safe place for youths in an otherwise dirty, degraded, urban mess that even the police had refused to enter since the race riots four years earlier.

She knew that now that the sun was down, she had to keep moving. The bitter cold and the creatures of the evening were not her friends.

"This is for you, Mandy," she whispered, in her usual soft, Etonian style, and off she briskly walked in the direction of Spencer Place.

Spencer Place was once an affluent street. The large brick houses formally housed white-collar workers, men of the city, because of their close proximity to the central business district. Now litter and the faeces of urban, homeless dogs covered the entirety of the street. It was known to be a Jamaican enclave. The Yardies, Jamaican gangsters, derived from the name they'd given their beloved Jamaica, The Yard, controlled the streets. Drugs, violence, and prostitution were the only commodities they dealt in.

She knew it was too cold for most of them; only the most desperate of girls, the lone walkers, would be out tonight. Most were too sick or apathetic to call her out on being on their turf. She sat on the steps of an abandoned house and waited. In the distance, a dark-coloured Ford Fiesta crawled towards the curb, and a thin, sickly-looking figure approached. After a few minutes of chatter, the waif walked around to the passenger side, and as she sat down in the passenger seat, her head disappeared below the windscreen. Less than three minutes later, the night walker was hobbling back to her corner, all the while wiping her mouth with her sleeve.

Hours passed. Cars drove by. Reggae played in a nearby house. Then she saw it: the lime-green Ford Cortina, the one mentioned over and over again in the file.

He parked on the opposite side of the street and turned off the headlights. She stood and turned her back to him.

She bent down and pretended to adjust her right boot, her ass pushed high in the air, then she turned and faced him. Even in her degraded, slutty clothing, she couldn't help but look magnificent. At five foot nine, her body was perfectly toned, her legs resembling a dancer's. Her porcelain skin shone under the dim, orange glow of the streetlights.

He turned on his headlights. They hurt her eyes. He approached cautiously and rolled down the window with the manual lever.

"Get in," he demanded with a smile. She stared at him for a few seconds studying his face.

Thick red and brown hair, mid-length beard . . . yes, it's him, it has to be. Peter Horton, she thought as she smiled longingly into his face.

"Get in the fucking car," he once again demanded, frustration seeping through his teeth. Before she even closed the door, he drove away, fast but not too fast down Round-hay Road towards the park. As they approached the car park of the wide, wooded expanse, she knew it was him. She was sure this was where he had taken the others. He turned off the ignition, followed by the headlights.

"Get your knickers off," he whispered as he looked straight into the night.

"I'm wearing fishnets," she answered, once again in her sweet, Yorkshire accent, making sure to include a slight quiver.

"Get your fucking knickers off!" He faced her, the fires of hell burning through his hateful eyes. She was genuinely shocked but composed herself as she hurriedly slipped off her stockings and held them tight in her hands.

He reached into the door panel on his right side and

turned back to face her, brandishing a claw hammer. She quickly, viciously head-butted him in the face, grabbed his right wrist and turned the hammer back towards him, breaking his nose as it made contact with the bridge. While he was stunned, she dove into the back seat and wrapped her stockings around his neck, just tight enough to restrict the carotid artery. He struggled, his hands reaching behind him in panic. He clawed at his throat, trying in vain to release himself. He gasped, groaned, and gurgled. His body went stiff as he arched his back. She felt him slouch.

She dragged him out of the car and onto the grass, scanning the darkness for any signs of human life. When she was sure they were alone, she went to work. She fumbled through her handbag. Paracord, scissors, and duct tape were all she needed. With her hands under his shoulders, she grunted as she lifted his torso and threw him face first into the boot. With the heavy work done, she slid his legs in, bending them to ensure he would fit perfectly. She bound his wrists and ankles, and wrapped a whole roll of duct tape around his head, leaving nothing but his ears and bloodied nose exposed, before slamming the boot shut. She pulled a navy blue pair of overalls and a pair of black pumps from her bag and quickly stripped off her wig, clothes, and boots, replacing them with the items she'd retrieved. With her previous clothing gone, she felt much more comfortable, her long, silky, dark-brown hair tied back in a ponytail.

She drove just under the speed limit through the decayed, urban landscape, knowing that home was just a few miles away. Soon, concrete and bricks were replaced by vast fields and trees as the road began to undulate through the country. Then, in the distance, she saw them: the large pair of wrought-iron gates, flanked by giant, stone columns. They appeared tiny in the distance, but as she approached, their sheer size became apparent. She flashed the headlights three times through the gates. In response, an old Range Rover sprung to life and flashed back twice.

Jenkins stepped out of the vehicle and ran to the gates. He grabbed them by the centre bars and pulled as hard as he could. As he let go, they crashed simultaneously against their respective columns.

"Did everything go to plan, m'lady?"

"Don't worry, Jenkins," she reassured him. "I'm quite all right."

She smiled gently and once again began to drive. The gardens were softly lit with white lights, as the manor remained small in the distance. Great oaks often blocked the view, but she knew that the gardens, the vast magnificent gardens, put the landscapes of Versailles to shame. As she pulled onto the gravel drive, she parked just twenty feet away from the great house at its centre in front of the massive oak door.

She sat and stared at the house. It was the one place that was truly home to her. It had been her family residence since it was first commissioned in 1765 by Edwin DeLacy, the first Baron of Britewood. His plantations in the West Indies and the spices and slaves they yielded generated untold wealth, and as a result, Britewood House would be forever the seat of the Lacy family, a name they had used since the start of the Great War.

It was built in the Palladian style, with eight gigantic Roman columns, spaced in perfect symmetry, along with wide bay windows and a backdrop of beautiful sand-coloured stone, mined from a local quarry. It was a listed Grade One building and one of the finest palaces in the north of England.

Jenkins appeared behind her in the Range Rover and drove towards the east of the building. She followed him out past the equestrian centre and towards the enclosed, multi-vehicle garage and carports. He parked the Range Rover in one of the ports and ran to the first door of the garage. He crouched and fiddled with the latch, until the door rolled violently upwards. Cautiously, she made a three-point turn and backed into the garage, as Jenkins pulled the door down behind her. He opened a lockbox on the wall, and with the touch of a button, the garage floor slowly began to descend until it came to rest at least twenty feet underground. An arched stone tunnel appeared in front of her. She drove through it and stopped right before the surgical table.

Jenkins was walking right behind the car. As it stopped, he sprung open the boot to the sight Peter Horton, writhing in fear and agony. Jenkins was a short man and appeared fat in his navy blue, double-breasted chauffeur's uniform. As he threw off his jacket, his massive barrel chest, thick arms, and cannonball shoulders appeared all the more impressive when compared to his slender waist. He wiped the sweat from his brow with his cuff and took a deep breath, before lifting Horton out of the boot with a vice-like grip on his torso and throwing him mercilessly onto the table. He secured Horton down with the leather straps that were attached to the table and pulled them tight. The final two straps then went across his neck and his forehead. Jenkins took a three-inch Swiss Army knife from his pocket and cut away the Paracord around his wrists and ankles.

"Will that be all, m'lady?" he asked. She nodded, and

Jenkins made an about-face and disappeared into the darkness of the tunnel.

While Jenkins had been preparing her guest, she'd prepared herself by slipping on a pair of blue nitrile gloves and a white surgical mask.

"First things first, Peter," she said as she turned and dropped the arm of the Linn Sondek turntable. The needle fell perfectly into the first groove of the record. Within a matter of seconds, the sound of Strauss's "Blue Danube Waltz" gently rose from hidden speakers. The violins shimmering in the key of A major calmed her as she unstrapped his forehead and began to pull the tape from around his head. His muffled screams hollered out once his mouth was exposed. He panted. With his nose broken and bloodied, he'd been close to suffocating during the bumpy journey to God-knew-where. By the time the last strip of tape had been torn from his skin, his screams were deafening.

"Is that how they sounded, Peter?" she whispered into his ear. "The young girls who you butchered?"

"I aven't done owt," he whimpered, blood and snot oozing from his nose as he cried.

"You mean you haven't done anything?" she replied. She took great joy from correcting something as trivial as his grammar.

He nodded rapidly. "Yea, it wasn't me! I swear, it wasn't me!" She smiled as she stared at him over her mask. She took the scissors from the stainless-steel tray at the side of the table and began to cut away his trousers. He cried uncontrollably while she cut away the rest of his clothing, leaving him naked on the table.

She retrieved a thick card file from the top drawer of the

first of three filing cabinets to the left of the table. She placed the file on his chest and opened it. The cover page consisted of the image of the crest of the West Yorkshire Police Constabulary and the words "The Yorkshire Butcher." She thumbed through the pages, witness statements, and descriptions resembling Peter, a perfect description of his vehicle, and copies of the alibi his docile, scared wife had given him to avoid arrest. Harrowing photos of young women who were dismembered, decapitated, and horribly disfigured followed, with the investigating officers' notes to accompany them.

She tore out a photo and held it in front of his eyes.

"This is Mandy, Peter, precious Mandy Phillips. My father paid her tuition to the School of Dance. You should've seen how wonderfully she glided across the stage. Her lines, oh her lines, Peter! But you did this to her."

"No!" he screamed over and over again, until she grabbed a black tourniquet from her tray and cinched it tightly around his right thigh. He went quiet for a moment, terror literally robbing him of his voice. She turned away, and when she turned back, she was brandishing a straight, surgical saw. He screamed one more time as she began to saw through his leg.

Over an hour later, Peter Horton lay delirious on the table, his arms and legs detached from his body. She gave him one more shot of adrenaline, and as the liquid coursed through his veins, he gasped and opened his eyes wide. She took off the mask and gently leaned over and kissed him on the forehead.

"Thank you, Peter. Tonight has been wonderfully cathartic," she said as she brought her face down to meet his.

"Lady Laura . . . Is it you?"

"Yes, Peter," she replied, "you lucky little boy. The last thing you get to see before Satan himself is the face of the Lady Laura Lacy."

She reached into her tray and retrieving a scalpel, motioned down towards his genitals and began to cut.

Two hours later, she was almost completely done with the clean-up. No blood was to be found, and Peter's dismembered body was neatly packaged in fifteen double-bagged parcels and stored in the boot of his car.

She enjoyed the clean-up as much as she'd enjoyed the hunting and the killing. Those hours of thrilling violence seemed to be balanced out with the ordered work of mopping, wiping, disinfecting, and ultimately discarding. She looked over the room for any signs of death. It wasn't exactly a room. It was more like a dungeon. Edwin, the first Baron of Britewood, had requested this secret place as a lair for his mistresses, who supposedly all loved to give and receive the ultimate in sexual torture. The tunnel had once led to a secret wooden door, out amongst the oak trees, but when the present Earl of Britewood, Lord Henry Lacy, discovered the tunnel, he built a shed over the entrance, which had recently been replaced by the enclosed garage and hydraulic lift, courtesy of David Jenkins. She pushed a button on the intercom, and Jenkins' voice came through the speaker.

"Your bath has been drawn. Are you ready, m'lady?"

"Oh, thank you, Jenkins. Yes, I'm quite ready! Will you please discard the car?"

She didn't wait for a reply to her question. Jenkins had never failed to disappoint in that regard.

She was proud of her lair—this secret, open space under

the great house. It was known only to her father, Jenkins, and her good self. The tunnel, the cabinets filled with all the tools of her deadly trade, the surgical table . . . they all delighted her.

Her favourite feature, however, was the open-walled dojo. The forty-eight tatami mats, purchased directly from Japan, were laid out on the floor and flush against the north and the east walls. The east wall was mirrored, while the north wall contained a kamiza, a Japanese alter to the Kami, the gods of the martial arts. To the left of the kamiza was a portrait of Kano Jigoro, the founder of Kodokan Judo; to the right, a portrait of Ueshiba Morihei, the founder of Aikido, and above it hung a portrait of Jenkins' teacher of the warrior arts of Budō, Abe Kenshirō. Jenkins had taught her Abe's art of Atemi-Ryu Jujitsu for almost two decades. It was a fusion of Judo and aikido. She loved it. It was a part of her now. Her technique was flawless and quite spontaneous. Jenkins had been given the title of Shihan by Abe. The title translated as *polished teacher*, but even Jenkins had to admit that she'd surpassed his skills.

Jenkins was already an experienced boxer in his youth. During the Korean conflict he had learned the art of Hapkido from the masters. Through his travels he'd learned the systems of Silat from Indonesia, the stick and knife fighting arts of Arnis from the Philippines, the battlefield arts of Muay Boran from Siam and of course, the use of the distinctively curved knife, the kukri from the feared Gurkha regiments of Nepal. He fused the numerous systems together to form one cohesive art, an art he named *Kasai-Do-Ryu Kenpo Ju-Jitsu*. The name translated to *the way of the flame*; beautiful, graceful, useful and supportive of life, yet deadly when the need arose.

Jenkins had taught Laura everything he knew and was thrilled with her own unique contributions to the art, so thrilled that he promoted her to the rank of *Judan*, tenth degree black belt and awarded her a certificate conferring upon her the title of *Nidai-Soke*, the second Grandmaster of the art. Laura hung the certificate directly under the kamiza in deference to the masters who came before her.

She walked up the stone spiral staircase, and when she reached the top, she pushed with all her might against the heavy, wooden door. As soon as she entered, she immediately pulled it until she heard the seal click into place. She was now in her bedroom, the great door disguised conveniently as a bookcase. Just one of six towering bookcases that covered the west wall. Bright green velvet curtains were tied back by golden tassels around the large bay windows and balcony. The moulding and panelling were painted in a brilliant white. The wooden floors were covered with a central Axminster carpet. The furniture, matching emerald Chippendale originals, had tiny, hand-painted swallows scattered here and there. The central piece was her bed, a grand, veiled, pristine, white-painted four-poster, used by her own great grandmother, Her Royal Highness the Princess Mary, daughter of King George V. Her portrait hung elegantly facing the bed, its gilt frame only adding to the majesty.

She stripped off her overalls then her underwear and carried them through the large, white wooden door and into her private, bathroom en suite. She opened the laundry chute in the south wall and threw them in, the heavy brass door slamming shut as she let it go.

She locked the door and stepped carefully into the hot bath. Jenkins had added Epsom salts and essence of lavender to soothe her aching muscles and relax her. This was her favourite room in the whole house. It was safe—after all, there was only one door in and out. It was symmetrical, with two identical vanities flanking the central window, which was adorned by white, silk curtains. The commode stood against the south wall and the shower cubicle stood against the north. A rug, similar to the one in the bedroom, was placed directly behind the bathtub and in front of the door. The bathtub was one of Lady Laura's prized possessions. It stood on four dainty white legs in the centre of the room. It was white, a brilliant white, and although it looked smooth and feminine, it was made of porcelain-covered iron and could survive a bomb blast. It reminded her very much of herself.

She languished in the bath until the water became lukewarm and the skin on her fingertips began to wrinkle. She stood and grabbed her towel from the standing rail next to the tub, patting the excess water from her body. She paused for a moment in front of the large, free-standing mirror and observed her body. She knew she was beautiful and took pride in keeping herself toned and strong, but she was all too aware that her femininity was her true power, so she took great pains to ensure that she did not become too muscular.

At thirty-two years old, she'd been doing this for exactly ten years (even though her first kill was ten years before that), and she had the scars to prove it. They were inevitable. The five-inch wound on the left side of her ribcage was stark-red and deep, impossible to hide due to her fair, ivory skin. The marks on her back, from beatings and fights, appeared as blue and scarlet islands on a pristine map and numbered in the dozens. She examined her face—not a scratch. As long as her face remained untouched, she could go on until her thirst was truly quenched.

Her father, Henry Lacy, the Eighth Earl of Britewood, had been a soldier and had a distinguished career in the Durham Lite Infantry. Captured by the Germans in January 1945, he'd been sentenced to death at Colditz, but by that spring, with defeat in the air, the Nazi Command released him to the Swiss as a gesture of good will. After all, the grandson of George V and the nephew of the king was the ultimate prize for all parties. As the Second World War came to a close, Henry resumed his career, and when the Special Air Service was reformed in time for the Malaya campaigns, he eagerly began training, eventually passing selection and being badged as a captain in the most elite military unit the world had ever known, the 22nd Special Air Service regiment.

Years later, he begrudgingly retired as a Lieutenant General and took the role as Patron and Honorary Commander of the Territorial Army's reserve unit in Yorkshire, B Squadron, 23 SAS(R). It was a role he still kept and would keep as long as he lived. Along with the role came an office in the regiment's secure armoury in Armley.

The armoury had been built in the early nineteenth century as a textile mill and had remained so until 1969 when the heir to the dynasty, Sir Anthony Loughton, sold up and partnered with a member of an illustrious family of financiers, in the managing of a hedge fund. Before the sale, he graciously gave the building to Her Majesty's forces, and they, in turn, assigned it to 23 SAS.

The regiment referred to it simply as The Mill. It was an ominous building, red brick turned black from smog and general dirt stemming from the various industrial complexes nearby. Three storeys high, each storey twenty feet tall, its many windows had been tinted black on the outside, and most had been fitted with ducts connected to charcoal filters on exhaust pipes to quickly purge the air of the gun smoke that was constantly generated within. Its inner courtyard consisted of a rappelling wall, a killing house, and six shooting lanes. It was perfect for the job at hand.

The Mill was located on an island between the Leeds and Liverpool Canal and the River Aire and could be accessed by canal road only. This made it almost impossible to breach, by any insidious element, and the river was used as a venue for maritime exercises.

When Laura was eighteen, years after the Incident and the fever had first been noticed by Jenkins, Lord Henry proposed that she be made mascot of the regiment. The soldiers and officers jumped at the idea. The thrill of belonging to an elite unit, coupled with the chance to hang out and flirt with Lady Laura, made drill weekends all the more enjoyable.

After a while, she began training with them in close-quarter battle, room clearing, green ops, and, of course, black ops. The men began to respect her athleticism, her intestinal fortitude, and her sheer tenacity. Women were forbidden from joining the regiment, but behind the great walls of The Mill, the men had pledged complete loyalty and secrecy, and the day she was awarded her very own honorary sand-coloured beret by Lord Henry himself, with the winged dagger and legend *Who Dares Wins* embroidered upon it, all the men, without exception, applauded with joy and pride. They'd accepted her as a trooper, and that was no common occurrence.

The public knew of her role as mascot. They knew she spent time with the men, but of course they didn't know what that time truly consisted of. Whenever her cousins, or patrons of the various charities she supported, noticed her scars, she would tell them that she'd fallen while running with the lads, or had been kicked by one of her beloved horses in Britewood's Equestrian Centre.

It was two o'clock in the morning, and as Laura lay on her bed in one of her sheer white silk negligés, she pondered the evening ahead. Horton's demise had been thrilling, but tomorrow's kill would be magnificent.

Everything had been planned meticulously. Her source of intelligence from the West Yorkshire Police Constabulary was Detective Inspector Billy Smythe, a gruff, no-nonsense old-school copper, who, as captain of the regiment, was also its commanding officer. He knew that Laura was the president of SLC, Search for Lost Children, a charity which had morphed into a crusading group to prevent, stop, and expose human trafficking. Smythe had been the leader of a task force for years and had presented his findings, un-officially of course, to Laura for her perusal. One of the suspects of human trafficking, unbeknownst to the public, was renowned broadcaster, philanthropist, and popular television star Sir Giles Gessup.

Nobody knew Laura's intentions. Not even her father or Jenkins. She knew that her father was a friend of Sir Giles, and therefore didn't want to involve him in such things until she was sure of his guilt. As for Jenkins, well, his first loyalty was and would always be to Lord Henry.

She closed her eyes and slowly slipped away, calm and thoroughly at peace with herself.

She woke up late the next morning. After a breakfast of boiled eggs and soldiers, she returned to her lair and worked on her kata, before her usual forty-minute run.

This was the night. Everything had been arranged, rethought, and planned again. There was now no doubt in her mind that Gessup was guilty. His fate had already been decided.

After lunch, she sat in her silk robe at her dressing table and stared blankly at the silver-framed photo to her left. Miss Johnson, her most trusted maid, stood behind her, brushing her hair meticulously from her scalp to the ends. Lady Laura wasn't a fan of photos in general. She preferred the gigantic, regal portraits, hand-painted and scattered around the manor. This photo was different. A simple closeup of her mother, Lady Alison Lacy, Countess of Britewood.

Alison was the daughter of a London barrister. Once a prospect for the Royal Ballet, she had given up her dance career to concentrate on writing. Her father gave her a modest allowance, which allowed her to follow her passion. Her life appeared idyllic. Her small group of illustrious friends would meet for afternoon tea at The Dorchester every Wednesday. She owned chic rooms in the West End, comfortable and conveniently situated close to the theatres she loved to frequent, and she relished her daily jaunts to the most fashionable of shops. Nothing was as it seemed, however, as behind her wide smile, the black dog of depression lurked and growled constantly in her head.

She'd met Henry completely by chance, in the waiting room of a Harley Street physician. Her father had contracted pneumonia, and as she waited with him, rubbing his back for comfort, Henry arrived for his annual check-up. As Doctor Brown entered the room in his white coat and asked Lord Henry to follow him, Henry noticed the distressed status of Nigel Howard and insisted that he be examined first.

Alison thanked Henry, and for the next half hour the two chatted and laughed and flirted, until Henry was sure that he wanted to spend the rest of his life with the beauty who sat beside him. Within the year, Alison Standish was pronounced the Countess of Britewood and was pregnant with her only child, Laura.

The black dog never left her. As she moved to Britewood House, she began to feel more and more separated from society and would spend her days with servants and, of course, her daughter Laura. She idolized Laura and taught her everything about being a lady. She would school her on etiquette and how to become and remain beautiful on the inside and outside.

Alison was overcome with loneliness when young Laura left to attend boarding school in London. Henry was often abroad with the regiment doing God-knew-what, and so, slowly, the black dog began to grow in both size and strength, until it became a terrifying hound. 1964 brought what Henry referred to as "The Incident." They didn't speak about it. They were forbidden to even mention it, but the damage had been done. Ten-year-old Laura had been exposed for what she truly was, and for Alison, it was all too much.

Laura overheard the whispers of Harris, the gardener and his grounds men concerning Alison's fate. A nine-year-old stable boy found her. He'd decided to go fishing in the secluded lake beyond the oaks, on the grounds of the Britewood estate. It was bitter cold and windy that day. The stable boy knew all the sounds of the woods and lake, so when the unfamiliar creaking, like a slow swing, came from behind him, he couldn't help but look. He stood, staring at her in horror with his mouth wide open. His knees began to shake. Within seconds, the front of his brown cotton trousers became black as urine soaked through them. Before him was the gorgeous yet morbid form of the Countess of Britewood, hanging by her neck from a low branch of an oak. She swung to and fro, gently at the whim of the wind. She would've appeared flawless in her ruby red evening gown and tiara, if not for her swollen, black tongue protruding garishly out of her mouth.

It was the only time that Laura had been devastated by a death. Of course, she blamed herself, but she had the perfect distraction for her grief. Her father agreed that he would direct Laura's apprenticeship—with the help of his trusted valet David Jenkins—in the warrior arts of killing, survival, and subterfuge.

"Will that be all, m'lady?"

"Yes, Liz," Laura replied, nodding gently and smiling through the mirror. She hadn't even glanced at the fabulous job Liz had done. She always gave her the perfect style for the occasion.

She watched from a balcony on the second floor. Across the dark and deserted expanse headlights appeared in the distance. Clive Loughton drove his brand-new black Jaguar XJ Sport well beyond the speed limit across the winding country roads, through the darkness. Laura glanced at her watch and smiled. She knew exactly how Clive and his ilk thought. He never really cared about being late. He considered tardiness his right as an alpha male. He usually considered himself to be at the top of the food chain. After all, he was tall, dark, handsome, and had many times been considered a dead ringer for a young Connery. As the only son of Sir Anthony Loughton, he was also wealthy, a trust fund child schooled at Eton; and, after dropping out of King's College through utter boredom, he decided to contribute to society by playing rugby for Harrogate and the odd game of polo here and there for charity. Women usually fell at his feet, but tonight, he would take a chance at the ultimate prize, Lady Laura Lacy and she relished the prospect of making him work for it.

Clive had met Laura at a fundraiser in The Royal York Hotel, and when she'd suggested he attend the Search for Lost Children gala at The Queens Hotel in Leeds, he jumped at the chance, asking if he could be her chaperone. For the first time, the prospect of meeting a woman made him nervous and Laura revelled in it.

The chief gardener, Harris, was waiting by the gate when Clive arrived. Harris pulled his tweed flat cap down to cover his eyes, the headlights of the car clearly bothering him. The frail Harris slowly opened each gate, purposefully taking his time at Laura's request. When Clive arrived, he sat for a few minutes in the driveway. Laura heard the faint sound of Lionel Richie singing "Hello" through the speakers. Laura knew instinctively that he'd chosen that particular tape to calm his nerves. She watched him as he rolled down his sleeves. He straightened his bowtie in the rear-view mirror and stepped out of the car before retrieving his black dinner jacket from the hook by the rear door. Jenkins opened the door to the estate slowly as Clive climbed the stairs.

"His lordship is expecting you, sir," Jenkins announced without so much as a smile. Clive nodded and proceeded inside.

Jenkins turned and noticed Laura grinning behind the support post at the top of the spiral staircase. He nodded, and she ran on tiptoes down the staircase, following Clive, hoping that he wouldn't sense her approach. He walked through the entrance of the great gallery, his black patent-leather shoes clicking on the Italian marble floor. To his left, a portrait of every master of Britewood hung below the cherubim moulding, a large gold frame adorning each one. To his right, portraits of every countess hung in the same manner. Directly in front of him was a large white-panelled door. Timber curtain swags, designed and inspected by Chippendale himself, supported the heavy red-velvet curtains around it, and they were held back by golden tassels. He'd surely heard of the protocol concerning Lord Henry's study door as a child. If the curtains were closed, Lord Henry was not to be disturbed, but if they were open, a knock on the door was all it took to be welcomed inside.

He knocked on the door, and a voice inside responded with a boom. "Enter!"

The door opened with a deep, ominous creak. Clive began to close the door, but Henry stopped him. "Leave it open," he said. "This old room gets stuffy." Henry kept his eyes on Clive, but in his periphery, he noticed his daughter crouched behind the large heavy wooden door frame. In the entrance of the study, two leather coffee-coloured couches faced one another in perfect symmetry, an Axminster rug between them. Bookcases covered the left wall, stacked with leather-bound books and the occasional photo in a silver frame. The right wall consisted of three, glass-panelled patio doors, surrounded by curtains similar to those at the entrance. The moulding was large and floral and was painted pristine white. A magnificent portrait of George V in full military regalia hung on the wall behind the desk, but the desk was the true treasure.

The HMS *Resolute* had been rescued from the treacherous North Atlantic waters by a U.S. whaler in the mid-nineteenth century. When the ship arrived back in Chatham Dockyard, it was decommissioned, and its decks were stripped and handcrafted into three unique desks. One, the Grinnell Desk, was given to the captain and later donated to the New Bedford Whaling Museum in Massachusetts. One of the others took the shape of a writing desk and was placed in Her Majesty's study in Balmoral, while the last, the most magnificent and ornate of all, was presented to the president of the United States by Queen Victoria herself. Known as The Resolute desk, it had been used by numerous presidents in the Oval Office, including the man of the hour, President Ronald Reagan.

Her Majesty's desk had remained in Balmoral until Her Majesty Queen Elizabeth heard of the retirement of her first cousin Henry. Upon his last day as Commander of the regiment, she gave orders for the men to secretly replace his own fold-away table with Queen Victoria's desk. It was his pride and joy. When he invited various guests to his study, he gauged their awareness and knowledge of history by their recognition of it.

"M'lord," said Clive, as he bowed his head. Henry, already standing, reached across the desk and held out his right hand, which Clive shook firmly.

"Henry Poole," Clive said, motioning to Henry's waistcoat.

"Indeed," Henry replied. Laura winced at the thought of Henry's internal reaction to Clive's acknowledgment of his Henry Poole, Savile Row suit. But Clive had made a faux pas by failing to notice the significance of the desk. She knew that Henry would now consider him to be superficial and ignorant, not a match for his daughter.

"How's your father these days?" asked Henry.

"He's doing well. Still working in the city, and just finished redesigning Sandlewood's interior."

"I look forwards to my invitation when it's completed."

The Loughton family had bought Sandlewood Castle in North Yorkshire from a Carmelite Order. It had been built as a fortress in the Middle Ages and most recently used as a convalescent home by the order, until the upkeep became overwhelming and the Order caved to Sir Anthony's decades-long request to purchase the estate. Henry loathed how the nouveau riche tried to emulate the noble classes, with the purchase of illustrious estates, only to crassly modernise them to appeal to the popular culture.

Laura slipped on her shoes as she lingered outside her father's office door.

"Jenkins will escort you to the gala this evening in the Silver Shadow," Henry stated.

"There's no need for that, sir," Clive answered matter-of-factly.

"You have a reputation as a drinker, Clive. I'll not have my daughter put at risk by a rash decision you might make!"

"Come now, Father, I'm sure Clive will be the perfect gentleman!"

Both men looked towards the doorway. She noticed Clive's face flush red as his heart raced, and was sure he held back a gasp when he saw her. She wore a black velvet, long-sleeved Christian Dior gown. It hugged her form perfectly. Her hair, long and dark, was neatly swept back and laced into a single braid, which was draped over her left shoulder. She chose her plain black, kitten-heel shoes, designed to mitigate her height, by the recent, up-and-coming graduate of Hackney College, Jimmy Choo. The focal point of her ensemble was the one-off Garrard necklace of diamonds and South Sea pearls, presented to her by the Sultan of Brunei on one of his few state visits. The matching pearl-and-diamond earrings completed her accessories. She placed her small black Louis Vuitton clutch under her left arm and glided towards Clive in the manner that only the women educated at the best finishing schools know how to move. He stood motionless as she straightened his bowtie and brushed off the front of his starched white shirt. She then touched each cheek to his and feigned a kiss as she did so. With Clive's back facing him, Henry scowled at his daughter. She returned it with a kiss and a glib smile in his direction.

"Have a good night, my Little Boots," called Henry.

Laura rolled her eyes, not even bothering to chastise him. She hated that nickname, but Henry had addressed her that way since she was a child.

As they left the manor, Jenkins waited by the 1965 navy blue Silver Shadow, the spirit of ecstasy flying proudly on the bonnet. It was the second one produced by Rolls Royce and delivered straight from the factory to Lord Henry at Britewood. It had been part of the household for twenty years, but it was still very much in showroom condition. Jenkins opened the rear passenger door for Laura, as Clive opened the door for himself on the driver's side. As Jenkins drove away, Laura, with the touch of a button, closed the newly fitted, electric privacy screen, between the back seat and the driver. Clive began to speak, but she quickly held her right index finger up to his lips. "Shush now, Clive!"

She found him physically attractive, as most women did, but she knew that attraction would disappear if he opened his mouth too often. He nodded and rolled his lips into a smile. She reached down and gently grabbed his left hand with her right and placed them both on his left knee. They sat in silence. Every once in a while, he would glance at her profile; she knew and liked that he was watching her, but she maintained a straight gaze.

They arrived at the Queens Hotel to a gaggle of paparazzi. Camera flashes lit the air, randomly and frequently. As Jenkins opened the car door for her, she waved and beamed at the crowd. She graciously parried the microphones even as they were pushed into her face, moving forwards with ease along the scarlet carpet. Clive followed, and although he nodded and smiled at random onlookers, he seemed to acknowledge that this night belonged to her. The people of Leeds loved her. Smiling, she linked arms with Clive. He returned a smile as they walked towards the ballroom.

The ballroom was as grand as they come, a huge space

with a central, extravagant chandelier. A stage adorned with red velvet curtains had been erected at the front with an orchestra ready to play just beneath it. Shirley Bassey would be the headliner, and a bevy of lounge singers, crooning everything from Tom Jones to Frank Sinatra, would be making an appearance. The crowd was loud with a thousand conversations. They comprised the cream of British society. Politicians, famous actors, popular artists, venture capitalists, and of course, the hangers-on filled the room. As Laura and Clive made their way to their table at the front, others began to notice them, and within seconds, a roar of applause cheered them, or her.

She hated these soirées. The dress-up, the pretending, she hated it all. Tonight was more tolerable, however . . . She and her father had founded SLC as a charity for two reasons: the first had been to genuinely help young victims of human trafficking, but the second reason, the most powerful motive for Laura, was to identify, find, and administer the ultimate punishment to the perpetrators.

She spotted Billy Smythe quite easily. He was seated at a table with two men in full police uniform. She could see that Billy hated these affairs as much as she did. His hulking six-foot-four frame was visible through his tuxedo and his pristine white dress shirt and bowtie, making him appear ridiculous given his cauliflower ears and bulbous, crooked nose. As her commanding officer in the regiment, she'd primarily seen him in camos, or his regimental tracksuit while boxing or running. Occasionally, she'd seen him in his dress uniform or a Marks & Spencer off-the-rack suit. He glanced up from his conversation with the uniformed men and ran his hands through his greased black hair and caught

Laura's eye. His scowl turned to a slight smile. She discreetly waved back.

She looked around and found Gessup's table without much effort. The unknowns crowded his table, asking for autographs and photos. He repulsed Laura. He quite literally made her skin crawl. His white tuxedo was matched with the most absurd pink dress shirt. His bowtie was large and made of maroon velvet. He wore red, circular sunglasses and his stark-white hair was parted in the middle and rested on his shoulders. His whole outfit matched his larger-than-life persona.

Gessup had begun his career in 1947, when he'd opened Britain's first disco in Leeds' famous Mecca Nightclub. Through the years, he had made it into the highest ranks among entertainment broadcasters in Britain. The public loved him. His charity work involved running marathons, volunteering in hospitals, and of course, attending fundraisers such as this. Laura had known him since childhood, but as a child, she remembered her mother and nanny ushering her out of the room when Gessup visited Britewood.

In his investigations, Smythe had labelled Gessup as a "person of interest" many times, but the evidence against him was circumstantial at best. The most damning link to Gessup in all of Smythe's findings was his frequent visits to La Maison de Merci school and orphanage on the Channel Island of Jersey. The Metropolitan Police had raided the orphanage just three years earlier and brought to justice an elite group of millionaires, who'd been paying the headmaster and staff to sexually torture the children in the most sadistic of ways. The nineteenth century mansion was nestled securely in the woods, making it ideal for their plans. The staff and more than twenty members, among them society's most illustrious sons, were ultimately convicted. Some of the children were found mentally and physically traumatised, others were missing, and some were only discovered as random bones in the wooded grounds after the excavation and ultimate demolition of the property. Gessup was once again named in many briefs, but the lack of evidence against him either meant he was innocent or cunning in the extreme. *The Daily Mirror* published an article concerning Gessup's link to the scandal, but after winning a fifteen-million-pound libel suit against them, no reporter dared mention his association with the place again.

How peculiar, Lady Laura whispered under her breath as she noticed the man seated to the right of Gessup. *Sebastian Davenport.*

Davenport was a tall, thin man with pale skin, high cheekbones, and a sharp, pointed nose. His blond hair was receding and combed back into a distinctive widow's peak. He would've appeared to be a perfect Aryan Dracula, if not for the black patch covering his left ocular cavity, the result of an incident in Buenos Aires two weeks prior to the start of the Falklands campaign.

Davenport appeared shifty to Laura, his one blue eye constantly moving in all directions, noticing everyone and everything. Davenport had made many trips to Britewood over the previous decade. Her father would always cite "business" when he locked the door of his study, allowing him and Davenport to speak in secrecy. Davenport had been known for over five years as "C" by the intelligence community. He was the director of the Secret Intelligence Service, and as such, coordinated all of Britain's dirty work in the international world of espionage. As she watched them closely, Laura shuddered to think that Davenport might be using Gessup as an asset of some kind.

The lights dimmed, and Gessup took to the stage.

"Distinguished guests, ladies and gentlemen, welcome to the first Search for Lost Children annual gala. Please put your hands together for the fabulous Shirley Bassey."

The crowd stood and erupted in applause as the orchestra began the music from the opening credits of *Goldfinger*. *Diamonds Are Forever* came next, and as the Bond ensemble continued, Clive ordered two vodka martinis. Laura smiled as the waitress brought their drinks, but internally she squirmed with embarrassment. *Does he really consider me his Bond girl, the woman who'd beg him to crawl between her open legs?* she thought while she took her first sip of the vile drink.

When Bassey completed her first set, Gessup once again took the mic.

"When anyone so much as thinks about philanthropy, grace, and charity, one of the first names that comes to mind is the Lady Laura Lacy. As patron of The Search for Lost Children, the Lady Laura has worked tirelessly to ensure that, as far as possible, all the children saved from human traffickers have an education and a loving, caring home. Please warmly welcome to the stage, the woman herself, the Lady Laura Lacy."

Once again, the crowd stood, their cheers and claps were deafening. As she stood, Clive covertly slapped her on the bottom. She was furious, but controlled herself and instead of unleashing her fury, she winked at him and smiled. Laura seemed to glide onto the stage. She smiled, nodded, and graciously waved.

"Thank you kindly, Sir Giles." He tried to approach her, his arms extended, but she stepped back, avoiding him, but placated him by blowing a kiss in his direction. "Over the past two years, my eyes have been opened to the suffering caused by human hands. Our work with both the West Yorkshire Police Constabulary and the Metropolitan Police has been instrumental in bringing the perpetrators of child sex trafficking to justice. The most rewarding aspects of our endeavours, however, have been our successes with the victims themselves. Young people, many of whom were broken and lost, have been given opportunities, love, and encouragement through our many programs. I, as the patron, am just a small part of this wonderful machine. I would like to thank every member of this audience for your generous work and donations. Without you, none of this would be possible."

She bowed once again, and Gessup joined her onstage. He introduced the next act, a Sinatra impersonator. They linked arms, and he escorted her from the stage. As they arrived back to her table, Laura introduced Sir Giles to Clive.

"Pleased to meet you." Clive stood and offered his right hand.

"Same," replied Gessup, quickly shaking Clive's hand and then refocusing his attention on Laura.

"It's been a long time, Laura. When are we going to spend time together?"

"Hopefully soon, Giles," she replied, "I'm just so busy at the moment, but soon, I promise." She chuckled to herself at Gessup's question. Even though he made her skin crawl, tonight would be the night they'd spend quality time together.

If only he knew what she had in store for him. As a young, prepubescent girl, she knew that Gessup was extremely attracted to her, even though he was over thirty years her senior. She also knew that he was culpable in the Jersey affair and that he knew some of the key players involved in the ongoing trade of innocent children. Tonight, she would proverbially kill two birds with one, or maybe two, very sharp stones.

As the evening wore down, Laura observed Billy and Sebastian at the bar. She tried to read their lips but was frequently interrupted by well-wishers and fans asking for magazines containing her image to be autographed. She could see that Billy looked worried and tired. She'd never seen him like that before. Her concern increased when she saw the smug look on Sebastian's face. She decided to leave. Laura and Clive said their goodbyes and headed into the night air of Leeds. It was bitterly cold, and although they hadn't brought coats due to Jenkins' door-to-door service, Laura decided they'd take a walk in the City Square across the street from the party. Jenkins spotted them, and as he turned on the ignition, Laura held up her hand and the ignition was instantly turned off. She grabbed Clive by the hand and ran him across the street.

"Where are we going, Laura? It's bloody freezing."

"We're going to visit the Black Prince." She pulled him close and kissed him on the lips. "I'll warm you up," she teased.

Clive beamed at what he considered a promise of sex.

As they walked towards the centre of the square, Clive studied the nymphs. The large, bronze statues of naked women holding torches over their heads lit their immediate surroundings.

"You seem to be more interested in them than me, Clive?"

"Never," he replied, playfully pulling her close to him.

"Clive, meet Edward, the Black Prince."

Clive looked up to see a massive bronze statue of a crowned warrior mounted on horseback. It appeared even larger, due to the stone pedestal it was mounted on.

"He reminds me of you a little," she offered.

Clive smiled.

"Thanks," he replied, "I'm quite the horseman."

Laura meant what she said, but it wasn't a compliment. The statue was big, expensive, and impressive looking, but was useless—cold and stiff, very much like Clive.

Jenkins drove them back to Britewood. Clive exited the car and ran around to Laura's side door.

"I guess this is it?" asked Clive holding her hand.

"Yes, Clive, until next time," she answered as she walked backwards up the stairs, teasing him with a blown kiss. Jenkins opened the door for her and closed the door on Clive, leaving him to the night.

Laura ran to the second floor and peered out of a window, her image hidden by the heavy velvet curtains. She watched Clive sit back into the driver's seat and close the door. She heard the car whimper as he turned the key in the ignition. He tried again, but the car was dead. He turned on the headlights, then turned them off to confirm that it wasn't the battery. After a few more tries, he sheepishly knocked on the door of the great house. A few minutes later, Jenkins answered in obvious annoyance.

"It's my car, Jenkins, I . . ."

"Is that you, Clive?"

He looked up to the top of the staircase and his eyes widened. Laura was a sight to behold. Her hair hanging loose, she wore a black, open silk robe, over a black-lace negligé. The moonlight from the window behind her shone through the clothing, revealing her form.

"Clive, whatever's the matter?"

"It's my car, Laura. It's new. I can't for the life of me understand why . . ."

"Jenkins, show Clive to the yellow room."

"Yes, m'lady," Jenkins answered matter-of-factly and walked up the stairs, followed by Clive. Jenkins walked past Laura, but when Clive reached her, she took his fingers in her hand. He pulled gently away and followed Jenkins down the wide corridor to a room on the left. As he looked back towards the staircase, Clive caught a glimpse of Laura watching him.

Laura had instructed Jenkins to show him around the room. It was grand, with a four-poster bed at the centre. Its drapes and the dressers and cabinets were bright yellow, obviously lending the room its name.

A few minutes later Jenkins left the room. He walked down the corridor towards the stairwell, where Laura was still standing. He reached into a cabinet by the stairs and brought out a bottle of Bollinger and two champagne flutes.

"Is it ready?"

"Yes, m'lady," Jenkins replied. "I injected it down through the cork."

Laura walked down the corridor and tapped on the door. There was no reply, but she heard the faint sound of the shower running in the bathroom. She quickly entered the room and placed the bottle and glasses on the bedside table before taking off her gown and lying on the bed. When the shower stopped, she propped her head up with her left hand, her elbow braced against the mattress.

Clive walked out of the bathroom. He was naked and drying his hair with a bath towel. He instantly saw her and stood still in astonishment. She looked him up and down, before her eyes came to rest right between his legs. As she stared, she smiled. He was thick, toned, and quite hairy. She would've mistaken him for one of the lads in the regiment, but for the fact that he had no visible scars on his body. She could see that he was already beginning to get erect. She motioned with her index finger for him to come closer. He robotically stepped forward. As he reached the bed, she grabbed him by the waist, pulling him onto the bed and mounting him. She hoisted up her negligé and felt the bulge of his groin prodding against her. The only barrier was her lace panties.

She reached for the bottle and popped the cork. Champagne splashed onto her chest and over his neck as she giggled and poured the liquid into the two glasses. She took one of the glasses and, propping up Clive's head, poured the liquid into his mouth.

He grinned and tried to grope her, but she parried each attempt as if playing a game of *Pattycake*.

Within seconds his eyes began to glaze over and his outstretched arms flopped onto the bed.

"Isn't this wonderful, darling?" she said as his eyelids fluttered to an eventual close.

"Oh yes, Laura, my love, it's . . ."

"Clive?" She slapped his face to see if he'd react. "Clive, are you in there?" She knew full well he was out.

She reached down and grabbed his testicles. "Maybe next time," she sighed, "but tonight, you're just a handsome alibi."

She left the room and ran down the corridor to her bedroom. She sprung the latch to the hidden door behind the bookcase and, after closing it behind her, scurried down the winding stone stairs towards the brown Ford-Cosworth. Jenkins was preparing for her most daring personal mission to date.

"What the hell was in that bottle, Jenkins?"

"Methaqualone. It's a sedative."

"Yes, Jenkins, it is. It knocked him out in less than two minutes. How long will it last?"

"You obviously gave him quite a dose, m'lady, probably until at least the late morning."

"Good. Keep an eye on him. If he stirs, there's chloroform in the bottom drawer of the first filing cabinet. Oh, and don't forget to replace the spark plugs in his Jag."

Jenkins nodded.

"Where's the cellular phone?" She scanned the room for the device.

Jenkins opened a cabinet door by the surgeon's table and retrieved a beige, plastic brick and handed it to her. She looked it over, while pressing a button that caused a red light to appear. It was her new toy. The Motorola DynaTAC 8000X was a revolutionary step in the field of communications: a mobile telephone that would allow her to make a call to and from almost anywhere.

"Is it fully charged?"

"Yes, m'lady!"

Laura dismissed Jenkins with a wave without even looking in his direction, and he left through the tunnel.

She unlocked a large steel locker and retrieved a rucksack from under a row of hanging navy blue overalls. She opened it and rummaged through it, quickly taking a mental inventory of its contents. When she was satisfied, she pulled the drawstring to fasten it, buckled down the front flap, and secured the phone in one of the side pockets.

Next, she peeled off her negligé and pulled on one of the overalls. It fit snugly. She pulled closed the long front zip, which stretched from her navel to her neck, and patted down the fabric Velcro flap to cover it to avoid any chance of light reflection. She reached into her right thigh pocket for a thin cotton ski mask and pulled it tightly over her head, adjusting her ponytail to avoid any serious discomfort.

She was still barefoot. She walked towards the dojo and bowed to the kamiza before stepping onto the mats. She glided to the mirror and stared at herself intensely. This was the real her, the monster behind the pretty façade. She pushed her face against the mirror and kissed her own reflection. She bowed once again before stepping off the mat and heading back to the locker, from where she grabbed her tabi boots, the split-toed boots worn by Japan's legendary Ninja. She carefully eased them on and secured them with their extra-long laces, crossing them multiple times up her shins, before tying them up just under her knees.

With the rucksack placed at arm's reach on the backseat, Laura fired up the powerful engine of the Cosworth and made her way through the tunnel. There was no turning back now. This night would send ripples through British society, and the domino effect could be catastrophic for her, her prey, or maybe both.

Horsforth was such a sleepy suburb. The crime rate was almost nonexistent. As Laura drove through Town Street, she knew that she would not see a single soul. Everyone was sleeping safely in their beds. Everyone except Sir Giles. Laura delighted in the fact that very soon he'd be screaming just like the others.

She smiled at how quaint the whole place was. All the buildings, both commercial and residential, were made of the same beige sandstone. The years of smog and grime had changed their colour to a light brown, which only added to the draw.

She arrived at the modest, detached house on Hall Lane, parked at the curb, and watched for several minutes.

To the casual onlooker, it was bizarre to think that a man as wealthy as Sir Giles would live here, but Laura knew his motive well. Gessup had been born in the house. His father and mother, Harold and Sally Gessup, bought it in 1919, the year before he was born. Harold had been a Tunnel Rat during the Great War, and when his service was finally over, he began what was to be a profitable turfing business. Harold tried to be a decent family man, but his outbursts were scary and bordered on murderous. By 1924, Giles was used to the regular beatings. Even as a five-year-old, he felt content in the fact that when he was being beaten, his mother was left alone. Things came to a head, however, in the spring of 1926, when at school he'd been instructed to go to the headmaster's office by his kindly teacher Mrs. Johns. Giles was told that he wouldn't be going home that day, or any time soon, for that matter. For the next five and a half months, Giles would attend Grangeview Orphanage while his mother recovered from her wounds.

Giles knew that bad things had happened to him at Grangeview, but had trouble remembering anything from that time. The local constabulary took him home that day. They dropped him at the curb, when they saw his mother at the open door waiting. Sally ran to the gate and fell on her knees to embrace him. She squeezed him so tightly that he thought he was going to pop. When he saw the bandage around her throat, he tugged at it curiously. She gently peeled his hand away and slowly shook her head.

"Mummy will have to keep this on for a while," she croaked.

"Why are you talking funny, Mummy?" The innocent question instantly brought her to tears.

"Mummy had an accident." Her words were hardly intelligible, but the answer didn't really matter to him. He knew that his mother was suffering, and that, for him, was almost too much to bear.

"Where's Daddy?

"Daddy's gone, Charlie," she cried, "from now on, it's just you and me."

As childhood advanced, life for Charles Giles Gessup didn't get any better. The kids at school would mercilessly bully him about his dad being locked up in the nuthouse— Strangeways, a maximum-security prison for the criminally insane. They also teased him about his mother. Words like "whore" and "prostitute" were thrown at him constantly. He never retaliated against his tormentors. He knew everything they said was the truth. After all, how else could she pay the bills, now that Harold was imprisoned? He'd seen some of the men who regularly visited. He'd even answered the door to a few of them. Most of them looked ordinary enough. It was only when he listened from his bedroom that Charlie knew that something was amiss. Sometimes his mother would scream, sometimes she would giggle, and yet other times, all he would hear would be a faint knocking sound on his bedroom wall.

As Charlie grew, he began to work, first as a Lipton Tea boy, then a coal miner. His wages paid the bills, and he managed to cover their expenses without his mother having to "work" anymore.

When Charlie began his job as a DJ in the Mecca nightclub in Leeds, he was spotted by a talent scout and in no time began a broadcasting career for BBC Radio, which resulted in both fame and fortune.

He dropped the name Charles, at the request of the BBC Controller. He didn't like the name very much and used the chance to create a new, more vibrant and powerful self.

Sally loved her house and wanted to live there forever. Giles chose the life of a bachelor and servitude to his mother, whom he now affectionately nicknamed The Countess. He bought the house for her outright and gave her everything she requested.

In January of 1967, the Countess died peacefully in her bed. For Giles, the grief was overwhelming. He kept the living room and her bedroom exactly how she left them. All of her belongings—clothes, books, keepsakes—remained untouched. He would remain in the house with his memories of her. He'd promised her he'd never marry. He didn't mind, really; after all, grown women weren't his cup of tea.

Laura had been in the house twice the previous month. Each time through the unsecured kitchen window. She'd thought about doing it in the house, so that Giles could expire in the same place in which he had been born. She soon saw through her own sentimentality though. His would be a noisy death that would surely attract attention.

She grabbed the rucksack, walked to the side of the house, and jumped over the small wooden fence. She opened the bag and retrieved just two objects, the phone and a large hypodermic needle attached to a syringe. After propping the rucksack against the wall, she stood on it to comfortably reach the kitchen window. She softly pried the window open, climbed inside, and stood on the countertop next to the sink. The stairs creaked and she knew it, so she exaggerated each step, twisting on the balls of each foot as it landed.

She listened at his bedroom door and heard the soft grunt of snoring. Next to his bedroom was his office. She slowly opened the door, closed it behind her, and made her way to his desk. His phone was perched right on its edge. This would be the most strategic location for her to hide. She sat behind the desk, turned the phone on, and dialled Giles' phone number.

She heard the sound of fumbling coming from the next room. Within seconds, Gessup came bursting into his office, pulling his red, silk robe awkwardly over his paisley-patterned flannel pyjamas. He stumbled towards his desk, still half-asleep, and grabbed at the receiver. He had overestimated the length of the cord, causing the phone to fly off the desk and bounce numerous times on the carpet. As he reached down to retrieve it, Laura seized the opportunity and stabbed him in the right buttock with the needle, pumping every drop of the liquid into him through the syringe. Gessup let out a high-pitched scream and fell against the door. He landed on his side and massaged his right buttock.

The blue-clad figure rose from behind his desk. Gessup rubbed his eyes and strained to focus, bewildered as to what was lurking in his house. He stared, open-mouthed, as the monster stepped towards him. He reached out and began to squint. His eyes closed, and he fell to the floor motionless.

He tried to focus in the dim light, but his vision was blurry. He had a headache. He tried to rub his head, but couldn't move either hand, and he wondered why he was so cold. As his vision returned, he looked towards the wall directly in front of him. As he came further to his senses, he realized he was completely naked and strapped face down onto his desk. His legs were hanging from the back of the desk, one free and one strapped so low that his big toe was touching the floor.

"That's right, Sir Giles," said a soothing voice from behind him, "I'm almost done."

"Laura, is that you?"

"Yes Giles, it's me," she replied, while strapping his leg to the table leg.

"Why am I tied to the . . ."

"*Shhhhh*, just relax while you can, Giles." Laura moved to the head of the table and squatted down until they were face to face.

"Tonight will be painful for you, Giles. Your pain, how-ever, can be mitigated by the truthfulness of your answers to my questions."

"Questions, what questions, Laura?"

She walked around the desk to her rucksack. She opened it and retrieved a two-foot-long retractable steel stake and a rubber mallet. Gessup strained his neck to follow her with his eyes. She moved directly behind him out of view. He felt something cold touching his anus, then, with a strike of the mallet, felt the stake driven at least three inches inside him.

He screamed in pain and shock.

"What's your part in it all, Giles?"

"Please, Laura, no, are you out of your mind?"

"I know you were involved in La Maison de Merci, but it's still happening, Giles. I want to know the whos, whats, wheres, and hows, Giles; and unfortunately for you, this is the most expeditious route to the truth."

"I don't know what you're talking about." He cried through his words and struggled in a futile attempt to free himself.

Laura once again stepped out of sight. Giles felt the stake being forced further inside him. He screamed and sobbed uncontrollably.

"Please stop," he cried, "I'll tell you anything, just please stop."

Laura retrieved a file from the side pocket of her rucksack. It resembled The Butcher file from the previous evening. This time, however, the word in bold on the cover was Grangeview. She laid it on Giles' back and began to turn the pages.

"Grangeview, you went there for a while, didn't you, Giles?"

Giles nodded and strained to look at her. She walked around to the head of the table and placed the file between his shoulder blades.

"One hundred and three young children between the ages of four and eleven within a two-year period, Giles. They've just disappeared. All of them abducted from their guardians, from their homes in the dead of night. The one thing which links them all is the fact that they've all come from turbulent homes, and they've all been residents of Grangeview."

Giles shook his head violently, in panic.

"Where are they, Giles?"

He once again began to struggle and scream. Laura calmly walked to the rear of the desk and hit the stake with the mallet. This time blood shot from the wound and covered the front of her overalls. Giles screamed and then whimpered. She didn't react at all. She just nonchalantly walked back to her previous position at the head of the table.

"You will tell me, Giles," she whispered in his ear.

"They're taken to America."

"Where in America?"

"I don't know."

"Who takes them?"

"I don't know who he is."

Laura began to walk towards the rear of the desk.

"No, please," he sobbed. "I really don't know who he is, but he's Irish, from the north, I think. I only know him through phone calls. The staff at Grangeview, just . . ."

"What are they used for, Giles?"

"You're in way over your head, Laura. These people are above the law. They'll kill us all if they find out about this."

"Do you think I care about the law, Giles? Is what I'm doing to you lawful? When I find out who else is involved in this, their fate will be as harsh as yours. Now tell me, how does this Irishman know who to target?"

"Okay, okay!" He was whimpering now, snot and saliva streaming from his nose and mouth. "I visit there twice a month. I ask to be introduced to all the children who'll be released within the week. I make a mental note of their names; then when I'm alone in the headmistress's office, I write down their information from their files. The Irish bloke calls me in the evening of my visit, and I pass on the information. I don't physically do anything. Please, Laura, just let me go. I promise I won't say a word to anyone. I'll stop visiting. I'll do anything, Laura, please."

She giggled at him. Her nitrile gloves sticky with blood as she reached under the table and grabbed him by his genitals.

"This is what you wanted, when I was a young girl, isn't it, Giles?"

He groaned in pain, or maybe pleasure, in response.

"Unfortunately, Giles, it didn't happen then, and it's not happening now."

She retrieved her rucksack from the floor and rested it on the desk. She felt around inside and plucked out her Kukri. She drew it from its scabbard, grabbed Giles by the hair and swiftly cut through his throat. He struggled for a few seconds before his head dropped down below his torso.

Laura wiped the blade off on the curtains. There was blood all over her workspace and a thick pool of it under Giles' head. She put the Kukri back in her rucksack and placed it comfortably on her back.

She stood in the centre of the room and began to process the information she'd just received.

An Irishman, from the north, she pondered to herself.

She knew that if this guy was trafficking children to America, he had to be in some way flagged by the police. Maybe the Royal Ulster Constabulary had him on their radar. Then again, he was currently on the mainland, and local, so maybe the West Yorkshire Constabulary knew of him. She thought about asking her proxies to ask around the Irish neighbourhood, the bars, working men's clubs, and even Catholic Churches. She couldn't do it. She was far too well-known and blue-blooded to be trusted.

Laura surveyed the room. It was a mess. There was no way she could dispose of the body without the chance of being noticed, so she left him just where he was, in the heart of his own home. She scanned the room one more time to ensure there was no evidence of her ever being there, and she swiftly left.

She peeled off her overalls and wiped herself down with a towel, before slipping into a small, black negligé and tiptoeing to the yellow room. She softly slipped between the sheets. Clive stirred and turned towards her, placing his arm across her torso, his naked body pressed against hers. She sank into his embrace and smiled contentedly.

Tomorrow was Sunday. She'd see Billy Smythe at Britewood Chapel for the morning service. She'd invite him for Sunday lunch, as was the norm. And when Henry fell asleep, as was his Sunday habit, she and Billy would discuss the Grangeview affair and the Irishman.

Two

Sunday, November 24, 1985

"HOW MUCH DID I DRINK LAST NIGHT?" CLIVE STRAINED to sit up, rubbing his head.

"Quite a lot, I should suspect," replied Laura as she tried to pull him out of the bed. "You have to leave, Clive. It's Sunday. Daddy and I are going to church and hosting lunch. It won't look good if you're here in this state."

Clive dropped back down onto the bed. "Just leave me here. I can't stand. I've never had a hangover like this before."

"Okay, just stay here, but try and be out before we get back. Jenkins has fixed your car."

"What was wrong with it?"

"I don't know. Do I look like a mechanic?"

Laura met her father by the door in the lobby. She chose a tweed matching skirt and jacket with a silk, salmon-coloured blouse for church. It projected country life and business all at once. Her father donned the same Harris tweed suit he'd worn the day before but chose a beige shirt and sky blue tie. Jenkins was waiting with the rear door to the Silver Shadow open as they exited the manor.

"How did things go last night, my dear?" asked Henry matter-of-factly.

"As you'd expect. The usual." Henry nodded and appeared completely disinterested.

They arrived at Britewood Chapel within a few short minutes. This was village life in Britain. The quaint building looked picture-perfect, with its steeple enclosing a bell, which only rang on Sundays and the holy days of Christmas and Easter Monday. A small group of congregants waited, speaking with the Reverend Wiggins, who looked rather studious in his round-rimmed glasses and cassock.

As they walked from the car to the chapel, all eyes followed. Smiles and handshakes engulfed them. These people reminded her of pigeons, annoying but harmless. She played the game and graciously reciprocated their sentiments.

Laura and Henry made their way to their usual reserved pew at the front. Smythe followed them with his wife Tracy and sat directly behind them. Laura turned and nodded at Billy who nodded back. She'd always been amused seeing his massive shoulders taking up half the length of the dainty wooden pew of the chapel.

The sermon was long and painful to sit through. Reverend Wiggins, although learned, was not a natural speaker and would regularly stutter, or simply lose his place in his notes. More than once, Laura nudged Henry awake.

When the service was over, Billy pulled Tracy towards him and whispered in her ear. "I need you to do me a favour, darling."

"Go on," she said.

"I need you to distract Lord Henry when we get back to the manor. Laura and I are trying to arrange his birthday party and need him out of the way."

"Okay, but how do I do it?"

"Tell him you've heard that he has one of the Resolute desks and you'd love to see it. He'll get a kick out of showing it to you."

They arrived back at Britewood House at the same time. Instantly, Tracy made a beeline to Henry.

"Lord Henry," said Tracy as she approached Henry in excitement.

"Yes, my dear?" he asked in his usual fatherly manner.

"I hear you have Queen Victoria's Resolute desk?" said Tracy.

"Yes indeed. Come with me, it's in my study," replied Henry, obviously impressed with Tracy's eagerness to view such an historic treasure.

Laura and Billy watched them enter the house and close the door.

"What's going on, Billy?"

"Let's take a walk," Billy suggested as he motioned towards the equestrian centre. "Where's Horton, Laura?"

"Who?"

"Don't be so bloody pompous!" There was a slight panic in his voice.

"What's going on, Billy?" she asked again. This time, she changed her affect instantly as the soldier in her rose to the surface.

"It's Davenport. He has this fucking crazy notion that

you've done something to get rid of Horton, and he knows that I gave you the case files."

"How would he know about the files?"

"Because I fucking told him."

"Are you working for that idiot, Billy?"

"Yes, of course I am, and I'm in over my head."

"What? How?" Laura was genuinely confused. She knew that Billy was as straight as they came. The idea of him working for the spooks in the Secret Intelligence Service was truly beyond her reasoning.

"It was after Mountbatten's death. When the IRA bombed his yacht, I began to filter intel to Davenport about the local Irish community. Just the usual: names, addresses, descriptions. He didn't assign me to an operations officer. I went through him alone. Obviously, I'm not supposed to be passing intel to the SIS. If the brass found out, I'd be fired from the constabulary. As for the Army, I'd probably get court-martialled."

"What do you want from me?" asked Laura.

"I don't want anything, but if you did, say, dispose of Horton, he wants you to work for him."

"No, no, no, Billy. I won't. It's not me. I can't!"

"Did you kill him, Laura?"

"Yes!" she said. "It was him, Billy. You know it was him."

The colour drained from his face. "Is he the only one?"

Laura slowly shook her head. Billy sat on a bench next to a stable and held his head in his hands. "All the files I've given you for SLC, have you been using them to track suspects?" he asked, his head resting firmly in his hands.

"Yes."

"Did you kill them?"

"Yes."

Billy groaned as he rubbed his eyes slowly. His breathing became erratic. "You're telling me you're a serial killer?"

"I prefer the term *vigilante*."

"I should turn you in," he snapped back.

"But you won't."

"Laura, he's suspected you for a while now. He may have only one eye, but he seems to see everything. He wanted me to tail you, but I refused. I told him we didn't have the resources, and that, quite frankly, it was illegal without just cause. We did, however, have a man surveilling Horton's house. So, when he didn't arrive home on Friday evening, I just knew that Davenport's hunch was right. How many suspects have you killed?"

"I don't know. More than ten, less than a hundred."

"What? Oh, my God!"

"Don't be so dramatic, Billy. They're no great loss. The world's a better place without them."

"So, Horton was your last?" asked Billy nervously.

Laura stayed silent and bit her lip.

"Horton was on Friday night. Have you killed someone else since then?"

She shrugged.

"You were at the gala last night, with pretty boy."

"Yes, Billy, but we left while the night was young," she said, her mouth curling into a subtle smile.

"Who the fuck did you slot?"

"Billy, I found a link between the missing children and . . ." She cut herself off.

"Who was it, Laura?" Billy raised his voice. The horses began to stir.

"Sir Giles, I killed Sir Giles."

Billy looked at Laura in horror.

"Grangeview, the orphanage. All the missing children had, at one time or another, resided there. Giles was a patron of Grangeview and had been a resident himself. After the Jersey affair, I knew he was in some way culpable," she explained with the clarity of a tutor.

"You murdered the most influential entertainer in British history, Laura. You don't even know for sure that he was guilty."

"Oh, yes I do, Billy." Laura's quiet voice calmed him somewhat. "He admitted it."

"What, Laura, did you torture him?"

"I interrogated him."

"Fuck! You tortured him, Laura."

Laura studied his face. He was smart, and she knew that he was now engaged in the game of chess she'd instigated. Most of the intelligence she'd received about her victims was from him, so he would be implicated if she was ever discovered. She also knew how protective he was of the Regiment and his country. If any of this ever leaked to the press, the Regiment's reputation would be stained, and the very foundations of Great Britain would be rocked. She made the choice to include him in her findings. Maybe now he would be more willing to facilitate her missions or, rather, her compulsions.

"He was working with an Irishman, a man from the north," she said.

"What were they doing?"

"Giles would visit the children and find out who was due to go home. He'd research their home lives and make a decision as to which of them were the easiest to kidnap, who wouldn't be all that missed. Then, this Irishman would call him. He'd relay the intel and then the Irishman or someone else would kidnap them in the dead of night."

"There were just over a hundred kids, if I recall?" said Billy, searching his mind for the exact number.

"One hundred and three, to be precise," Laura responded without missing a beat.

"Giles is connected to Davenport. I think Sebastian was using him as an asset. I don't know how much of all this Sebastian knows. He has eyes everywhere, and, for all we know, he's got someone tailing you," said Billy with concern in his voice.

"You're speaking like you don't want me to be caught, Billy," said Laura jovially.

"I think we both know that if *you're* caught, we're *all* caught. I don't know how to deal with this, Laura. I knew you were different, but I didn't know you were this different. Have you ever thought about seeking some kind of help?" he asked.

"Help with what?" she responded in confusion.

"Laura, you're killing people, for Christ's sake!"

"People die every day, Billy. The people I kill are monsters. Society's better without them," she shrugged.

"Does your father know about this? Does he know about Horton and Giles?"

"God, no! He knows what I do but doesn't know who I do it to. He just leaves me alone, generally. I think he likes to pretend I'm normal."

She stared at Billy and thought about how long she'd known him. She remembered how quickly she'd mastered her chosen craft and how eager she'd been to perform. She knew that Billy had been frustrated by the knowledge that she would never be publicly recognized for her skills. In all her time with the Regiment, she knew that Billy had never been prouder of a trooper than he was of her. She considered Billy a noble and just man and knew that the copper in him would probably want to arrest her. She wasn't above the law, but she spoke as if she was and knew that this would be deeply disturbing to him. Was it hubris, or was it a keen sense of justice that drove her to target these men, those who the law had failed to capture? Not even she knew. Maybe it wasn't a bad idea at all, if Davenport used her? Maybe she could be of use to the country? Maybe by being such a monster, she could actually make the world a better place? She was confused and knew that Billy was even more confused, but the one thing she knew for sure was that she couldn't stop now.

"Laura, let's meet with Davenport, but we need to tread lightly when it comes to Giles. Hopefully he doesn't know. Where did you leave the body?" he asked.

"I left it in his house. The whole place is a bit of a mess, I'm afraid," she responded.

They arrived back at the manor just in time for lunch. Mrs. Wilcox and her daughter Debbie had cooked a fine meal. Roast beef, potato gratin, garden peas, baby carrots, and gravy made with pure beef stock were on the menu. Henry was thrilled to have the Wilcox family on staff. They always performed like a well-oiled machine.

Sandy Wilcox had been the cook for over twenty years,

but when her husband Tony quit Barnsley colliery after continual bouts of bronchitis, Henry suggested he tend to the vegetables in the gardens and help with the stables. The fresh air and manual work helped his lungs, and the yield and quality of vegetables made the lunches and dinners of Britewood feasts like Henry had never tasted before. Debbie was the most recent addition to the Wilcox family. Her mother schooled her intently on all the traditional Lacy family recipes, to ensure that they'd be enjoyed by at least the next generation.

The lunch was full of small talk and nervous laughter.

"Well, Lord Henry, Laura was fantastic yesterday evening. Sir Giles gave her a glowing introduction," said Billy.

Laura quickly turned her head towards Billy. *What the hell is he doing?*

"Ah," said Henry, instantly coming to life, "my good old friend Giles. I haven't seen him in weeks, but we have dinner plans on Friday." Henry picked up his entrée fork and stabbed a piece of beef. Billy looked at Laura for a response, but all he got was a raised eyebrow.

"Billy tells me you were with Clive yesterday evening," said Tracy. "Should I get Billy to buy me a new hat?"

"I don't think you'll be seeing me in a white veil any time soon," said Laura, "but a new hat does sound good. Maybe we could go shopping together?"

"I'd like that. Perhaps to Harrogate, or even London? I hear the trains are a wonderful adventure these days," said Tracy, getting excited.

"I knew I shouldn't have given you that Barclaycard," said Billy, as he turned towards her.

Tracy ignored him. "Was the event a success last night, Laura?" she asked.

"Very much so," said Laura. "Many people donated, but the media exposure was far more valuable."

"Good," said Tracy. "I was actually meaning to speak to you about volunteering. I don't get out of the house much, so I think it'd be a good opportunity for me to broaden my horizons."

"I agree," said Laura. "Maybe you could help me organise events and assist me in general? We could have so much fun."

"Oh, I'd love that, Laura," said Tracy.

"Okay then, leave it with me. I'll be sure to include you in any upcoming plans."

Jenkins entered the dining room and made his way over to Henry. Henry waved him towards the table and leaned in close, while Jenkins whispered into his ear. Henry nodded and waved Jenkins away.

"It would appear that we have another guest," he announced as he stood up.

Sebastian Davenport casually opened the door and strolled in. Henry shook him firmly by the hand.

"Please, Sebastian, take a seat next to Laura," Henry directed.

Before sitting, Sebastian reached over and shook hands with Billy. "Good to see you again, Billy, we didn't get much time to talk yesterday."

"Indeed," replied Billy, forcing a smile.

Sebastian reached out and shook Tracy's hand. "Tracy," he beamed, "it's been such a long time." Tracy smiled. "Lady Laura," he said as he held out his hand towards her, "you performed majestically last night. Who was that handsome devil with you?"

"Just a family friend," she answered.

Sebastian settled into his chair. He helped himself to the serving platters, generously spooning a little bit of everything onto his plate.

"So, Laura, anything new with you?" he said non-chalantly, before taking in a forkful of mashed potatoes.

"Not really," she said, "life is rather mundane."

"Well, that needs to change," he said as he faced her, "I'm sure you could find something thrilling to fill your evenings."

Laura rolled her eyes at him. She viewed him as a typical Eton-educated bureaucrat. The kind that did far too little work for a fat check at the taxpayer's expense.

"Maybe I could find something for you. I think we'd make a great team, don't you?" he said, smiling from ear to ear.

"Of course I do, Sebastian," said Laura theatrically, "but alas, I've just remembered, my social calendar is completely full for the foreseeable future."

"I'm sure it is," said Sebastian smugly. "I believe it was Poe who said that there is no exquisite beauty without some strangeness in the proportion. What's the strangeness in your proportion, Lady Laura?" An awkward silence descended upon the room. He faced her, his one blue eye observing her face for a reaction.

Laura smiled and fluttered her eyelids. "Hopefully, you will never find out."

They ate. Nervous small talk and laughter scattered around the table.

That smug bastard, she thought as she crunched through another al dente carrot. *Does he not know I could dispose of him just like the others? Maybe I should get it over with.*

Rhubarb and apple crumble completed the lunch, and, as the guests said their goodbyes, Sebastian approached Henry. "May I have a word with you in private, Henry?"

"Of course, dear fellow," said Henry.

Laura and Billy glanced at one another other. They said their goodbyes. Laura shook Tracy's hand and kissed her on the cheek. As she shook Billy's hand, she pulled him close. "Call me later," she whispered, and Tracy and Billy walked away to their waiting car.

Laura watched Henry and Davenport walk through the great gallery and into Henry's study. She heard the door slam and the bolt lock.

Henry was nervous. He wasn't used to feeling that way in his own house, especially in his own study. As far as Henry was concerned, Sebastian had broken a cardinal rule and insulted a member of his family in his domain. It was obvious that Sabastian neither respected nor feared his position. Henry chose to proceed cautiously.

"Henry," Sebastian began, "our American project is in need of some new talent."

"Who do you have in mind?"

"Who do you think?"

"Well, we have plenty of talent in the Regiment. They're fit, eager, and obviously many of them will be willing to do anything to help with the cause."

"I *do* have someone in mind." Sebastian sat down and crossed his legs, resting his elbows on the arms of the guest chair. He knitted his fingers together and looked at Henry quizzically.

"Go on!" said Henry, his expression serious and sombre.

"Let us not pretend anymore, Henry. You and I know all too well what Laura is. There's nothing to fear or be ashamed of. As a matter of fact, it's bloody wonderful!" Sebastian leapt from his seat and began strolling on the Axminster, with his hands behind his back.

"No, Sebastian, I don't think you quite understand . . ."

"I understand all too well. She's a master of pretence, Henry. A stone-cold killer, who'll fit in pretty much anywhere and won't stop until the job's done."

"I can't allow it, Sebastian. I have plenty of talent to draw from, anyone but Laura!" Sebastian stopped in his tracks and faced Henry straight on.

"She has no choice, Henry. She's killed many, many monsters. Justice is on her side, but the law most definitely is not."

Henry sat at his desk as his face grew pale.

"What are you saying, Sebastian?" he asked with a slight tremble in his voice.

"I'm telling you, Henry, that we'll protect her, allow her to carry on with her various crusades. My God, man, we'll even help her! But in return, on occasion, she'll do a little work for me. Heck, Henry, she'll even enjoy it, and she'll be doing it for British interests."

"How did you know?"

"Well, now that the cat's out of the bag, I don't mind telling." Sebastian leaned in. "Your valet, Jenkins, confided in me on one of my visits years ago about his service in the Parachute Regiment. He informed me that he'd failed on his second attempt at SAS selection, and although he'd failed, you'd chosen him as your valet because of his sterling record of service to Her Majesty's forces. Of course, it's a severe blow to any man's ego to fail such a course, especially when it's his ultimate goal. But to see a woman pass such a thing, especially when she's led such a privileged life, can be severely humiliating. I offered him a chance to be an Operations Officer, and he gladly accepted. Don't think for a second that he's been disloyal to you, Henry. He holds you in the highest regard. All he's ever done is pass on certain pertinent information concerning Laura, Billy, and of course, your good self."

"I considered him family. We talked about the most delicate affairs. I trusted him with everything, including my daughter in her youth . . . but he's a bloody traitor," Henry softly muttered.

"No, Henry, he's anything but a traitor. He's been of great service to Her Majesty's government. Most of Laura's kills have been fed to her, indirectly of course, by me." Sebastian paused. "The reason I'm presenting this to you today is that Laura has recently gone too far. If I had known beforehand, I would've stopped her, so I can't completely blame her. I should've done my due diligence."

"What are you talking about?"

"Last night, she tortured, then murdered, Giles Gessup."

"That's not possible."

"Yes, Henry, it's more than possible. It actually happened. It was a monstrous scene right there at his home for all to see. One Police Constable fainted when he saw what she did to his body. But don't worry, my dear friend, only a few of us know it was her."

"Why? He was a valued friend. What could he possibly have done?"

"Giles was working on our American project, Henry. He was an intricate cog in the machine. The foreign diplomats you had approached, those who could help us economically and militarily, all needed a slight nudge to comply. Giles was essential in the compliance stage of our project. God only knows why she would want him dead, I mean, in the long run we'll all benefit from Giles' work. She obviously had her reasons. Who knows, maybe she's just bonkers?"

"I thought we were paying them off. I mean, most men have a price."

"Let's just say we prefer to use leverage over cash."

"What are you talking about, Sebastian?"

"Henry, we have a piece of property secluded away in a mountainous area of western America, far away from prying eyes. It's heavily guarded and safe. Within its walls, we offer all the desires that society frowns upon. We've also procured a herb from South America. It was originally harvested as a truth serum, but when crushed and burned, the inhalation of its smoke will make the most disciplined of men do unimaginable things. What our guests don't realize is that all the rooms are fitted with cameras, clandestinely, with lenses as small as a fingernail."

"Where does Giles fit into this?" Henry asked as he began to tremble.

"Do you remember Giles' charity work for Grangeview, Henry?"

"Yes." Henry steadied himself on his desk.

"Well, the rumours associated with Giles were, for the most part, true. He had what might be considered a fondness for children, young children. It was a compulsion he really couldn't control, although he did try. We would allow him to feed his compulsion, as long as he helped us in the procurement of the former children of Grangeview."

"Why children?" asked Henry.

"Some of the most influential people in the world can be convinced to do the most unimaginary and terrible things under the right conditions Henry and as you know, leverage can be a powerful tool in geopolitics.

Henry let out an audible gasp and covered his mouth to catch himself. "You're a monster!" he whispered, horror welling in his eyes.

"No, Henry. Calm down, let's look at the big picture. These children are all lost. Their lives have already been ruined. They'll be nothing but a burden on society in the long run. This way, they'll be of some use. Their sacrifice will be of great use to the nation and will make the lives of all our citizens safer, more prosperous." He smiled as he watched Henry's reaction.

"Get out of my house." Henry stood and pointed at the door, his face devoid of emotion.

Sebastian paused for a moment. "I know this is probably a bit of a shock, but we're so close, Henry. We may just be able to end the Cold War with this. We'll have Russian, Chinese, and Saudi diplomats at our feet. Laura will be the icing on the cake." Henry remained silent, still pointing towards the door.

"Think about this," said Sebastian gently. "I'll call you in a few days when you've thought things through. Your family will be propelled by this operation Henry. Laura will take her place with the ruling elites. She's the only one worthy of such prestige."

Henry watched Davenport as he left the house and sat in the driver's seat of his green MG convertible. He saw Davenport retrieve a handkerchief from the pocket of his waistcoat and gently tapped the cavern under his eye patch, wiping away the excessive moisture. He opened the glove compartment and pulled out a packet of rose tobacco and his clay pipe. He filled the bowl and lit the tobacco, puffing on the pipe as he did so. He took one more look at Britewood House, smiled, and drove off through the gates.

Three

LAURA ARRIVED AT JUST AFTER TWO O'CLOCK IN THE afternoon. Her heart beat with excitement touched by melancholy as the limousine dropped her off at The Dorchester on London's Park Lane. This was her treasured tradition. Usually, the tea party was held on the Friday before Christmas, but Henry asked Laura if she'd mind if it was scheduled a week earlier this year.

Henry, as usual, had arranged everything. Afternoon tea for four at three o'clock in The Promenade, a table for four for evening cocktails at eight o'clock in The Spatisserie, and two two-bedroom suites connected, so the girls could mingle freely.

Today, however, was Thursday. As was custom, Laura would meet her best friend from St. Francis Preparatory School, Jenny Waldron, and spend the evening reconnecting before Sara and Nicola arrived the next morning. Jenny held an irreplaceable piece of Laura's heart, as the two had been there for one another when they each needed someone most.

Laura checked in and hurried to her usual suite on the third floor. She walked to the window and marvelled at the view of the magnificent plane tree at the edge of the hotel's front garden. She scanned the entirety of the suite. Everything was as she remembered. The mahogany trim and furniture contrasted with the well-polished brass rails, fused to create a 1930's ambience. She touched the eight-hundred-thread Egyptian cotton sheets, and then smoothed them back over the bed.

Her luggage arrived moments later, and, after tipping the bellman, she changed into her comfortable pink Lycra leggings and a soft Benetton T-shirt. She grabbed her small Puma shoe bag and made her way to the fitness centre to blow off some steam.

She unzipped the bag and retrieved her Sony Walkman. She checked if there was a tape inside. Duran Duran's *Arena* popped out to her pleasant surprise. She placed her head-phones on and secured the Walkman to her fluorescent green belt as she stepped onto the treadmill. She pressed play and "New Religion" blasted into her ears. She began to run, preparing herself for an emotional reunion.

Forty minutes later and five miles in, she lowered the speed to a walking pace and checked her watch. It was three-fifteen. Jenny would be there by five. She grabbed her belongings and hurried up to her room.

She was well aware of Jenny's financial difficulties, so she made a point to dress down when they met. She waited in the lobby in a white Topshop trouser suit and black satin blouse. A plastic, black-and-gold brooch, which came with the shirt, was affixed to the top button where usually a tie would be. Her hair was pulled back in a ponytail. She wore plain, black slippers. Jenny was five-foot-four, and she wanted to be as close to her height as possible.

Jenny arrived in a black, floral-printed Laura Ashley dress with a thin, plastic belt tied around her waist. As she walked through the doors, she saw Laura. They ran to each other, and embraced.

Laura held Jenny by the waist and looked at her. "It's so good to see you my friend. You are as beautiful as always." Jenny's perfectly combed bobbed blonde hair rested symmetrically on her shoulders. Her sky-blue eyes and flawless complexion were both striking and soothingly familiar.

"How've you been?" asked Laura softly.

"Just the same, but better now, after seeing you," replied Jenny before sinking her head into Laura's shoulder. Laura swayed her gently and stroked her hair.

"Are you hungry?" asked Laura, as she always did when they met.

"A little," replied Jenny in her standard manner.

Laura and Jenny were seated in The Spatisserie as was the norm, and they ordered their traditional first meal of French onion soup, followed by rare petit filets with tiramisu and breakfast tea for dessert. They sat at their table after the meal and finished off their bottle of Château de Rothschild.

"How are you coping?" asked Laura with concern.

"I'm okay, I suppose," answered Jenny.

"Have you spoken to anyone, or sought help?" Laura asked as she leaned closer to Jenny.

"You ask me the same question every year, Laura. I'm okay, I'll never tell anyone anything. Everyone has their cross to bear, and we have ours."

Laura nodded and softly grasped Jenny's hand across the table and began stroking it with her thumb.

"You know you have my full support if you ever want to talk with a therapist. It could give you some relief. And, if you ever need anything, Jenny, I . . ." Laura was interrupted midsentence.

"The same goes for you." Jenny looked into Laura's concerned eyes.

Laura waved her hand in dismissal. "This is enough, you know me. I have my own ways of fighting my demons. I'm fine. I was thinking, though, maybe I can have you moved closer to the manor. The estate has many cottages, and I'm sure we could find someone close, who's in need of a decent secretary."

"I'm okay, Laura. I appreciate the sentiment, but I want to stand alone. I'd hate to feel like I'm a burden or beholden to you.

"Nonsense," said Laura. "you're my friend. You're more than my friend."

Jenny reached across the table and touched Laura's fingers. "I love our get togethers, Laura," she said, "but sooner or later, I want to build a life of my own. Let's cherish and celebrate these gatherings. If I moved closer to you, you might get tired of me."

"I'll never tire of you," whispered Laura.

"Have you found anyone?" asked Jenny.

"What do you mean?"

"A man, Laura, have you found a man, someone who's suitable for marriage?"

"Good heavens, no," said Laura. "They're all either useless and full of arrogance, or quite the catch, but afraid of their own shadows."

"Yes, I know what you mean. But I do get lonely, and I

long for someone to spend my life with. Although, I worry about what would happen between us if one or both of us gets married."

"I'm sure we'll be able to make time for each other, Jenny. Stop worrying. Come now, let's get out of here . . ."

When they arrived back to the suite, Laura took Jenny by the hand and led her to her bedroom. Behind closed doors, where they both felt safe, Laura looked down at Jenny's unclothed body. The cheeks of her backside still had the deep, straight red scars from the beatings she'd received as a young girl. They were a constant reminder of her suffering, of their suffering.

Laura wondered how things might have been if Mr. Clark had never entered their lives. Her mind flashed back to another place and time. Spring, 1963. Laura was ten years old. St. Francis Preparatory School in Kent was the finest school for girls in the whole of England. She'd been there for two years when, at one morning assembly, the dashing Mr. Nigel Clark was introduced as the school's new head-master. A graduate of King's College with a first in economics, Nigel was as clever and charming as he was good-looking. He was tall and broad, with shoulder-length sandy-blond hair, which reminded Laura of the Hollywood actors she'd seen on her rare visits to the cinema.

She was flattered that he remembered her name, and she noticed how the other girls would swoon when he would treat them to readings of *Romeo and Juliet* in English class. Mr. Clark made her enjoy school all the more. That was until he invited Laura and her best friend to visit him alone at his home. Nothing was the same after that. His unforgivable violence and predatory greed stole their childhood.

Fortunately, Henry sensed something was terribly amiss and Laura confided in her chauffeur. At her request, he trained her in the dark arts. With her new skills, she was able to eviscerate her headmaster the way she did to so many men after him.

That night she made her first kill, Laura left Mr. Clark's house empowered. She became fearless. She liked her new self and knew that the frightened little girl she'd once been was gone. Girls like Jenny had to be protected, and she was the one to do it.

The trauma however, remained. If it weren't for that monster, Laura's mother might still be alive. She might not be afflicted with her unquenchable thirst. She might just have grown into a normal woman.

Laura pulled Jenny close and fell asleep in her arms, training her mind on all that was good. Tomorrow would be a joyful day for them. By five o'clock, they'd be bonding over finger sandwiches and pastries and marvelling over the gossip from the last year.

The women awoke a little after nine. Jenny took a shower, while Laura put on her metallic blue Lycra workout leggings. The phone rang. Laura had been charging it on the dressing table since the night before. It had just enough juice to take a call. She heard the frantic voice of Billy Smythe as she answered.

"Laura, thank God. You need to come home immediately," he demanded.

"Why? What on earth's the matter?" she asked, feeling her stomach drop.

"I can't explain, just hurry. I'll send a car to collect you."

The phone fell silent. She knew this was something serious. She tried calling her father on his phone in the manor. There was no answer. She tried to call Jenkins in the servants' quarters, but again, no answer. She rushed into the bathroom and told Jenny she had to leave.

"Whatever's the matter?" asked Jenny in distress.

"I don't know," replied Laura, "but whatever it is, it's urgent. Tell the girls to carry on without me. Tell them I'm sorry." Laura embraced Jenny's wet body, grabbed her things, and bolted out of the suite towards the lift.

By the time she reached the lobby, a Metropolitan Police Rover SD1 was waiting in the front drive. The bellman filled the boot of the car with her luggage and the driver approached her frantically.

"I'm Police Constable Ramstone, ma'am. I've been asked to take you anywhere you direct me."

"We're going to Britewood House in Leeds," she said as she climbed into the passenger seat. Ramstone grabbed an A-to-Z directory from the glove compartment and began to thumb through the pages. Laura snatched it from him and threw it onto the back seat. "Just drive," she ordered, "I'll give you directions. Head north on the A1!" The car screeched out of the driveway with its blue lights flashing and sirens screaming.

A police cordon met them at the entrance to the grounds. The gates were already open, so a constable pulled up the yellow tape just enough for the car to drive under. Laura could see him transmitting on his radio through the rear-view mirror as they passed.

As they approached the house, they were met with a

flurry of activity. Police officers were everywhere, and crime scene investigators swarmed the grounds with cameras, sticks, and shovels. Smythe was talking to a uniformed officer, but when he saw Laura arrive in the squad car on the driveway, he ran towards her.

"Laura," he said with tears in his eyes, "it's your father." Laura ran through the yellow police tape and the great gallery. Yellow tape blocked the door to Henry's study. A constable stood guard and caught her as she ran towards him. Smythe ran behind her and grabbed her around the shoulders, holding her back. "You can't go in there, Laura. It's a crime scene."

Laura sobbed and sank into Billy's arms. "I want to see him!" she demanded.

"He's gone, Laura, he's gone!"

Sandy Wilcox and Liz Johnson sat with Laura in the kitchen. Liz held Laura in her arms and stroked her hair as she whimpered softly. Sandy kept herself busy making tea and preparing soup for the staff and police officers.

Billy walked into the room and sat across the table from Laura. He glanced at Sandy and Liz, and within seconds the two left the kitchen, closing the door behind them. "I know you're hurt, Laura, but we have to talk," he said as he reached over to hold her hand. "This was a professional hit; you may be in danger. We've got to take precautions and get you to a safe house."

Laura pulled her hand away and shot out of her seat. "I'm not going anywhere!" she screamed as she clenched her fists. "What the fuck happened here, Billy?" She collapsed back into her chair.

Billy moved his chair close to her and once again took

her hand and began to explain. "It wasn't just your father, Laura. Jenkins and Davenport were also shot to death. They were all found in your father's study. Jenkins and Davenport were both shot in the face. Your father seems to have put up a fight. It looks like he was shot at close range in the chest. The killer locked the door on them and left."

Laura wiped the tears from her eyes and composed herself. "Did you find the key to the study?" she asked.

"No," said Billy, "the killer must've taken it."

Laura shook her head and looked Billy straight in the eyes as she began to make sense of her thoughts. "Daddy would usually lock the door from the inside when he was in his study and leave the key in the door. When he left the room, he'd lock the door from the outside and take the key with him. The killer must've known that they'd all be in the study at the same time. Billy, the killer had to know about this meeting. Maybe he'd been with them."

"Just what I was thinking," replied Billy.

"What about the weapon?" she asked.

"No weapon was found as of yet, but the exit wounds would suggest a 9mm round. Did your father keep any handguns?"

"Yes," answered Laura, "he had a few handguns. I hadn't seen them in a few years. What about the rest of the household staff?" she asked.

"They were all out in Leeds," replied Billy.

"What?"

"Yes, according to the staff, Lord Henry had arranged tickets at The Odeon in the city centre followed by dinner and bed and breakfast for them at the Queens Hotel. Mrs. Wilcox told us that Henry had instructed her to prepare a tray of cold cuts for him for dinner and cereal for breakfast this morning. Apparently, Henry wanted to give them an early Christmas treat before the rush of the season. It all checks out. They watched the four o'clock screening of *A View to a Kill* before heading off to the hotel. They arrived back just after nine o'clock this morning and noticed instantly that the front door had been left open and Sebastian's car was still on the front drive. The curtains were back across the door of your father's study, so when he didn't answer Mrs. Wilcox's knock, she got concerned. She went to the outside and managed to glance in through a crack in the curtains of the patio door and saw your father, Davenport, and Jenkins sprawled on the floor. Mr. Wilcox smashed open a window to get to them. Thankfully, he had the common sense to leave them alone for the crime scene team to study. Mrs. Wilcox called emergency services, and by ten-thirty, everything was locked down. As soon as I found out, I called you, Laura. It looks like your father wanted to clear the house before he met with Sebastian."

Laura looked up, and for the first time since learning of her father's death, Billy saw the warrior in her return. "We have one lead!" she said.

"Go on," said Billy as he leaned in close.

"The Irishman. Giles told me he received calls from him regularly," she stated.

"We need to access his phone records. We just have to match the dates of his visits with calls received on or after those days and see if anything pops out on us. I'll get right on it. Are you going to be all right, Laura?" he asked, as the compassion returned to his voice.

She nodded. "I need to look through the study, Billy. Will you allow it?"

"Of course, one of my men will be waiting at the door in case you need anything." Billy kissed her forehead and left the house.

The constable pulled the tape from the door when he saw Laura walking towards him through the great gallery. He opened the door and held it with his right arm as she slid by him. He closed the door behind her, leaving her alone with the memories of her father. She was left in almost complete darkness. Even in the evening, the study was usually lit by the white lights of the grounds, but for some reason, the curtains around the patio doors were closed. She switched on Henry's desk lamp and stepped over the thick, dark red stains on the floor to get to the doors. She pulled back the curtains and looked for the golden tasselled ropes that usually held them back. *Where are they?* she thought as she searched behind the curtains. She couldn't remember ever having seen the curtains drawn.

She once again scanned the room and noticed something missing. A silver framed photo of her and her parents had stood on the top of the central bookshelf opposite the patio doors. It'd been there since she was a child. She couldn't see it. She grabbed the guest chair at Henry's desk and placed it in front of the bookcase. She climbed on the chair and reached up and felt around on the top. She found the photo and propped it back into its place.

There didn't seem to be anything else amiss in the room. She sat behind the desk in her father's chair. Then it dawned on her. At the moment, there was no male heir to her father's title, including the house and the grounds. The

Crown would have to perform a detailed investigation into who her father's closest male relative was. She knew that his fortune would be left to her, along with the house in Essex and the flat in London's West End, but sooner or later she'd have to leave the house and clear her lair underneath it. She wondered if Billy and the lads in The Regiment could help. Britewood had been her home since birth. It was the one place that reminded her of her mother. It would break her heart to leave.

Over the weekend, Laura had told the staff not to disturb her in her room. Sandy left a tray outside her bedroom every four hours, for breakfast, lunch and dinner. The staff had assumed that she had been mourning.

Each morning at seven, she'd retrieve the tray from the floor outside her room and devour her breakfast: scrambled eggs, wheat toast, and orange juice. She'd then leave the tray outside and lock the door, then descend the stone staircase to her lair. She'd start the day by weight training, concentrating on light weights with many reps, then work on the katas, the pre-arranged fighting patterns taught to her by Jenkins. She'd then spend five three-minute rounds on the heavy bag, and finally take a five-mile run in forty minutes on the treadmill to finish her workout. She'd open the filing cabinets and plough through all her old files concerning Jersey and Grangeview. At one, she'd return to her room to eat lunch. More eggs, this time boiled, foie gras with Jacob's Cream Crackers, and a bottle of Perrier. She'd return to her lair again, and after another five-miler, she'd concentrate on projectiles, throwing knife after knife, all shapes and weights against a heavy balsa wood target from twenty-five feet, hitting the centre ring every time. Then it was back to the files until dinner at six. After dinner, she'd lie in her bed and think about it all. Her mother, father, Jenkins, and Jenny weighed heavily on her mind.

On Tuesday morning, she opened the door and bent down to grab her tray, but was met instead by a pair of familiar, shiny brogues.

"How've you been, Laura?" asked Billy.

"Billy, sorry about my appearance," she said. She was wearing a pair of navy blue gym shorts and a wrinkled T-shirt, with the word *relax* written across it, a reference to the song by Frankie Goes to Hollywood.

"I've seen worse," replied Billy as he perused the room.

She was thankful she'd locked the secret door of the bookcase before Billy's unexpected arrival and hoped that she hadn't overlooked anything unusual.

"Are you going to get ready?" he asked.

"For what?"

"The reading of the will, Laura. Don't tell me you'd forgotten?" said Billy, while shaking his head in disbelief.

"That's tomorrow, isn't it? What day is it?" She searched Billy's eyes for answers.

"It's Tuesday," he said.

"Fuck it, I thought it was Monday!" Laura had lost track of time. She pushed Billy out of her room and towards the staircase. "I'll be down in half an hour," she said, as she slammed the door in his face.

Laura left the house and found Billy on the front drive, standing beside his black Audi Quattro. It was a cold day, so Laura wore her black Chanel bouclé wool skirt and jacket with black leather gloves. Her outfit was finished by her black Frederick Fox saucer hat.

They drove into Leeds city centre and parked outside the grand stone Duke House on Wellington Street. A sign hung over the door: *Mosley and Fletcher, Solicitors at law.* Billy opened the door for Laura, and she walked into the lobby. A young woman ran from behind her desk and curtsied frantically as she began to speak. "Good morning, m'lady," she began, "it's such an honour to meet you. I'm so sorry about your dad, I mean, Earl Britewood, I mean, His Lordship. I really hope..."

"Thank you," Laura cut the girl off midsentence. "I believe Mr. Mosley is expecting us."

The girl nodded and knocked on a mahogany door. The door immediately swung open, and Arthur Mosley walked out to greet them. "Hold all my calls, Gemma," he instructed. "I'll be busy for the next hour or two."

Arthur Mosley was a short, rotund man. With his wispy white hair, droopy face, half-moon glasses, and pin-striped suit, he resembled Churchill in more ways than one. His office was typical for an elderly solicitor. Mahogany panelling covered the walls, most of which were obscured by giant bookcases filled with leather-bound editions of various law books.

"Lady Laura," he began, "it's been such a long time. I'm sorry we have to meet under these circumstances." Laura nodded gracefully, and he continued. "This gentleman with you is obviously Captain Smythe." He extended his hand to Billy. "Your father told me that should anything happen to him, young Billy, as he called you, would accompany you to my office. I just need a few signatures, and you can be on your way, unless you have questions?" He peered over his glasses, glancing back and forth at the two of them for a response. "Very well, then, join me at my desk."

His desk was cluttered with books, files, and documents, but his hand immediately rested on a briefcase lying dormant at the centre. He opened it and took out a file before closing the case and placing it on the floor.

"It'll be no surprise that your father left all his worldly belongings to you. His personal wealth, offshore accounts, and property he accrued personally is all yours. A signature here, here, and here, is all I need. Captain Smythe, if you wouldn't mind signing in the witness boxes also?" Laura and Billy did as they were instructed and handed the document back to Mosley.

"What of Britewood House and the title? Do we have even the slightest inkling as to whom it will pass?" asked Laura.

"Yes, Laura, we may have, in fact, found an heir. Your father and I have spoken about this at great length in the past; we haven't been in agreement as to the legality of the sentiment of the document."

"Then who do you suppose it might be?" Laura raised her voice as her nervousness turned into frustration.

Mosley paused, took off his glasses, and rubbed his eyes. He once again picked up the briefcase and opened it. This time, he retrieved a pair of white gloves from inside and put them on. He pulled out a thin, ledger-sized cardboard box, and scanned it for an opening. He struggled with the contents for a while, but eventually managed to pull out what appeared to be a thin, leather-bound dossier. Laura saw the letters *G* and *R* embossed in gold, along with the roman numeral three.

"This is the patent for the First Earl of Britewood, my dear," he said as he tapped on the manuscript. "I will have to study this document in great depth before any decision is made. The process may take months."

Laura turned her head to Billy, who touched her arm in reassurance under the table. She composed herself. "How long am I to remain at Britewood?" she asked.

"Again, this process will take time, so until a decision is made, you may stay and use the manor as your home," answered Mosley. "One more thing, will you be transferring your affairs to another solicitor or retaining my services, Lady Laura?"

Laura rolled her eyes. "The family has used you since the fifties, Mr. Mosley, why fix it if it's not broken?" She reached across the desk, grabbed Mosley's face, and pulled him forwards before kissing him on the forehead. Mosley beamed.

Four

Wednesday, December 25, 1985

LAURA SAT AT THE DESK, HER FATHER'S PRIZED possession, and pondered all of the events of the previous few days. Her father's dress uniform was on a coat hanger on the curtain rail covering the patio door leading to the gardens. It had been retrieved from the dry cleaner by Mr. Wilcox and looked as magnificent as ever. She held Henry's sand-coloured beret in her hands and focused on the cap badge. Below the depiction of a winged dagger, the legend *Who Dares Wins* was embroidered on a scroll. Laura read it over and over again until it became her mantra.

A voice came from the doorway. "It's strange to see this door open," said Billy, leaning up against the frame. Laura, startled, jumped to her feet and brandished the Japanese tanto knife that had been harmlessly lying on the desk. "Damn it, Billy, you scared me," she said as she replaced the knife and sat down.

Billy walked towards her and dropped a manila envelope on the desk. "I got the ballistics report back," he said, as he sat opposite her at the desk. "All three victims were shot with the same 9mm. The weapon hasn't been found. Jenkins and Davenport were shot from approximately three feet away in the forehead while facing the door and your father was shot in the chest at point-blank range. Due to the residue on your father's hands, we're led to believe that he struggled with the killer and was holding the weapon when he was killed. It looks like he put up a fight."

"That's odd," said Laura. "Why would the killer shoot Jenkins and Davenport from the door, but follow Daddy behind his desk to kill him? I mean, obviously this guy is a crack shot. He pulled off two perfect headshots. Why wouldn't he just kill Daddy the same way and be done with it?"

Billy nodded. "I agree, it's odd, but maybe he wanted something from your father. Is anything missing from the study?"

Laura shrugged. "I really couldn't tell you, Billy. It was his personal space. I still can't bear to go through his things. I will tell you one thing, he kept this study in meticulous order, so when you allowed me in here alone on Friday, I found it strange that our family photograph was lying face down on top of the bookshelf. He always wanted it at eye level, and I still can't find the golden ropes and tassels to tie back the curtains. I'll just have to have the servants order more."

Billy picked up the manila envelope, opened it, and pulled out the contents. "These are Giles' phone records," he said, handing the papers to Laura. "Look at the highlighted number. I got the dates of Giles' visits to Grangeview from the administrators of the school, and he was called by this number late at night on every one of those dates, between ten and eleven o'clock."

"Who does the number belong to?" asked Laura.

"It's a phone box on York Road," answered Billy. "We went there and dusted the receiver and door handle for prints, but, considering the location, it was as clean as a whistle. We couldn't pick up anything worthwhile. This would suggest that someone's recently wiped it clean."

"So, once again, we're screwed," said Laura as she pounded the desk with her fist.

"Not quite." Billy smiled. "The phone box is ten feet from The Woodpecker Pub. As you know, The Woodpecker is frequented by many of our Irish Republican acquaintances. I went there today to ask the landlord Roy Gallagher if he could help me with my inquiries, but the guy doesn't want to talk."

"Oh, really," said Laura, appearing nonchalant. "Then it looks like we should follow other lines of inquiry, doesn't it?"

Billy rose to his feet. "Be very careful, Laura," he said. "The Woodpecker's full of IRA. Many of them are being watched by MI5. One false move could have you making enemies of people on either side."

"I'll bear that in mind," said Laura as she smiled from behind the desk.

Billy shook his head. "Roy Gallagher lives alone in the flat above the pub," he said. "When the pub closes at eleven, there's only him and the two barmaids left inside, until they finish counting the cash and doing the clean-up. Both women will leave by the front door at just after midnight. Merry Christmas, Laura." Billy turned and walked away through the great gallery.

Laura reached for a copy of *The Yorkshire Evening Post*

and pulled out an advertisement she'd seen earlier for The Jolly Giant toy shop. She pulled the rope behind the desk to activate the service bell. Sandy Wilcox arrived a few minutes later. Laura handed her the paper. "I need Tony to pick up two of everything on this advertisement as a gift to St. Gemma's hospice. I'll be going there tomorrow, so I need him to go now. It's Christmas Day, so the shop's only open for two more hours."

"Yes, m'lady," replied Sandy.

Two hours later, Tony Wilcox returned with three large sacks full of toys. He took them to the study and, as instructed, placed them on the couches. Laura thanked him and when he left, she began searching through each sack. Within a few seconds, she found what she'd been looking for. She took the two child-sized Darth Vader helmets to her desk and cut open the plastic wrapping of one of them. The helmet came with a voice modulator, which, when activated, would change any voice into a deep, robotic voice similar to Darth Vader's. She inserted two AA batteries into the mouthpiece and began to speak into the mic. "Who dares wins," she said. She pulled the modulator from the helmet, and after retrieving a black ski mask and sewing kit, she stitched the electrical box into a ski mask, just under where her mouth would be. She pulled the mask over her head and spoke into it. "Who dares wins. Who dares wins," she repeated, happy with her creation.

Wilcox used the dark blue Nissan Bluebird for his trips to the garden centre. It was scratched and dirty both inside and out. It was, however, perfect for reconnaissance. Laura sat in the car outside The Woodpecker Pub, looking through her binoculars from York Road. She was ready, but not as ready as usual. Normally, she would meticulously plan her hunts, sometimes taking weeks to assure herself that her plan was as fool-proof as possible. This time, she would just have to wing it.

It was eleven-fifteen. The local drunks were leaving the pub and gathering outside. Some were singing Christmas carols, some chatting, others laughing and roughhousing. She observed the windows. They were single-paned with wooden frames. The odds were that they were lever-locked from the inside. She knew she could enter the pub through any one of them within thirty seconds or less. She scanned the building for an alarm box and couldn't see one.

By midnight the crowd had disappeared. Two women left the building by the front door and walked away, across the road towards the city centre. The lights of the pub went off, leaving the building in total darkness. A few seconds later, a light in a window above the pub came on, and the shadow of a figure in the room could be seen moving around.

Laura exited the car and ran towards the building with her head down. She squatted next to the building, as close as she could get to the wall without touching it. She strode towards the first corner of the building, keeping a low profile. She looked around the corner, and, when she was sure no one was there, she ran to the second corner. The third corner took her to the rear of the building. She was relieved to see a high fence running parallel to the back of the building. It was more than enough to conceal her from any unwanted attention. The first window she came to was frosted glass. It was a window to a toilet. She took off the small backpack, unzipped it, and retrieved a short rope attached to a small, black suction cup and a metallic cutting tool attached to the opposite end. She stuck the suction cup to the window and pulled the rope tight. Laura held the blade against the window and etched a perfect circle around the suction cup, using the rope as a guide for the radius. She then pulled the suction cup and a circle of glass came away from the window. She reached in through the circle and felt around for the lever. When her hand found it, she raised it and the window opened without a sound. She crept in through the window and found her footing on a countertop. She looked through the open door to her left and noticed a staircase next to it that was dimly lit at the top. Without another thought, she jumped from the countertop and made her way to the staircase, tiptoeing as she ascended each step.

The bedroom door was cracked open, and light was coming from under the door of the bathroom en suite. She noticed the outline of a lump in the bed. *This will be easier than I thought,* she mused as she retrieved a syringe from her backpack. She moved towards the bed and carefully pulled the top blanket away from the motionless lump in order to expose a piece of flesh. The door to the bathroom swung open, and Roy Gallagher stood naked in the doorway, his muscular six-foot-three frame cutting an impressive silhouette against the bathroom light. "Who the fuck are you?" he screamed as he saw the black-clad figure bending over his bed. A woman's voice screamed as she jumped up.

Laura stabbed the naked blonde in the neck and depressed the plunger. The woman was instantly knocked out cold, but Gallagher grabbed a small rounders bat from beside the bed and ran at Laura, striking down towards her head. Laura raised her arm and the bat crashed down on it. Pain seared through her body, but she instinctively kicked him in the groin and ran for the door. Gallagher followed her to the door and pushed it closed as she pushed to open it. With his free hand, he grabbed her by the neck from behind and smashed her forehead into the door, breaking a door panel in the process. Laura screamed with pain. He threw her violently onto the bed as the limp blonde bounced along helplessly with the impact. He jumped on top of her and pulled the ski mask from her head. His face lit up when he saw her, and he became erect.

"What do we have here?" he asked in his heavy Derry accent. He began to pull open her overalls exposing her breasts and grabbed at them with his left hand as he held her tightly by the throat with his right. Laura reached up and stabbed him in the eyes with her thumbs. Gallagher screamed in pain and let go of his grip to her throat. She reached up with both hands and grabbed his head, pulled it towards her face, and bit his nose. Gallagher screamed as she shook her head frantically. She bit harder and harder until his nose came away from his face. Gallagher gurgled and fell off the bed, clutching at his bloody face in absolute terror. He rolled forwards onto his knees into a foetal position. Laura spat his nose onto the floor and composed herself for a few seconds. She reached for her rucksack and grabbed her old and trusted kukri from inside it. Covering her breasts, she stood over him and raised the knife above her head. With one swift and violent motion, she brought the knife down through his back and straight into his heart. Gallagher slumped and fell prostrate onto the floor. As she pulled the knife out, thick, black blood pooled under his body.

She walked into the bathroom, washed off the blade in

the sink, and wiped the red sludge from her gloves with a hand towel. She checked herself in the mirror and smoothed out her hair. She began to shake and threw up into the toilet.

She sat down on the seat of the toilet and began to weigh her options. Billy would instantly know this was her handiwork. She didn't have time to clean up. She was wearing disposable nitrile gloves, so there wouldn't be any prints. She'd been sure not to leave any footprints in the blood after the melee.

She walked back into the bedroom and noticed the blonde unconscious on the bed. Laura put her ski mask back on and pulled out four zip ties from her rucksack. She secured the woman's ankles to the bed frame and her wrists to the headboard. Laura looked around the room for a cup or vase, anything that would hold water. She walked back into the bathroom and picked up the small waste bin. She turned it upside down and an assortment of used condoms, sticky tissues, and hair fell to the floor. She filled it with ice cold water from the bath faucet.

Laura climbed onto the bed, mounted the woman, and threw the full bucket of water onto her face. The woman gasped for air and squirmed from side to side. It took a few seconds for her to get her bearings, but when her eyes focused on Laura's terrifying appearance, she began to scream. Laura placed her hand over the woman's mouth, and her electronic voice boomed from behind her mask.

"Be quiet, and I won't harm you," she said in her Darth Vader voice.

"Please don't hurt me," the woman whimpered.

"What's your name?" asked Laura.

"Angie . . . Angie Kennedy," the woman responded, clearly panicked.

"I need to ask you a few questions, Angie."

Angie nodded.

"Are you Roy's regular girl?" asked Laura.

"Yes," replied Angie.

"Are you in a relationship with him, or are you a prostitute?"

"We're in a relationship."

"Angie, do you know of anyone here with ties to America?"

"The lads who don't have convictions go back and forwards to New York all the time," replied Angie, confusion evident on her face.

"What about the phone box outside? Did anyone make a habit of using it regularly?"

"Only Danny Buckley," replied Angie. "He used to tell people that it was his office and would get mad if any of the locals used it."

"Where is this Danny Buckley?"

"No one knows," said Angie. "He was usually here every night of the week, but he disappeared on Friday the thirteenth and hasn't been seen since. We joked about the date, he went missing for a while, but now people are worried about him."

Laura intuited that Danny had disappeared the day her father was murdered. That was obviously no coincidence. Danny had to be found.

"Does Danny have any associates here at The Woodpecker?" asked Laura.

"None, other than the drug addicts he sold heroin to, he seemed to just hang around and drink with everyone else at the pub, but it's weird that Joe went missing the day after Danny."

"Joe who?" asked Laura.

"Joe Byrne. He was around here every night too. He's a scary man. Roy wasn't scared of anyone except Joe. I think Roy was giving him protection money."

"Tell me, what do you know about both of these men?" demanded Laura.

"I swear, I don't know anything else. I've told you everything I know," sobbed Angie.

Laura jumped from the bed and scanned the floor. She reached down and picked up a small, sticky piece of flesh and wrapped it in a tissue she'd plucked from a Kleenex box on the nightstand next to the bed. She couldn't leave his nose on the floor, especially with her teeth marks in it. She then grabbed her kukri and walked over to Gallagher's lifeless corpse. She turned it over and began to cut the flesh from around the area where his nose had been. She once again placed the flesh in a tissue and put both pieces into her rucksack.

Angie watched in terror.

"Where's your handbag?" asked Laura.

Angie motioned with her eyes to the right of the bed. Laura bent down and rummaged through its contents. She picked out what appeared to be an electric bill. She held it close to her face and stared at the address on the envelope for a few seconds. She dropped the letter on the floor and cut a piece of wool from the blanket on the bed and pulled a bottle full of liquid from her bag. She unscrewed the top of the bottle and poured chloroform onto the wool. Laura once again mounted Angie. "If you tell anyone about this conversation, I'll find out, and I'll kill you in your bed at home. Do you believe me?" she asked, her robotic voice emotionless.

"Yes," said Angie through her sobs.

Laura held the woollen rag over Angie's face and Angie once again went limp as she fell unconscious. Laura cut the zip ties from her hands and feet and escaped into the night from the window she'd entered through.

Laura pulled off her ski mask and entered the phone box. The internal walls were decorated with depictions of genitalia, crude remarks, and phone numbers. A well-used phone book rested on a shelf under the phone. Laura scanned the walls for any pertinent information, grabbed the phonebook, and walked to her waiting car.

It was eight the next morning. Laura sat at the desk in the study hunched over the stolen phonebook, when Billy stormed in. He slammed the door behind him and approached the desk.

"What the fuck did you do?" he shouted with a mixture of horror and concern.

"Please, sit down, Billy, I have something to show you," she said softly, seemingly oblivious to his question.

"You left a witness, Laura," continued Billy. "The woman's in shock. She hasn't spoken a word since we found her. Damn it, Laura, she's at St. James in the psychiatric wing. Oh, and what did you do with Gallagher's nose, for God's sake?"

Laura once again ignored Billy's questions and placed her right index finger on a page of the phonebook. "I took this from the phone box outside the pub. I was told last night that a somewhat infamous Irish Republican, by the name of Danny Buckley, uses the box as a personal office. As you can see, the pages are full of scribbled notes and phone numbers. I spent most of the night looking through it, and I came across this."

Billy focused his eyes on the page. "It's obviously an American phone number, 0-0-1 is the prefix for the States."

"I called the number with the Motorola about an hour ago. It rings to a phone box in California—Seal Beach to be exact. It rang for nearly ten minutes until someone answered. The gentleman who did answer was quite obviously inebriated, but I did get to extract some useful information from him. Apparently, the booth is less than ten feet from an Irish bar named Sullivan's. In fact, the whole of the city's main street is full of Irish bars, many of which are staffed by people from Ireland, or at least of Irish descent."

"I know Danny," said Billy, the frustration returning to his voice. "He's a vicious little cunt. We've picked him up a good few times for grievous bodily harm and drug dealing, but each time, the CPS refuses to prosecute. Word is that he's got someone protecting him. This could actually explain a few things. I'll have a unit pick him up."

"Don't bother," said Laura matter-of-factly. "He's gone."

"Gone where?" said Billy.

"He's just gone. He disappeared the evening of Father's death. He and another fellow by the name of Joe Byrne."

"Joe Byrne," repeated Billy, his eyes widening at the mention of the name. "He's a major player in the Provisional

IRA. He's the quartermaster of the Armagh Brigade. We've been working with MI5 on a few operations, and each time he's evaded us. He's smart. If he's involved, I can guarantee this one will be tough. It could be that after finding out about Giles, they killed your dad, Sebastian, and Jenkins and ran off to California."

"Either that, or they've also been killed. Do you have any intel on them, Billy?"

"After the stunt you pulled last night, Laura, I'm hesitant to include you in anything. Why don't you just leave this to us?" Billy implored.

Laura smiled. "So that's a yes, I presume?"

Billy nodded. "I'll bring the files we have on both of them tomorrow, and we can look through them after the funeral."

Reverend Wiggins stood at the open doors to the chapel as a gold carriage led by six black Arabian stallions arrived. Record crowds lined the streets of Leeds to pay tribute, as the carriage was driven from internment in Leeds city centre to Britewood House. Laura followed the carriage in the back seat of the Silver Shadow, driven by Billy, who was wearing his army dress uniform.

Six SAS troopers stood by with the reverend to act as pall bearers, as Billy led Laura into the chapel. They walked slowly, arm in arm, down the centre aisle. Laura looked over the crowd. The chapel was packed with all demographics: military types, aristocracy, business tycoons, house servants, and politicians. Tracy was seated in the front row, and Billy kissed her as he took a seat beside her. Laura sat to his immediate right. Along with her fitted Givenchy skirt and jacket, Laura wore a black, veiled hat. She glanced over her right shoulder and noticed Anne, The Princess Royal, who was sent as a personal emissary of Her Majesty. Anne smiled and nodded sympathetically in her direction. Laura returned the nod and then looked over her left shoulder. Sir Anthony and Clive Loughton were sitting directly behind her with another man. Clive smiled, Sir Anthony closed his eyes and nodded reassuringly at her, but the other man, the one she'd never met, looked right through her, his wispy white hair, slender face and sunken eyes ominous in the light of the church candles. Her initial impulse was to avert her eyes, but she forced herself to stare at him for just a few seconds more.

The choir sang "Jerusalem" as the troopers slowly carried the coffin into the chapel in perfect step to the beat. The coffin was placed on a pedestal in front of the altar. The good Reverend stuttered through his sermon. Her father's friends and colleagues—the crème de la crème of British society—eulogized him. Then it was Laura's turn. She collected herself for approximately five minutes and took her notes up to the lectern. She pulled her veil back over her hat, exposing her face to the congregation. She scanned her papers and then folded them and placed them in her handbag. She cleared her throat while placing her fist against her mouth and began.

"My father, the Lord Henry, Eighth Earl of Britewood, was as good a man and father as there ever was. He was a soldier, a statesman, a writer, a diplomat, a loving husband, and a splendid father. He was everything a man should be. I can only hope that I can be half as effective as he was in managing the affairs of his position. His death mirrored his life: valiant, daring, and courageous. He didn't leave this world without a fight, and neither shall I. His faithful valet, David Jenkins, has been left in the care of his family. His service to my father and me will not be forgotten. I promise you all that whomever is responsible for their deaths will pay the highest price. I will not rest until the perpetrator is caught and punished to the fullest extent of my law. Thank you all for being here today. I know my father is appreciative of your kindness as he sits at the right hand of his father."

As the coffin was led out to the family mausoleum, Laura walked behind it, with Billy trailing behind her. The rest of the congregation followed. "*My* law?" Billy whispered into her ear.

"Yes, you know what I meant," she replied.

As the coffin was placed on the marble slab, in the gigantic, stone tomb, a regimental piper played "Amazing Grace."

The reception was held in a ballroom on Britewood Estate. Sandwiches, pies, and desserts crowded tables along the western wall, as guests mingled around the twenty-five circular tables, which were filled with an assortment of wines provided by the Rothschild Vineyard from the south of France. Clive Loughton approached Laura and placed both hands on her hips as he whispered into her ear from behind, "I'm here for you, Laura."

Why not just bash me over the head with the nearest Moët bottle, carry me up the stairs, and plough me like a caveman? thought Laura, as she turned away from the stench of cigarettes on his breath.

"Oh, thank you, Clive," she replied. "It's so reassuring

that you're here, now that Father's gone." She turned to face him and kissed him on the forehead. *Maybe I'll let him do me tonight,* she pondered as she stared him in the face. *It'll be fun, and I could do with the stress relief.*

"Laura?" came a voice from behind her. She turned and saw Billy waving a manila envelope in her direction.

"I have to go, Clive," she said as she tore herself from his arms.

Billy sat across from Laura at the Resolute in the study. He watched her as she flipped through the two files he'd given her. Her eyes darted across each page and eventually came to rest on the photos of the two suspects. "Obviously, Danny is a minor player in the IRA. It looks like he's under the command of this Joe character," she said as she looked up at Billy. He nodded in agreement. "Joe seems smart. He's careful. There are only two photos of him here, and both are difficult to make out. He could be in the ballroom right now, and I wouldn't be able to recognize him. I understand why MI5 and your team haven't got him banged up at Her Majesty's pleasure yet, but this guy, Danny, why isn't he in prison? I mean, each time he's been arrested the proof of his guilt has been overwhelming, but each time, apart from the petty stuff, the CPS has refused to prosecute. I just don't get it." Laura shook her head in disbelief.

"I don't either," answered Billy. "We've pretty much given up on Danny. As far as I'm concerned, he's being protected by someone."

"What do you think about their connection to the bar in California?" asked Laura.

"They might be there."

"I could do with a holiday," she said, widening her eyes and flashing a smile.

"You're not serious?" Billy retorted.

"Why not? After all, I can work over there in almost complete anonymity." There was a knock on the study door. "One second," shouted Laura, as she stuffed the files back into the envelope. "Come in!" The door opened slowly and in walked Jenny.

Laura gasped. She leapt from her chair and ran across the room to greet her. They embraced, and Laura kissed her on both cheeks.

Laura turned her head towards Billy. "Billy," she said with pride, "this is my good friend, Jenny Waldron." Billy held out his hand to Jenny. When Jenny reached forward, he took her hand and kissed it while bowing his head. "Leave him alone, Jenny," said Laura, "he's taken." They all laughed.

"I'll leave you ladies alone," said Billy, "you've obviously got some catching up to do." When Billy closed the door behind him, Laura locked it, closed the curtains on the French doors, and dragged Jenny onto one of the leather couches, where they collapsed into a deep embrace.

"I didn't think you'd come," said Laura, as she stroked Jenny's hair.

"I wouldn't leave you like this. I know how much your dad meant to you."

"How did you get here?"

"I took the train from Manchester and caught a bus from the station."

"How long are you staying?

"As long as you need me," replied Jenny, as she tilted

back her head and looked into Laura's eyes.

"I have to go back to the reception." Laura stood to go. "Come with me. I'll introduce you to a few people. Then afterwards, we can spend some time together."

Clive Loughton was busy chatting to one of the female service staff when Laura arrived in the ballroom. The server giggled as Clive whispered into her ear. As Laura approached, the server replaced her smile with a serious expression and curtsied before hastily leaving the area.

"Clive, this is my good friend, Jenny Waldron," said Laura, pretending to be oblivious to Clive's encounter with the server.

"Pleased to meet you, Jenny," said Clive. His gaze widened as he saw the beauty before him. Laura knew that Clive would find Jenny attractive and would probably try to seduce her. She knew that if Clive succeeded, she'd be hurt and jealous, but didn't know why. Would it be the betrayal by Jenny, or that Jenny had used Clive's body the way she wanted to? In either case, Laura resisted her feelings of jealousy. She knew that her relationships with Jenny and Clive would only distract her from the work at hand. If they got together, this would allow Laura to continue her work without distraction. "Clive, will you please show Jenny around for me, while I take care of the other guests?" she asked.

"Of course, I'd be delighted," replied Clive, and the two walked away together.

Billy and the man with the sunken eyes were chatting next to the fireplace when Laura approached. Billy, without hesitation, introduced them. "Sir Geoffrey, may I introduce you to the Lady Laura?" Sir Geoffrey kissed Laura's hand.

"Geoff Marsden, m'lady. Pleased to meet you. Your father and I served together in the Regiment. He was a dear friend."

Laura nodded. "The pleasure's all mine."

The three of them chatted for almost an hour, until it was time for the Princess Royal to leave. It wasn't long before the house was empty, save for the staff, Jenny, Billy, and Laura. Clive left with Sir Anthony, but before he left, Laura noticed him discreetly grab Jenny by the butt and whisper in her ear. Jenny smiled coyly in return. The rouge left on Clive's collar was enough to convince Laura that they had both betrayed her. She knew what kind of an animal Clive was, but the slight by Jenny hurt.

Jenny sat with Billy and Laura by the fire and stared hypnotically into the crackling flames. After what seemed like hours, Laura broke the silence. "Thanks for being here today, Jenny," she said as she patted her on the knee. "I'll have Bob Wilcox drive you back to the train station. You should be able to catch the seven-fifteen to Manchester."

Jenny appeared shocked. "I thought you might want me to stay a few days?"

"No, Jenny, I don't need anyone but the staff and good old Billy here at the moment. Anyone else is a distraction." Laura rose and motioned for Jenny to stand. Laura walked Jenny to the front door, where they waited in silence for Wilcox. A few minutes later, the Range Rover arrived on the front drive, and Laura opened the rear door.

Jenny attempted to kiss Laura on the cheek, but Laura pulled away. "I guess this is goodbye, then?" asked Jenny.

"Yes, I guess it is," replied Laura as she waited for Jenny

to climb into the back seat. Laura slammed the door and walked back up the stairs without looking back as the vehicle drove off down the driveway and out of the front gates.

Laura took her place next to Billy by the fire. "Do you fancy a holiday in California?" she asked.

Billy shook his head and rolled his eyes.

"We could catch them, Billy, and bring down the whole house of cards." Excitement welled in her voice.

"How can I just leave, Laura? What about work, the Regiment, my family? What the hell would I tell Tracy, that I'm going hunting for the Earl of Britewood's killer and to thwart a child-trafficking ring involving MI6? Come on, Laura, be serious!"

"Yes, I see how difficult things could be for you." She paused and looked up, searching for answer. "Regardless, I have to go. It'll probably be better for me to do this alone anyway."

"What do you think of Geoffrey Marsden?" asked Billy, changing the subject.

"He seems like a good enough chap," she answered.

"He's Sebastian's replacement at the Secret Intelligence Service. He's the new C. He's known your father since they passed selection together in the Regiment; they served together in Malaya and Borneo. He was an Operations Officer with SIS, when your father was still in the Regiment, and they worked closely together in Ulster," explained Billy.

"Why have I never heard of him?" asked Laura. "Daddy introduced me to most of his contacts, I'm sure."

"Who knows?" replied Billy. "What I do know is that Sir Geoffrey was involved in operations that only the Cabinet knew of. Maybe your father thought it best to keep him away from you."

"I'm going to need a travel agent. I believe Executive Solutions is the preferred agency of Prince Michael of Kent and was used by the Duke of Windsor when he gave up the crown for that floozy Wallace. I'll use them. Do you know anyone in Southern California, Billy, anyone who could help me when I'm there?" she asked.

"Not off the top of my head, but I'll make inquiries."

When Billy left, Laura took out a pad of paper from the desk drawer. She thought for a while, then began to compose a list of everything she'd need for the journey. She began with her personal items: cosmetics, shoes, clothes, not forgetting the one- and two-piece swimsuits she'd bought from Selfridges for her many jaunts to the Maldives and West Indies. Then it was on to her operational items: weapons, ammunition, sedatives, even explosives had to be packaged correctly and sent in sealed containers.

She tapped her pen on the pad for a few seconds, deep in thought. *How will I get this all into the States without scrutiny?*

She spun the rolodex on the desk and stopped at the letter *M*. Her finger flicked through the contacts until a familiar name caught her eye. She picked up the phone receiver and began to dial. Within seconds, her call was answered. "Arthur Mosley, Solicitor-at-Law, Gemma speaking, how may I help you?"

"Yes, this is the Lady Laura Lacy. I'd like to make an appointment with Mr. Mosley at his earliest convenience."

After securing her appointment, she descended into her lair. She opened her lockers and selected all the equipment she'd need. She pulled out multiple pairs of overalls, tabi boots and socks, a dozen or more ski masks, and her gas mask, lining the equipment up against the stone wall. Then she moved to the locked wall containers. She selected multiple cases of 9mm and 45-calibre ammunition and stacked them in boxes along the wall and then moved on to her weapons safe. She typed in the combination and pulled on the great door. From a rail of handguns, she picked out a Browning and a Colt 45. From the hooks above the rail, she pulled down an SLR and an HK MP5 SD. She performed a function check on each one, and, once she was satisfied with their condition, she placed them in a rifle case and locked it with a padlock.

She slipped off her shoes and bowed before stepping onto the dojo mat. She pressed the centre mirror, and it opened, becoming a door. She stepped into her walk-in storage room, which was filled to capacity with Japanese weapons. She took from the walls a *katana*—the long sword of the samurai, a *tanto*—a Japanese knife that she placed in her jacket pocket, and four egg-shaped containers containing *metsubushi*, the blinding powder often used by medieval ninjas while trying to escape. She paused and marvelled at the curved blade of the kukri hanging from the weapon rack. She grasped it by the yak bone handle and turned it over to observe how the light reflected from the blade. This was the tool that had brought out her strength as a child, and hopefully, in the distant land of America, it would help her deliver justice for the many missing children she was on a quest to find. Of course, she sought revenge for her father's murder. She placed these favoured items into a black silk drawstring sack and pulled the strings tightly.

By the morning of Boxing Day, Laura was hammering the last few nails into a six-foot-square cargo box in the garage. The secrecy of her lair, coupled with the convenience of the garage's hydraulic floor, had made the packing quite simple.

Liz Johnson and the Wilcox family had been preparing for Christmas since the beginning of the weekend. It was perfect timing. The season provided the diversions to allow Laura the space and time to prepare.

Laura arrived at exactly ten in the morning for her meeting with Mosley. She walked in through the front door to find the reception desk empty. The door to Mosley's office was open, and from the smoky smell of Cohiba cigars, Laura knew that Mosley was close by.

"Good morning, m'lady," said Mosley as he popped his head around the door frame. "Excuse the lack of formality, but due to the season, I've given Gemma the week off."

"Good morning, Mr. Mosley. That's quite all right. It's probably better given the circumstances. Do you have everything I requested?" she asked.

"Yes, of course, but it was like pulling teeth getting the pen pushers in the Foreign Office to do anything even remotely like work in the Christmas season. Please take a seat," he said as he held the back of the leather guest chair at his desk.

When they were both seated, Mosley fumbled around in a drawer, brought out a silver ashtray, and rested his cigar on its edge, before digging through another drawer to pull out a manila envelope. He opened it and poured its contents onto the desk. "Here's your passport and the documents and seals for your diplomatic bag. Make sure the seals are placed on your containers correctly. They're tamperproof, but only if they're correctly used. Executive Solutions have also arranged a house for you in Huntington Harbor, a few miles south of Seal Beach; a first-class ticket to John Wayne Airport in Orange County; and a suitable vehicle, as you requested, which will be waiting for you in the garage when you arrive. As for your diplomatic bag, or in your case, cargo crate, you'll have to collect that from the port in Long Beach when you get there. Customs will need to see your diplomatic papers in order to release it to you. I will have these diplomatic papers sent, via registered mail, to your Huntington Harbor address."

"Great job, Mr. Mosley!" she said. "Do you have the other things that I requested?"

"I do," said Mosley, as he peered quizzically over his gold-framed, half-moon glasses. "Your father often had me take care of, shall we say, unordinary tasks, and I never asked questions. I'm extending that courtesy to you." He reached into the desk drawer once again, but this time didn't fumble. Instead he stared straight into Laura's face, grabbed an envelope, and tossed it onto the desk. She reached for the envelope, and, after receiving a paternal nod from Mosley, opened it and emptied the contents onto the desk. She picked up the paper driver's licence and read the name aloud. "Jane Bogart," she said in obvious disappointment.

"It's a name that popped into my head, m'lady. There's also a standard British passport. You'll be travelling under this passport. You'll have to fill out a visa waiver as you enter, this will be enough to get you a California Driver's License, but you can drive with that one for up to thirty days under California law. I've also instructed Executive Solutions to rent the house and car in that name. Be aware though, m'lady, that your diplomatic documents are in your real name. It's your title and your father's connections that secured them. If you're trying to fool anyone in a position of power, they'll possibly still know that you're at least in the U.S."

"Thanks, Mr. Mosley," said Laura, standing to leave.

Mosley stood, too. "I've taken the liberty of adding a few more things, m'lady."

"Oh, really? And they are?"

"In the sealed cash envelope attached to the passport, there's the phone number of an old friend of mine. He owns a haulage company. When you receive your diplomatic papers through the post, he'll meet you at the port of Long Beach and have your crate transported to your house. He'll do his best to ensure that the truck's not followed." Mosley then presented one final, large envelope, pulled out the contents, and handed the pile to Laura. "What you have in your hand are two, life-sized California licence plate stickers, with the appropriate registration tags. They'll come in handy, should you wish to conceal the licence plate of your car."

Laura stuffed them gleefully into the manila envelope with all the other items, leaving her diplomatic papers on the desk for Mosley to post. She kissed the fingertips of her right hand and then touched them to Mosley's forehead. "Thank you, Mr. Mosley, you are a darling," she said as she walked towards the door. Mosley picked up his cigar, and as he puffed on it, he disappeared into a cloud of thick, grey smoke.

Five

Friday, December 27, 1985

IT WAS ELEVEN O'CLOCK IN THE EVENING WHEN JOE
Byrne walked through the entrance of Leeds Bradford Airport
and noticed a uniformed police officer chatting to a cute
cashier at the bureau de change. They were obviously flirting
and deep in conversation. *Time to fuck up this wee piggy's
chat-up session*, he whispered to himself in his Belfast brogue
as he approached the cop from the rear. "Excuse me, mate, I
need to know where to check in," he said.

"Check-in's over there, Paddy," said the cop, pointing to the
check-in desks and immediately turning back to the cashier.

"No, mate, I need to check in with this," he said as he
waved his diplomatic passport. The cop turned and immediately focused on Joe.

"Are you the private jet fella, Mr. Wiggins?" he asked.

"Aye, that I am, big man," replied Joe with a wink at the
cashier. She smiled in return, and the cop's face turned red.

"Er, okay, sir, please follow me," said the cop. "Do you
have any luggage?"

Joe motioned at the black canvass duffle bag, which
was slung over his left shoulder. "Just this, but don't worry

yourself, big man, I got it." Joe read aloud the nametag on the cop's uniform. "Smith, that's an unusual name for an Englishman, isn't it?"

Smith ignored the sarcastic remark and walked towards a door labelled *Authorized Personnel Only*. Joe followed Smith through the door and down a corridor, which led to a flight of stairs and out onto a runway where a Gulfstream IV waited.

Two figures were in the doorway at the top of the mobile stair ramp. Joe strained his eyes just enough to recognize the slender frame of Geoffrey Marsden. He didn't recognize the second, larger man.

"I'll leave you here, sir," said Smith, and without waiting for a reply, he disappeared up the staircase.

Joe walked towards the plane and scanned it from nose to tail, before ascending the stairs. "A brand new G4," he said, as he passed Geoffrey and walked down the centre aisle of the aircraft. "I feel special."

"As well you should," said Geoffrey, following behind Joe aboard the aircraft. He sat down on a large, beige leather chair, before pouring himself a flute of Moët. "Champagne?" He lifted the bottle from an ice bucket.

"Don't mind if I do," said Joe, as he sat in the chair at the other side of the table.

"The flight will take approximately thirteen hours," said Geoffrey, as he poured another serving of champagne. "We'll have plenty of time to chat about what's expected of both of us."

"I wait with bated breath," said Joe sarcastically.

A second man approached Joe. He was a large, ominous-looking hulk of a man, completely bald, with a linear scar from the top of his head to the centre of his right eyebrow. Without saying a word, he grabbed Joe's duffle bag, opened it, and dumped the contents into the aisle.

"What the fuck are you doing?" asked Joe in complete disgust, as the man moved Joe's clothing around with his foot.

"He's doing 'is job," replied Geoffrey.

The man picked up Joe's toiletry bag and looked through it before zipping it back up. He nodded at Geoffrey, who nodded back.

"You can put your things away now, Joe," said Geoffrey cordially.

Joe shook his head and let out a sigh before scrambling to his feet and stuffing his belongings back into the bag. He sat down as the plane began to move up the runway, and both men secured their seatbelts. Joe looked back and saw the bald man sitting in the farthest booth to the back of the plane. As the plane began to ascend, the twin Rolls-Royce RB.223 Tay turbofan engines hummed louder and louder, until the plane levelled out at approximately thirty-five thousand feet.

"Your colleague, Danny, has been a great asset, and I can assure you that his work for us has had only a positive bearing on his relationship with you and your organization," said Geoffrey as he nodded at Joe.

"I understand that," said Joe. "He explained all that to me before he left."

"Do you know where he went?" asked Geoffrey.

"No," said Joe. "Sebastian promised him protection, so Danny got nervous and tried to contact Giles when he found Sebastian was killed. Of course, Giles didn't answer his calls. When Danny read in the *Evening Post* that Giles' house was being treated as a crime scene and he was missing, presumed dead, he decided to confide in me. He told me he had to leave but wouldn't tell me where to. He told me that his work with the security services was important and that I had to make contact with you guys. He said that he would contact me with instructions when he was settled."

Geoffrey listened intently. "It's perfectly understandable that he got cold feet, but his work is far too important to us. This is crucial timing. We obviously ignored the other, let's say, criminal enterprises he was involved in, gave him a salary, and turned a blind eye to the colleagues he asked us to leave alone, you included, as long as he did as instructed. The same deal will apply to you, if you agree."

"And if I don't agree?" asked Joe.

"I think you know what the alternative will be. You've dealt with us long enough to know how we operate."

"So, what exactly did he do for you guys?" Joe inquired.

"What did he tell you he did?" countered Geoffrey.

"He told me that Giles would give him the names of various children, the kids who wouldn't be missed, the vulnerable ones, and he would find an opportunity to snatch them. He'd get them fake passports and then pay a local woman, Angie Kennedy, to pose as their mother and take them to America." Joe took a sip of champagne.

Geoffrey paused and took a slow drink from his flute. "Did he tell you what the children were used for when they got there?"

Joe could feel his blood begin to boil. "He said they were taken to a place in the mountains where dirty bastards, the kinds who have controlled the world since the dawn of man would have their way with them and be secretly filmed. Is it all true?"

"Quite so! It all sounds a little sordid, but when we have that kind of leverage on influential world leaders, politicians, and titans of industry, you can understand the benefits to us and our interests."

"Yes, but if you want me to take over from Danny, why are you taking me to America? Why don't I just continue where Danny left off?" Joe didn't want to go to America, that much was clear and the thought of this particular mission made him sick to his stomach.

"We'd prefer to show you our operation personally. We also have a possible problem we need you to sort out for us," said Geoffrey.

"What do you mean?" asked Joe, leaning forward. The hairs began to stand up on the back of his neck.

"As you know, Angie Kennedy is one of our agents. She's been with us for quite some time. She was visited by an individual close to Henry Lacy. The visit happened at the time of your friend Roy Gallagher's death." Geoffrey searched Joe's face for a reaction.

"Was this the fella who killed Roy?" asked Joe, his voice taking a serious tone.

"This person is no fella, Joe, it's the daughter of the late Lord Henry."

"No way." Joe chuckled in disbelief.

"I'm dead serious, Joe. She's a killer, and a cold killer, at that." Geoffrey looked Joe square in the face, as if to reassure him that this was no joke.

"We're talking about Lady Laura here, right?" Joe smirked.

"Joe, we have reason to believe she's going to the U.S.,

and if she does, she's going to try to foil our little operation. We can't let that happen. We know she was in London at the time of her father's and Davenport's deaths, so she's not a direct suspect, but she may have gotten someone else to do her dirty work and that person could be the man who's the chief investigator in the case. If she believed her father was a part of all this, she's capable of anything."

"This has to be a joke," said Joe, his voice becoming serious.

"No. We believe she's been drilling regularly with 23 SAS and that the lads have accepted her as a trooper. We also believe that Sir Giles and Peter Horton were two of her many victims."

"That's fucking stupid. There are no women in the SAS, and she's a fucking royal. Christ, Princess Di and her go shopping together," said Joe, perplexed by the situation.

"Angie called us and is now in witness protection. She told us how a woman in black overalls and a ski mask, using some kind of electronic voice changer, had attacked and killed Gallagher. She told us all the gory details. Whoever this was bit off Gallagher's nose and then cut the flesh around it and took the flesh with her in order to avoid being identified by her teeth marks. The knife she used was a kukri, common among the Gurkha and SAS regiments. We believe it's Laura Lacy, Joe. You should know that she questioned Angie, who was with Roy in his bed that night, about you and Danny. Now that Danny's gone missing, there's nothing to say she hasn't killed him too."

"Why would she question Angie about me?" asked Joe.

"You and Danny are colleagues. She probably just assumed that you and he were partners in the operation."

"You want me to *kill* Laura Lacy?" said Joe.

"Not quite. We'd like to chat with her first. She obviously knows about our operation and isn't too happy with it at the moment, but if she's convinced how crucial this is to national security, she might just come on board. With her public profile and her skills, she could be one of our finest assets."

"So . . . you want me to kidnap her?"

"Possibly. We'll let you know what's expected of you in due course."

Joe yawned and stretched his arms out. He ran his fingers through his thinning black hair. "I'm knackered," he said.

"There's a bed through the door at the end of the aisle. Why not sleep for a while?" suggested Geoffrey.

"Aye, I think I'll do that," said Joe as he stood up and stretched.

Joe walked into the bedroom and closed the door behind him. He threw his duffle bag on the bed and walked through the sliding door into the water closet, which contained a small sink with a mirror and a toilet. He looked at his face. His eyes were bloodshot and the whites were now a pronounced red, dimming the blue centres. His cheeks had always been red, but now they were heavy and accentuated the bags under his eyes. He splashed water on his face and dried it with a hand towel that had been resting on top of the toilet. He shrugged off his mid-length, black leather jacket allowing it to drop onto the floor and kicked off his black Bally loafers. He carefully unbuttoned his white Topman shirt and hung it on a hook mounted on the door and dropped onto the bed.

As he laid there, he stared at his shirt and thought of his

mother. She'd bought him the shirt last Christmas, just a month before the tumours in her lungs had taken her. Now it was Christmastime, and here he was, flying to America, on a brand new, luxury private jet, with men he would've gladly garrotted just days earlier.

The bald man viciously shook Joe out of his slumber, and Joe jumped out of bed with his fists clenched. "Time to get up, we've arrived," said Geoffrey from the doorway. "I'm sorry about my man, he never did have a gentle bedside manner."

Joe relaxed his frame and dressed himself before following Geoffrey off the plane, while the bald man followed behind. Although it was dark, it was warm, so Joe slipped off his jacket, securing it under the strap of his duffle bag, which was slung over his left shoulder.

"Where the fuck are we?" he said.

"We're at John Wayne Airport in Southern California," Geoffrey answered with a grin.

"They named the airport John Wayne. I'm liking this place already," said Joe as he slapped Geoffrey on the back.

They entered the airport through a small side door and flashed their diplomatic passports at the immigration officer, who stood at a small counter inside. The officer nodded approvingly, and they made their way to the arrivals lounge.

There were only two people waiting: a small, stocky man of Latino heritage, with wavy black hair and a mouth that curled down at the sides, giving him the appearance of a continual scowl. The other was a tall blond man with sharp, Germanic features and piercing blue eyes. The tall man held a small, handwritten sign, which read *Derek Wiggins* across it. "Mr. Wiggins," he said in a cheery voice as they approached him.

"Yes, that's me," Joe said. He looked directly at Geoffrey and whispered, "I wish you'd let me choose a name for myself. Derek Wiggins sounds like the name of a supermarket butcher."

"I'm Matt Norton, and this is my colleague Juan Gazzano. We'll have your back while you're here," said the blond, as he presented his right hand. Joe shook his hand and then held his hand out to the shorter man. Gazzano just stared at him. "Don't mind my friend Juan, here, he's just quiet."

Joe turned towards Geoffrey, who shrugged. "Go with them. They'll take you to your lodgings and show you around," he said. "Get him to the office by eleven tomorrow."

"Will do," replied Matt, as he grabbed the duffle bag from Joe's shoulder.

All five of them walked out through the glass exit doors. Geoffrey and the bald man got into a waiting limo and drove away. Joe, Matt, and Juan walked across the street and into the first parking structure. Matt opened the trunk of a dark blue Ford Mustang and threw the duffle bag into it. Joe got into the front passenger seat and Juan slid into the back.

They drove in silence. The car sped north on the Pacific Coast Highway and made a right turn on Superior Avenue. They drove past a series of plush condominiums, and in less than a quarter of a mile, they took another right and approached a large, iron security gate. Matt wound down his window and typed a code into the keypad and the gate slowly opened, the soft sound of its motor buzzing as it did so.

As they pulled into the driveway, their headlights exposed the large, beautiful gardens. Fountains stood thirty feet apart, over undulating lawns, and the building stood majestically behind them. The building itself was designed in the fashion of an eighteenth-century French château. It was comprised of one hundred and twenty-eight condominiums, with two full gyms, two Olympic-sized pools, and tennis courts, which flanked the building in perfect symmetry.

They parked in a numbered parking space in the first lot. "Here we are," said Matt as he turned off the engine.

"This is my lodging?" Joe asked.

"Yep. Welcome to Versailles. Grab your bag and follow me," said Matt as he climbed out of the vehicle.

Joe grabbed his duffle bag from the trunk and followed the others to a side door. "The code to enter is nineteen fifty-four," said Matt as he punched the numbers into a keypad. "Apparently, that's the year this place was built, by some old actor called Cagney or something," he continued with a shrug.

"Jimmy Cagney?" asked Joe in surprise.

"I think so," replied Matt.

They all crammed into the narrow lift, and Matt pushed the button for the third floor. They exited and turned left. Matt took the key from his pocket and opened the first door on the right. The condo was no larger than an average hotel room. The kitchen was on the immediate right. As they entered through the doorway, they saw a door leading to the bathroom. The sparsely furnished living room followed. There was a black leather two-seater couch; a comfortable-looking, fabric covered chair; and a mahogany cabinet, containing a new Philips multi-stack sound system. A curtained-off space provided a modicum of privacy for a twin bed and closet. The place was small, but the view was magnificent. The rear gardens, with the backdrop of the vast Pacific Ocean, filled the window.

"This is my number. If you need anything, call me, but don't call me for any stupid shit," said Matt as he threw his plain, white business card on the coffee table in front of the couch.

"Got it," said Joe.

"Be ready by ten-thirty," said Matt. "Mr. Beck doesn't like it when people are late."

"Got it," replied Joe, as he unceremoniously walked the two of them to the front door. He ushered them out and quietly closed the door behind them. He sighed deeply and ran his fingers through his hair. He walked towards the window and stared into the distance and continued staring until the sun rose.

There was a loud bang on the door. Matt pushed it open and it slammed violently against the wall. "You ready?" he asked as he looked around the room. He was wearing skin-tight Levi's 501s and an equally tight bright blue polo shirt. His partner followed wearing a similar outfit, the only difference being the colour of his shirt. Pink was all the rage.

"Sound the alarm, it's the sausage jockey squad!" yelled Joe as he stifled his laughter.

"What's that supposed to mean?" asked Matt, who was hovering over Joe's seat in the living room.

"Shut your mouth, pretty boy," replied Joe as he stood from his chair, pushing Matt across the room. "Yeah, I'm ready, and watch your tone. I'm the big man in this room, got it?" He pointed at Matt's face. "Now, let's go see this fella Beck, whoever the fuck he is."

Matt and Juan looked at one another in shock and watched Joe walk out the front door.

"Well, are you coming or what, lads?" he asked as he turned back to them. They hurried out the door behind him without another word.

Joe walked towards the car and stood by the passenger side door. "We don't need the car, we're going right there," he said as he pointed through the gates to the large glass skyscraper across the street. Joe followed Matt and Juan across the street and through the double doors of the building. Two uniformed security officers stood behind a desk in the foyer, and they both nodded at Matt as the three of them walked by. The three passed the reception desk, and Matt winked at the receptionist without stopping. She smiled.

The door to the lift opened when Matt arrived. Once inside, he placed a key into a slot and pushed the button for the seventeenth floor. Matt stared at Joe, but when Joe stared back at him and tilted his head, Matt averted his gaze.

As the lift slid open, a beautiful reception area came into view. It was large with pillowy couches, coffee tables outfitted with heavy, glossy books, and reprints of paintings by Monet and Vernet on the walls. The bald man from the previous evening sat on a chair in the corner reading a magazine. He didn't acknowledge them.

Matt approached the receptionist—a petite, porcelain-skinned woman, her hair combed back in a ponytail. She was wearing large, black-framed glasses.

"We're here for Mr. Beck," he said.

"Yes, he's expecting you, go right in," she replied as she motioned towards the tall, stainless steel-covered doors.

Matt and Juan entered the office, followed by Joe.

Geoffrey sat in the leather-bound guest chair at the desk, and a thin, grey-haired man sat on the elevated, throne-like, intricately carved wooden chair behind it. "Come in, fellas, and grab a seat," he said as he pointed at the conference table to his left. Each man grabbed a chair from around the table, placed it in front of the desk next to Geoffrey, and sat down.

"I'm Ron Beck," said the man behind the desk, as he held out his right hand.

"Pleased to meet you, I'm Joe Byrne." They shook hands.

"No, you're not," Ron snapped back, causing the whole party to flinch. "You're Derek Wiggins while you're here, got it?"

"Got it," replied Joe nonchalantly.

"We've had a few fuck-ups over the last couple of weeks, but I'm not gonna let a couple of deaths and some cunt of a blue-bloodied Limey get in the way of what we've done, or what we're about to accomplish. You do as you're told, and you'll be taken care of. In fact, we'll all be taken care of. Do you see this?" asked Ron as he pointed to a large, framed map on the wall.

"Yep," replied Joe.

"That's what's at stake here. Right now, we've got leverage on some of the most important political figures in the U.S. That's given me a tremendous advantage when it comes to my business. Now, we're introducing foreign powers to our little project. So the potential—when it comes to a favourable geopolitical outcome for Geoffrey's friends in what was once Great Britain—is, shall we say, significant. This project is unlimited. There's just so much we can do here, to make the world safer and all of us wealthier. All we need from you is a constant supply of children, and we'll do the rest, got it?"

"Got it," replied Joe, with a forced smile.

"These guys will show you around and take you where you need to go," he said.

"I'm gonna need a car," said Joe.

"I'll tell you what you'll need," said Ron without missing a beat.

"Got it," replied Joe as he rolled his eyes.

"Okay, guys, let's get this show on the road. You know what to do," said Ron as he motioned towards the door.

"I guess this is goodbye, then," said Joe in Ron's direction. Ron nodded, and the party of three walked out of the office into reception. As they made their way to the lift, Joe glanced at the bald man, who continued reading his magazine, seemingly oblivious to their presence.

The three of them headed north on the 405 freeway and exited on Beach Boulevard in Huntington Beach, and took a left onto Westminster Avenue, stopping at the In-N-Out Burger drive-thru. Matt spoke into the intercom. "Three number ones with grilled onions and three Dr Peppers. We'll be eating in the car," he said. A voice repeated his order, and they drove to the window. Juan opened up the back door and walked out towards the restaurant.

"Where's he going?" asked Joe.

"He's going to the restroom. We're in for a long drive; if you need to go, go now," replied Matt.

Joe got out of the car and followed Juan into the toilet. Joe opened the door of a stall, but Juan grabbed him by the shoulder and shook his head no. Joe shrugged and stood at the furthest urinal. Although there were four urinals, Juan stood at the urinal right next to Joe.

"Oh, I see," said Joe. "Getting comfortable together, are

we?" Juan ignored Joe's attempt at humour.

They made their way back to the car, and Matt handed them each a tray consisting of a burger, fries, and a drink. "Eat up," said Matt before biting into his burger. "You're about to consume the world's best burger."

Joe unwrapped the burger on the tray and took a bite. "Jesus, you're not wrong," he said, his speech muffled by his full mouth. He grabbed his drink and sucked in a small amount of this liquid. It was ever so slightly bitter. *There's something in this,* he thought. He continued to eat the burger and every once in a while touched the straw of the drink to his lips pretending to sip. Within a few minutes, he pretended to doze off. Juan tapped him gently on the head.

"He's out," he said.

"Dang, it usually takes longer than that," said Matt, shaking his head in amazement.

Joe felt a cotton bag cinch around his head. He opened his eyes but remained absolutely still. He concentrated on the journey; the twists, turns and the climb. After approximately one hour and fifteen minutes the car came to a stop. There was mumbling. He heard the back door of the car open and felt cold air rushing over his hands.

"How long as he been out?" said an unknown voice.

"About an hour," replied Matt.

"Let's just make sure," said the voice and Joe felt a sharp prick in his neck.

He felt hands grabbing him and dragging him out of the car. He fought against the drowsiness, but fell quickly into unconsciousness.

Joe woke up, laying on a large, four-poster bed. The furniture around him looked like oak—two chests of drawers and a wardrobe against the far wall. The heavy, thick curtains were closed. A tapestry portraying what appeared to be a Bavarian mountain scene covered the wall next to the wardrobe, and the head of a buck, with excessively large horns, on a wooden shield, hung on the wall facing him.

He looked down at his naked body. The sheets were wet and unkempt. He looked over at the door, to what he believed was a bathroom. The door was partially open, the light was on, and he could hear someone inside. He placed his feet on the floor and held his head in his hands. It hurt, like the worst hangover of his life. He stood and steadied himself before walking towards the bathroom. He opened the door to find a tiny blonde girl, no more than ten years old, naked, shivering with her back against the bath and her knees pulled tight to her chest. He gasped, and the girl began to sob uncontrollably at the sight of him, terror evident in her face. He grabbed a towel and secured it around his waist and placed another towel over her arms and knees, tucking it under her chin.

"What's going on here, darling?" he softly whispered. She continued sobbing and hid her face in the towel.

"Get dressed," said a deep voice with an East London accent. He turned to find the bald man holding his clothes in the bathroom doorway. "I'll be waiting outside," he said as he threw the clothes on the bed and walked out the main door.

Shocked, Joe stood in the doorway of the bathroom and stared at the girl. Below the towel resting over her body, a pool of blood began to seep out beyond her feet.

"Holy Christ!" he shouted in panic. He stumbled into the bedroom and fumbled through his clothing, fumbling to get his clothes on as he struggled to distinguish each item. He left the room and tripped down the stairs, catching himself on the banister before falling. When he reached the bottom, Matt, Juan, Geoffrey, and the bald man were waiting in the lobby. The lobby was just like the bedroom: rustic, like an alpine cabin. Wooden floors covered with embroidered rugs and heavy, rough-cut furniture with stuffed animals in ornate cases surrounded him. Matt was giggling, but the others were staring coldly at him.

"Come on, we're done here," said Geoffrey, as he pulled up the collar of his overcoat. The bald man opened the door, and they all walked out into the darkness and heavy snow to their waiting vehicles. Joe looked up at the building and caught a glimpse of a figure standing on the turret of a roof, a sentry. The bald man violently pulled a cloth bag over Joe's head; from the rear, he pulled the drawstring tight around his neck. He then grabbed Joe's wrists and zip-tied them together behind his back, before stuffing him into the trunk of Matt's Mustang and slamming the door.

Six

Monday, January 13, 1986

LAURA STEPPED OUT OF ORANGE COUNTY'S JOHN Wayne Airport into the blinding sunlight and slipped into the closest waiting taxi. "I'm going to this address in Huntington Harbor," she said as she handed the driver a slip of paper.

"Okay," he replied. "Do you have any luggage?"

"No. Everything I need will be waiting for me."

"You from Australia?" he asked.

"No, I'm from England," replied Laura. The flight had been long, and she had work to do. She was both tired and anxious to get to work. The last thing she wanted was a chat with the first taxi driver she met.

"Are you on vacation?" he asked.

"Yes," answered Laura, believing that a monosyllabic answer would sway him from asking any more unnecessary questions.

"Would you like me to take you on the scenic route down PCH? It's a little longer, but it's got better views than the freeway," he suggested cordially.

"Just get me there as expeditiously as possible, please," Laura snapped back at him.

The driver nodded and proceeded towards the 405 South freeway. Laura had never been to California before. In fact, it was only her second visit to the United States. She marvelled at the sheer size of everything: the brightness, the palm trees, it was all so very splendid. The taxi exited the freeway on Springdale Street. They whizzed past apartment buildings and shopping parades and stopped at occasional red lights until they turned right onto Warner Avenue. Another right turn on Algonquin took them to Huntington Harbor. The houses were quaint as far as she was concerned, each one custom-made to suit the needs and tastes of the tenant. Palm trees lined the streets; playgrounds and parks were scattered here and there. It was clean and vibrant, and as they came to a stop on Carousel Lane and she opened the door, the smell of fresh sea air engulfed her nostrils.

She paid the driver with a crisp twenty-dollar bill and closed the door before turning to the house. It was a two-storey, colonial-style house, painted pristine white, with an attached two-car garage and a short driveway. She loved it. The house next door had been fashioned in the style of a gothic castle, but was made of wood—so cheap, grey cladding had been used to cover it. She shook her head at the realization that the bloody monstrosity would be her primary view from the front of the house.

She noticed a piece of paper stuck to the front door. The United States Postal Service had tried to deliver her diplomatic papers less than an hour before she arrived and, according to the notice, would deliver the package again the next morning. She retrieved the door keys from the lock box next to the front door and entered. A short hallway with beige carpets led to the living room, which was modestly filled with a black leather couch and matching La-Z-Boy chairs. Next to the empty fireplace stood a Sony Trinitron television on a black stand. Copies of Andy Warhol's most famous pieces hung on the walls, a stark and colourful contrast to the beige paint.

The kitchen was large and rustic, with a gigantic centre island, covered by a heavy wooden unvarnished top. She peered at the microwave, pressed a few of its buttons, and shuddered at the prospect of eating anything cooked in it.

The dining room was immediately behind the kitchen. An eight-seater dining table rested at its centre. A large Welsh dresser, containing black octagonal crockery and ample cutlery, stood against its only bare wall.

The patio door off the dining room led to the rear of the house, where a deck, fire pit, and plenty of patio furniture awaited her. She walked to the rear of the patio and relished the sight of the harbour. Almost each house had a small boat or yacht in the accompanying slip. She was disappointed that hers was empty, but then again, she wasn't there for a vacation.

She made her way to the upper floor. The master bedroom was en suite, and a glass door led out to a balcony with a small breakfast table and two chairs. The second bedroom was fitted out as a gym. There she took note of an exercise bike, treadmill, rack of dumbbells, and a flat bench with an optional incline, and a small two-tatami, mirrored studio space to finish it off. The third bedroom was for her clothing and accessories. Three mirrored closets were filled with casual, business, and evening clothes, something for every occasion. A chest of black matte drawers contained underwear, swimwear, lingerie, and accessories. From the third drawer, she pulled out a pair of blue cut-off Levi's. *They can't be any more than six inches long,* she thought to herself as she held them out in front of her.

She became startled when she saw her reflection in the floor-to-ceiling mirrors. She'd forgotten that Liz had bleached her hair and given her highlights. *Damn, you look wonderful, Laura*, she thought to herself.

She snapped back to her senses and got to work. She pulled a pair of dark blue Jordache jeans from a shelf in one of the closets and put them on. They were a perfect fit and clung to her legs like paint. Next, she chose a white, pinstriped Miller Ranch western shirt, leaving the top three buttons open. On the floor of the closet there was an array of shoes for all occasions. She slipped on a pair of blue and teal silhouette pumps. She didn't need it, but to finish her ensemble, she pulled a black leather belt from a drawer. The ornate, silver buckle was a perfect pairing for both her jeans and shirt.

She entered the garage from the door in the kitchen, where a silver Audi 5000S (Turbo) awaited her. She was pleased with the choice. It was low-key, fast, and reliable. She reached into the glove box and pulled out the Thomas Guide, thumbing through the pages until she found what she was looking for: Seal Beach Main Street.

She started up the car and edged slowly out of the garage. She was amused at the automatic transmission. *Stay to the right,* she thought. *The last thing I need is to break my cover and have to invoke diplomatic immunity after a head-on collision with some yank.*

She drove out through Algonquin, right on Warner, past the marshland, and took a right onto Pacific Coast

Highway. She drove past dive bars and sleepy mom-and-pop restaurants, until she came to the Naval Weapon Station, at which point the vista consisted of a vast barren grassland, surrounded by barbed wire on the right and the majestic blue Pacific Ocean on the left. At last, she turned onto Main Street and parked the car at the first empty parking space she found.

She exited the car and scanned her immediate environment. It looked like a typical American tourist town. She glanced at the pier at the end of the street, disappearing out into the ocean. She walked by quaint gift shops, restaurants, and bars. It was only two-thirty, yet the street was quite full of people in casual clothing. Couples walking hand-in-hand, children playing, and two surfers in wetsuits and bare feet running towards the ocean, laughing and chatting, giddy with their obvious joy of life. *Does anyone work around here?* she whispered under her breath.

She saw Clancy's Irish Pub to her immediate right and stepped into the doorway. The bar was empty. The lone bartender, a tall man with a broad chest and red beard, was polishing a glass as she entered. "How're ya?" he shouted towards her, in a pronounced northside Dublin accent.

"Good," she replied before walking out. She glanced across the street and saw the green and gold sign identifying Hennessy's Bar and Grill. She walked across the street and again walked in through the doorway and scanned the place. Two middle-aged men in Hawaiian shirts, board shorts, and flip-flops spoke loudly at the bar, while the female bartender read a magazine to stave off the boredom of her shift. There was no one else in sight. She crossed the street at a crosswalk and there, in front of her, was the place she'd been looking for. Sullivan's Pub was a large corner building with a fenced-off patio area consisting of eight round tables, each of which had a large green umbrella protruding through its centre. People sat randomly around the tables, a smorgasbord of demographics, eating appetizers and drinking an array of beverages. The phone booth was located just five feet from the front door.

She entered the phone booth and searched the walls for clues. Phone numbers, notes, and crude messages were plastered all over, no different than the filth written on the walls of the phone box outside The Woodpecker in Leeds. She concluded that men were the same creatures all over the world. Only one phone number caught her eye. It began with 0353 followed by the city code for Leeds. She found her spot and surmised that whomever was using this particular booth had, at some point, conducted business with Danny Buckley and possibly Joe Byrne.

She entered the pub and immediately saw two uniformed cops sitting at the bar. There were a few other people sitting at tables: an elderly man reading a book, sipping on what appeared to be an Irish coffee; a middle-aged couple drinking beers; a man with thinning, black hair sitting at the end of the bar reading a newspaper; and a party of six young women who were apparently tourists. The bartender, a short man of slight build with dark brown hair parted at the side, was deep in conversation with the cops. He looked up from his meeting. "Just grab a table, miss, Nicole will get you a menu," he shouted across the room.

The waitress grabbed a menu from under her station, but Laura held up her hand. "Don't worry," she said, "I'll sit at the bar."

The bartender stopped his conversation and stared at the cops and nodded his head at them. Both cops stood up. The shorter one remained quiet. He avoided eye contact with Laura as she watched them. He was dark-skinned and appeared to be of Central or South American descent. The second cop—a tall, slim, good-looking blond—winked at her. "Good afternoon, ma'am," he said with a smile. "We'll catch up to you later, Ken," he said as they both walked through the door and left the bar.

"Was it something I said?" asked Laura.

"No, they're just making their rounds," replied the bartender. "Ken Sullivan," he said while extending his right hand.

Laura gripped his hand. "Jane," she replied.

"You got any identification?"

"What for?"

"Just to check your age."

"Oh, I'm flattered, here." She pulled out the new driver's licence and extended it across the bar. Ken took it and examined the name. "Good to meet you, Jane Bogart," he said and winked at her whilst handing back the licence.

"What can I get you?"

"What do you have for wines?"

"House red or white."

"Surprise me," she said, rolling her eyes.

Ken opened a fridge and retrieved a bottle of Chardonnay. He polished a wine glass with a towel hanging from his belt and perused it for blemishes, before placing it in front of her and pouring her a completely full glass.

Laura knew she was somewhat of a snob and realized that her new middle-class persona, Jane, would have to be more forgiving of social foibles.

"Are you trying to get me drunk?" she asked through her laughter.

"No, ma'am," replied Ken. "I think my hand slipped." He gave her a wink.

She'd been watching his hands as he poured the wine. They were heavily calloused on the knuckles, and his fingers were slightly crooked. The small flag on the rear of the bar was partially obscured by the many trinkets on the shelves; the leprechaun figures, ceramic shamrocks, and the wooden harp all slightly obscured it, but the eagle, globe, and anchor it portrayed told her one thing: this guy was a United States Marine.

"Where are you from?" he asked.

"I'm from England," she replied.

"You on vacation?"

"Yes. I just came here to unwind for a while."

"You hungry?" He tapped his fingers on a menu on the bar.

"I could eat. What do you recommend?"

"Club sandwich, it's a bestseller."

"I'll have it."

"What kind of bread do you want it on?"

"What have you got?"

"Sourdough, wheat, rye, or nine-grain."

"Wheat."

"What side do you want?"

"What do you have?" sighed Laura.

"Fries, mashed potatoes, or potato salad."

"Nothing. I'll just take the sandwich."

"Okay. It comes with a soup or side salad."

"God, man, do these questions ever end? I'll have the salad."

"What dressing?"

"You have to be kidding! Okay, what do you have?" She shook her head in frustration.

"Ranch, blue cheese, Thousand Island, Italian, or good old oil and vinegar."

"I'll take the oil and vinegar, and please don't give me any more choices. I'm surprised you serve any more than a table a day with all the questions you ask."

"Got it. It'll just be a few minutes," said Ken as he tried to subdue his laughter. He wrote her order on a small hand-held pad and took it into the kitchen.

When he returned, he resumed their conversation. "How long do you plan on staying here?"

"I don't know. Probably until I feel replenished."

"Do you have anything planned while you're here?"

"No, as long as I'm in close proximity to the beach, I'll be fine."

Ken stared at her for a while, nodded, and began organizing the bottles on the shelves at the back of the bar.

"Who's that?" asked Laura, pointing to a photo hanging over the top shelf of the bar. It was a photo of what appeared to be an elderly Southeast Asian man, with a lei of flowers around his neck.

"Oh, that's an old friend of mine, but unfortunately, he's no longer with us."

"He must've been important to you, for you to have his photo in such a prominent place."

"Oh, yes. I owe him a lot," said Ken as he continued to rearrange and wipe the bottles.

"Did you serve together?"

"No, I met him the year I got out. I was a little lost back then. He put me back on track."

A bell sounded. "What's that?" she asked.

"That's your salad." Ken walked into the kitchen and came back carrying a bowl in one hand and a small, plastic container in the other. "Here's your salad." He placed the bowl in front of her. "Here's your oil and vinegar," and he placed the container down next to the bowl.

"Is it customary here in California to eat with one's fingers?" asked Laura.

"What?" replied Ken.

"May I have some cutlery?" she asked.

"Cutlery?" he answered, obviously perplexed.

"A knife and fork."

"Oh, yes," he chuckled.

He reached under the bar and pulled out a knife, fork, and spoon, wrapped in a napkin. Laura unrolled the utensils, inspected the knife and fork as she held them up to the light, and placed the napkin on her knees.

"Is everything okay?" asked Ken nervously.

"I suppose, but I'm trying to find anything other than lettuce in this bowl," she said as she picked through the green leaves with her fork.

The bell rang a second time. "That'll be your sandwich," said Ken as he walked into the kitchen. When he came back to the bar, he was carrying the sandwich and placed it to the right of her salad bowl.

"My god, man, what on earth is that?" She opened her eyes in surprise.

"It's your sandwich," replied Ken as he placed salt and pepper shakers right behind the sandwich.

"It looks like a brick. How am I supposed to get that thing in my mouth?" she asked.

"Most of the time people just squash them down as much as they can and kind of open their mouths real wide, I guess," said Ken as he scratched his head.

Laura pushed her salad bowl to the side, picked up her knife with her right hand, her fork with her left and began to cut the sandwich up and eat it like a meal.

"Yep, definitely not from around here," said Ken as he continued to organize his bar.

Laura ate half the sandwich and left the rest on the plate.

"May I have the bill?" she asked.

"It's on the house," replied Ken as he continued his tasks. He stopped for a second and turned to her. "I bought this bar because this town suits me. It's peaceful, and apart from Saint Paddy's Day and the summer, it's reasonably quiet."

"It seems like a lovely place to live," said Laura.

"I've been to many different places for one reason or another and there's nothing quite as peaceful as this. I'd like to keep it that way."

"Understood," said Laura as they stared intently into each other's eyes. "Thanks for the meal." She scooted off her stool.

"Do you want a takeout box for the rest of it?" he asked as he reached under the bar again.

"No, thanks. Maybe you can have it for dinner," she replied as she walked towards the door.

"Interesting woman," said the man at the end of the bar, as he folded his Orange County Register and placed it on the bar.

"Yes, Derek, she is," replied Ken, picking up the plate and ducking under the bar to drop the remainder of the sandwich into the trash can.

Laura paused with her hand on the door handle. *That's a Northern Irish accent,* she thought to herself and exited the bar.

Laura got into her car and drove back towards Huntington Beach on Pacific Coast Highway. A Crown Victoria police cruiser followed her and flashed its lights. She pulled off to the right and watched as the blond police officer she'd seen at the bar approached her on the driver's side. She rolled down the window. "Driver's license, registration, and insurance," he said. Laura opened the glove box and retrieved the documents from a small plastic folder. She calmly reached into her purse on the passenger seat and retrieved her licence. She handed the documents to the officer.

"Is there a problem, officer?" she asked calmly.

"You didn't stop at the stop sign at the end of the street before you turned onto PCH," he said, pointing his hand in the direction they'd driven from, while at the same time staring at her documents.

"Hmm, I could've sworn I did," she answered smiling up at him.

"Jane Bogart," said the officer as he read the name on the licence.

"That's right, Officer Norton," she replied, reading his name badge.

"What're you doing here in California?" He stared directly at her.

"I'm on vacation, but I'm seriously considering moving here to become a film . . . sorry, a movie star."

"Have you been drinking?" He pulled off his Ray-Ban aviator sunglasses.

"No," she replied.

"Didn't I just see you in Sullivan's, sitting at the bar?" he asked tilting his head.

"No, you must be mistaken," she answered without missing a beat.

"Yes, I guess I am," said the cop, as he put back on his glasses.

"May I go now, officer?" said Laura nonchalantly.

"Watch your step, Miss Bogart." He handed her back the documents.

"Will do," she replied as she watched him walk back to the car through her side-view mirror.

When she arrived home, she parked the car in the garage and walked into the house through the kitchen. The jet lag was beginning to hit her, so she decided to work out, in order to revitalise her body and clear her mind. She stripped down to her underwear, and after a short stretch, she began to run on the treadmill. As she ran, she replayed her visit to Sullivan's over in her head. The cops knew something about her from the moment they saw her. *Why else would they stop their conversation, leave the bar, and then pull me over on the way home to check my papers?* she thought. Then there was Ken Sullivan. *He seems on the surface to be a decent man, but why the cloak-and-dagger conversation with the cops and the talk of keeping his town peaceful?* It seemed to Laura that all three men were hiding something, but whether they knew anything about her mission was still a mystery. If the cops were involved, she knew she was in trouble and would need all the help she could get to find the children and get them to safety. She didn't know who to trust and therefore trusted no one, not even Billy. She knew that Davenport had got to him and knew all too well that he had a family, a career, and a sterling reputation. He had much to lose if he didn't play ball. The cop who stopped her now knew where she lived, and it had taken him less than a day to find out.

She completed her five-mile run in forty minutes and wiped the sweat from her body with a large, beige bath towel. She placed her hands on the floor placed the balls of her feet on the flat bench, raising her legs off the ground, and began to perform push-ups. Her chest hit the floor and her arms then locked out straight with every repetition. She averaged one per second and completed eighty. When she finished, she sat on the floor and placed her feet under the treadmill. She laced her fingers together behind her head for her sit-ups. Her elbows would hit the floor at the end of the downwards movement and then would touch her knees as she sat upright. She completed one per second and completed eighty, as she'd done with the push-ups. She completed three sets of each exercise. Two hundred and forty push-ups and two hundred and forty sit-ups. She completed her workout with a stretch, dropping into a perfect side-spilt with her forehead against her knee, then performed the same stretch on the other leg.

She showered, and after drying off, she slipped into a short, white silk kimono that had been hanging on the back of the bathroom door. She wrapped a towel around her hair and tucked it tight into place.

She laid on her bed and realized how alone she was. She hadn't felt this isolated in years. Her father was dead as was Jenkins, she'd been betrayed by both Clive and Jenny, and now she was alone in a foreign country with no one to trust and a formidable task ahead of her.

She pulled the towel from her head and stood as she

slipped off her kimono, allowing it to drop on the floor. She tucked under the comforter and curled into a fetal position on her right side.

She pondered how she would retrieve her diplomatic crate from the Port of Long Beach. Hopefully, the transportation company that Mosley had arranged would do the job without a hitch, but again, she was unsure and would not allow herself to trust anyone.

She felt uneasy and anxious, but within minutes, the jet lag took over, and she drifted off.

It was her first morning in the house. The postman arrived just after eleven o'clock. Laura signed for her package and opened the generic Royal Mailbox it came in. She examined the seal. It had been secured perfectly. She grabbed her purse and searched for the phone number Mosley had given her on her last visit to his office. There was no name on it—no address, no other information except the number. Even the scrap paper it was written on was generic. It was cheap, transparent stock with no watermark.

She called the number. Someone picked up, but there was no greeting, just the crackle of white noise. "Hello?" she said.

"Go ahead," came the deep voice on the other end.

"I have a package to be collected," she said.

"What time?" asked the voice.

"Two o'clock this afternoon." She was slightly unnerved by the curt questions.

"Park in the parking lot at customs at Long Beach docks," said the voice.

"How will I find you?" asked Laura.

"I'll find *you*," said the voice before hanging up.

Laura stared at her phone. She'd been apprehensive about her collection, but now she was anxious. Just weeks before, she'd had her father, Jenkins, and Billy Smythe to help her. Now she was all alone, with nothing but a scrap of paper to offer comfort.

She entered her car and once again took the Thomas Guide from the glovebox and thumbed through it. She mapped out her journey to the docks in her head. She surmised that it would take no longer than thirty-five minutes to get there, but first she'd have to stop somewhere close to affix the stickers to her licence plates. She didn't want to do it before her journey. She'd already been stopped once by the police, and trying to explain away fraudulent licence plates on a second stop would be a hassle. She looked at the route for a suitable place to stop and prepare. *There it is,* she thought as she tapped the page with her fingernail.

She ran up the stairs and sat behind her dresser. She took her time with her makeup. Subtle crimson lipstick, a hint of pink rouge, and dark-grey eyeliner was all she needed. She plucked a dark blue Chanel suit from the closet. She tucked her white silk blouse into her skirt and carefully slipped into the bespoke jacket. Her shoes were a perfect match for her suit, and she finished the ensemble with one-carat diamond studs and her diamond-encrusted Patek Philippe watch. The customs agents would be expecting a countess, so a countess she'd give them.

She checked her watch and made her way to the car. She performed a systems check. Left indicator, then right, brake lights, headlights—they were all in perfect, working order. If she drove just under the speed limit, there'd be no reason for the police to stop her.

She edged out of the garage and scrutinized the street. All the vehicles seemed to match the environment. There was nothing she considered suspicious. A black Bentley, a Mercedes here and there, a white Ford transit van, a station wagon. When she was satisfied, she closed the garage and put on her seatbelt.

She drove out of the harbour, left onto Algonquin and right onto Warner, past the marshland, and right onto Pacific Coast Highway. After a few miles, she turned left into the Seaport Marina Hotel's car park. This was the perfect place to prepare herself and her vehicle. She stepped out of her car and scanned the building, flagpole, and streetlights for any closed-circuit cameras. When she was satisfied, she opened the manila envelope and placed the licence plate stickers over the licence plates, ensuring there were no creases.

She once again perused her environment. There was no one around, only vehicles. Rental cars filled the majority of the car park: worn-out beaters at the far end were obviously employee vehicles, a work truck with lumber sticking out of the bed, and a white transit van. She focused on the van. *Was that the same van I saw on Carousel?* she thought to herself, as she sat down in the driver's seat and secured her seatbelt. She waited a few minutes and observed it through the rear-view mirror.

Slowly, she headed towards the car park's exit. She drove through Belmont Shore and stopped at the first light on the street. She checked her side mirror and there, just two cars back, was the van. She made a mental note of the licence plate and continued to drive. She drove onto Ocean Boulevard and the first light went red. The van was only two cars behind.

The light went green and she inched towards the second light. The second light turned red. She edged towards it, as if about to stop, but stepped down on the accelerator and gunned through the red light. Cars honked and swerved out of the way. She gunned through the third and fourth lights and screeched into a left turn on Pine, past the arena. She made another right and stopped for a few seconds. She checked all mirrors. The van was nowhere to be seen. She calmed herself, took a few deep breaths, and made her way to the docks.

A sign up ahead read *U.S. Customs.* She turned right and parked in the first lot, as she'd been instructed. She checked her watch—it was one forty-five. The lot was mostly vacant, a couple of eighteen-wheelers, a car here and there, some with federal licence plates. She checked the right-side mirror, and someone rapped on the driver's side window. Startled, Laura jumped in her seat.

She opened the car door and stepped out to meet him. He was short and of slight build, but his belly stuck out from under his blue-and-white plaid shirt like a soccer ball. His skin was dark, his face heavily wrinkled and accented by a long, grey handlebar moustache which hung at least two inches below his chin. He wore a pristine white Stetson hat.

"I'm Jesus Gonzales," he said in a deep Texan voice.

"Laura," replied Laura, as she extended her right hand. Jesus shook her hand.

"Go through the door marked *Customs,* and speak to Agent Shepherd. Present your paperwork. He'll take you to the dock. I'll meet you both there, and we'll get your package." Jesus walked backwards towards his Peterbilt truck.

Laura nodded and went through the door to customs.

There were two people in line. The lone agent behind the counter was dealing with a young female client's documentation, when he looked up at her. "Laura Lacy," he said as she entered.

"Yes," she replied, holding her diplomatic passport in the air. The agent dismissed the young woman at the desk and motioned for Laura to approach. She handed over her diplomatic paperwork. "Are you Agent Shepherd?" she asked.

"That's me," he replied, without taking his eyes off the document, "follow me." He flipped up the latch in the counter and walked out to the car park. Laura followed behind, and they walked towards a series of covered ports.

She instantly recognized her crate. "Everything seems to be in order, ma'am. Please sign here and here," said Shepherd as he circled two signature boxes on his clipboard and handed Laura his pen. Laura signed, and Shepherd left her alone with her crate.

Jesus approached in his truck. He backed it as close as he could to the port, jumped out of the cabin, and ran around to the rear. He pushed a button on the trailer next to the door. The door slowly opened, and a ramp extended from the rear and dropped. He ran up the ramp into the trailer and pushed an extra-wide pallet jack out onto the loading dock. He slid the jack under the crate and pumped the handle vigorously until the crate was suspended. With a little manoeuvring, he turned the crate around and pushed on the handle until it was in the trailer.

Laura looked into the trailer and noticed many shipments, packages, crates, and boxes. "I don't want to seem picky, Mr. Gonzales, but I need this crate delivered promptly," she said, trying to maintain her composure.

"Don't worry," said Jesus. He pressed another button, and the ramp receded into the trailer and the door closed. "It's two o'clock right now; your package will be at your house by three-fifteen."

Laura shook her head and jogged back to her car and started the engine. She drove back to the Seaport Marina Hotel, scanning the traffic and parking lot.

She safely arrived home and sat nervously waiting at the dining room table. It was two fifty-five. She promised herself she'd remain composed for at least twenty more minutes. She flipped through a copy of *Vogue*, which had been left, along with numerous other fashion magazines, by her handlers at Executive Solutions. She threw the magazine across the table and it bounced on the back of the chair across from her. *Did they really think this shit would interest me?* She leaned back in her chair and scowled at the smiling, upside-down face of the model on the cover.

There was a knock at the door. It was Jesus. "I thought I'd be delivering this to a castle," he said as he looked into the house curiously.

"What?" said Laura.

"I thought you were a princess or something," he said as he chewed on a toothpick.

"Not quite. I hope you're not too disappointed," she replied sarcastically and rolled her eyes.

"Makes no difference to me. Now, where do you want your package?"

"Put it in the garage," she ordered as she searched the street for the truck. "Where is it?" she asked.

"It's in the van across the street." He pointed at a plain van.

"You changed vehicles," said Laura in surprise.

"Yes, I took it to a warehouse, where I switched. There are trucks coming and going all the time, so it makes it difficult for anyone to follow or track the package."

"How very clever of you." She walked towards the garage and opened the roller door.

Jesus eased the crate into the garage with a pallet jack, while Laura watched the street for anything she considered suspicious. There it was, at the end of the street: the white Ford transit van she'd noticed before.

"Please wait here, Jesus," said Laura, and she took off towards the van. "I need to find out who these people are."

Jesus lost his footing on the pallet jack and hit the floor with a loud thud. Laura immediately rushed back to him. She helped him to his feet as he rubbed his head and winced.

"God, are you all right?" she asked.

"Yes, it's nothing," replied Jesus. "I guess I'm just a little clumsy."

Laura composed herself and looked out the window. The Ford Transit was gone.

Jesus walked towards his van, and when he returned, he was holding a crowbar in one hand and a mallet in the other. "These are on the house," he said before climbing back into the van. He tried to close the door, but Laura followed him and held it open.

"Here," she said, holding a hundred-dollar bill in front of him.

"It's all taken care of, ma'am," said Jesus. "Keep my phone number handy, in case you need something else moved." He smiled at her, slammed the door, and drove away.

Laura shoved the cash into her blazer pocket and scanned

the street one more time before closing the garage door. She grabbed the crowbar and mallet and eagerly stripped a side off the crate. She grabbed a weapon case and raced to her bedroom. She sat on the bed and opened the case to reveal four Browning handguns and four fifteen-round magazines. She locked back the slide of each gun, and after inserting a magazine into each one, she released each slide. She pulled out a cloth pouch from the case and opened it to reveal four sticky-backed magnets. She stuck one magnet on the frame of her bed, just behind her headboard. She repeated the process in her gym, kitchen, and living room, finding the most strategic place in each room to hide her weapons. She taped her kukri behind the sink in the bathroom. Although she'd used it many times, the most memorable times were in bathrooms.

The shed in the rear yard was large and resembled a Conex. It had a door and no windows other than the small, blacked-out window in the door. She walked inside and surveyed this symmetrical building with a central walkway. On each side of the walkway, waist-high, stainless-steel cabinets ran the length of the walls, the tops of which doubled as workstations. Above the cabinets, there were recessed chipboard-covered walls, with dozens of four-inch nails protruding from them. They were originally designed for mounting tools, but Laura would use them for weapons.

She filled the black cloth sword bags with the weapons and accessories from the crate and took them, one by one, to the shed. She organized and categorized them. She filled a cabinet with ammunition cans, containing nine-millimetre rounds for her Brownings and HK MP5s. She filled another cabinet with cans of forty-five-calibre rounds for her M1911s. She hung knives and swords next, followed by a few more exotic weapons, including her *kusarigama*, the long chain attached to a sickle she'd used only once before.

She locked the shed and pulled on the door to ensure that it was secure. She collected her overalls, ski masks, and tabi socks and boots and secured them in a closet in her dressing room.

Now she was ready. When she'd arrived, she'd felt vulnerable, alone, and, in many ways, helpless. Now that her familiar toys had arrived, she once again felt empowered. The day had been productive. She knew she was being watched, but the tactical advantages she'd afforded herself by her preparations eased her mind.

She drew herself a bath, adding Epsom salts and essence of lavender, the way Jenkins used to do it. It was hot, piping hot. She eased herself in, slowly. Tonight would be the true start of things. Tonight she'd start the ball rolling, until she found what she was searching for—the lost children of Grangeview and her father's killer.

Seven

Wednesday, January 15, 1986

STEPHANO ANGELO SAT BEHIND HIS DESK AND STARED at the corner of his office. The shriek of a skill saw and the monotonous hum of a mason drill blasted out from somewhere in the building. Ordinarily, the noise wouldn't have bothered him, but this was the third consecutive day, and he was ready to tear someone's head off. The building was brand new, but the finishing touches to The Seal Beach Police Department's new headquarters would take a few more weeks to be completed.

At thirty-six years old, Steph was the youngest police chief in the department's history and probably the most qualified, with a Doctor of Jurisprudence from UCLA. He was definitely the most experienced, having served four years in Vietnam, with the Army's 5th Special Forces Group (Airborne) before joining the Torrance Police Department as a patrolman, rising through the ranks the hard way to captain.

He'd only been Police Chief for two months, but it was beginning to feel like decades. He'd transferred from a high-octane, high-stress police department as a captain just three months prior. He came to the idyllic beach town in order take it easy and cruise into retirement. But when the former Police Chief Rooney committed suicide in his office next to City Hall with his service weapon, the City Council voted unanimously to give the job to Steph, whose youth, experience, education, and attention to detail made him the ideal candidate.

He glanced at his watch. It was one-fifteen, and he'd agreed to meet his old buddy Ken Sullivan for lunch at one-thirty, at The Harbor House Café in Sunset Beach. Steph took a comb and a handheld mirror from the top left drawer of his desk and combed his thick, black hair. Gazing into the mirror, he carefully carved out a perfect left side part and used the comb to sweep back the hair on the sides of his head. He straightened his tie and ensured that the Windsor knot was directly under the top button of his shirt before grabbing his jacket from the back of his chair. He walked through the office pool and noticed a cloud of smoke billowing from one of the cubicles.

"Put that fucking cigar out, Singer!" he yelled as he walked past the cubicle.

"Yes, Chief," came the response and a few heads popped up and looked around in curiosity.

"Anyone calls for me, take a message," he said to the desk sergeant as he walked out into the parking lot.

"Am I your secretary?" responded Sergeant McCall, sticking up his middle finger. Steph saw the gesture through the glass in the door before it closed and shook his head and laughed as he walked to his car. Detective Sergeant Mike Singer ran after him.

"Steph!" he shouted.

"What?"

"We still on for this evening? I have to let the wife know if I'm gonna be home for dinner or not." He tapped his watch.

"Wouldn't miss it for the world. See you at seven," replied Steph as he opened the door.

He slid into the driver's seat of the brand new, sky blue, unmarked Dodge Diplomat undercover unit. He reversed out of the car park and sped off, south on Seal Beach Boulevard, towards the Pacific Coast Highway. He opened the windows, pushed a cassette into the tape player, and Frank Sinatra's "Summer Wind" came blasting through the speakers. The vast expanse of the Naval Weapons Station came into view, and within seconds, he peeled through the green light, and the car screeched into a left turn onto the Pacific Coast Highway.

He caught a glimpse of the old water tower on the right side of the road, and just as he passed it, he swung a right turn and parked directly next to it, in front of the custom-built, single-car garage.

He walked the twenty-five feet to the diner and entered through the front door. "I'm over here," said a voice, and he turned to see Ken Sullivan sitting in the booth at the end, next to the dessert fridge.

"You're three minutes late," said Ken, looking at his watch.

"Fucking sue me," replied Steph.

"I'll let it slide this time, but if it happens again, I just might," said Ken.

"The usual, guys?" asked the waitress as she poured two cups of coffee.

"Yep, thanks, Susan" replied Ken without a pause.

The waitress brought the two cups of coffee from behind the counter and placed them on the table. She then disappeared through the doorway leading to the kitchen.

"Look at that body," said Ken. "How old do you think she is?"

"She's way too young for you, you dirty old bastard. She does have that Madonna look going for her though. I'm surprised the owners let her wear a skirt that short," Steph answered, shaking his head.

"I'm not surprised at all," said Ken. "Those legs are the reason you and I come here most days of the week."

"You said you wanted to discuss something with me," said Steph.

"Yeah, it's probably nothing," said Ken as he stirred sugar into his brew.

"Well, are you going to tell me, or leave me here in suspense?" Steph rolled his eyes.

"Okay, okay. Your guys, Norton and Gazzano, have been acting a little strange," said Ken as he took a sip of coffee.

"What do you mean by strange?" asked Steph.

"They came to me last month in the bar, and asked if some British chick had been in asking questions," he paused for a few seconds.

"What kind of questions?" Steph leaned in.

"They wouldn't say, but they had a photo. The chick was smokin' hot, you couldn't miss her. Anyway, a couple of weeks ago, this Irish guy comes in, his name's Derek Wiggins, but Norton and Gazzano seem to know him. Every time he comes in, they're in minutes later. They chat and sometimes go outside to talk. They definitely have something going on. This is the interesting part: yesterday, the three of them are in the pub. Your cops finish up talking to this guy Derek and then ask me again if I've seen this chick. As they're questioning me, who do you think walks through the door?"

"The chick," answered Steph.

"Damn straight," said Ken.

"And?" said Steph, eager for Ken to continue the story.

"Well, she walks in, sits at the bar, and orders a sandwich. She introduces herself, tells me her name's Jane Bogart," said Ken as he took another sip of his coffee.

"Is that it?" asked Steph.

"Not quite. As she sat down, Norton just nodded his head at her, wished her a good evening, and left. And Derek, who was at the bar, said nothing to her. He just listened to the conversation she had with me."

"I suppose that's a little strange," said Steph.

"A little strange. They've been looking for her for weeks, then on the day they actually find her, they just give her a time-of-day greeting and walk out. That's not just a little strange, Steph, that's totally bogus," said Ken.

Steph took a final gulp of coffee from his cup and held it up. The waitress grabbed the coffee pot and took it to the booth, filling Steph's cup. "Okay," he said. "I'll look into it."

A bell rang from the kitchen and the waitress walked behind the counter and grabbed two plates from the hatch and brought them to the table. "Two double cheeseburgers with fries and extra pickles?" she asked.

"Yep, that's us," said Ken, before picking up a handful of fries and forcing them into his mouth.

"How's the house, or whatever the hell it is, coming along?" asked Ken between mouthfuls of cheese burger.

"Just a few more finishing touches, and it'll be done," said Steph as he dropped his head and looked through the back window at the converted water tower.

"I'm surprised you got planning permission for that fucking thing," said Ken shaking his head.

"I know people," whispered Steph tapping his nose.

Ken looked at his watch. "I've gotta get outta here." He stood to go.

"All right, I'll see you at seven. Mike's gonna be there, too," and Steph threw a twenty-dollar bill onto the table.

When Steph arrived back at the department headquarters, he walked past the desk sergeant and once again saw smoke billowing out from Singer's cubicle. "Put that fucking stogie out and follow me," he said as he walked by Singer, who quickly stubbed out the cigar and followed him to his office.

"Close the door and sit down," said Steph from behind his desk.

"I can explain, Chief. I only punched him when he started talking about Mary," said Mike Singer.

"What are you talking about?" asked Steph.

"Is this about the incident with Murphy?"

"No. I have a job for you. What do you think about Norton and Gazzano?"

"I don't really know them. It's a bit weird that Gazzano can hardly speak English, but it is what it is," said Mike.

"I was just at lunch with Ken. He says that they've been inquiring about some British chick. They've been constantly asking Ken if he's seen her. Anyway, yesterday she turned up out of the blue. She's supposed to be a stone fox, but when she arrived at the bar, Norton and Gazzano just took off. Has there been anything out there about a good-looking British chick that I've missed? Any warrants, APBs, anything?"

Mike looked up in thought for a few seconds and then shook his head. "No, nothing that I know about anyway."

"Keep an eye on them, will you, Mike? But keep it low-key. There's something about them that I just don't like," he said quietly.

"Listen, we've worked together for over ten years," said Mike, looking Steph straight in the eye. "I appreciate you asking me to transfer to this department with you, but please, don't ask me to rat on other cops. You know me, and that's just not me."

"Sure, I'm just asking you to keep an eye on them," said Steph.

"Okay, I'll do it. Can I go now?" Mike stood to go.

"Sure," said Steph. "Oh, and bring your best game tonight. I'm stressed and I need someone to take it out on."

"I'm quaking in my boots," said Mike as he walked out of the office.

At six-fifty, Steph made his way through the front door of Sullivan's and walked behind the bar, past the keg room, and up the stairs. He opened a plain white door, and as he entered the room, he bowed deeply at the waist. The room was approximately twenty-five square feet, with light blue walls on three sides that were covered with photos, plaques, and various awards and certificates. The fourth wall was mirrored, approximately six feet up the wall. The space above the mirrors displayed eight identical black frames. Each contained a separate numbered list headed by the words Kenpo Karate. A ninth larger frame was mounted in the dead centre of the wall. It contained a similar but larger photo of an old Asian man, which hung behind the bar.

Mike and Ken were stretching on the floor when he arrived. They were each wearing a gi, the white, pyjama-like outfit traditionally worn by martial arts practitioners. Both men had their jackets wrapped closed and secured by a black belt.

Steph placed his sports bag on a bench against one of the mirrored walls, and took out his gi. He undressed down to his underwear. Ken was chatting with Mike as they stretched on the floor and caught a glimpse of Steph.

"Do you wear that cup to work?"

"Damn right I do," replied Steph. "Do you know how many times I was kicked in the nuts as a beat cop?"

"Yep, me too," said Mike as his knuckles made a loud, knocking sounds against his groin.

Ken laughed and shook his head before standing. "Okay, let's get started," he said as he clapped his hands and jumped to his feet.

They all stood facing the mirror, with Ken at the front and the two others flanking him in perfect symmetry.

"Down into your horse," said Ken as they all stepped out with their left feet, just a little wider than shoulder-width. Their feet were parallel to the side walls and their knees were bent deeply.

"Meditate," said Ken as they all placed their left hands

across their right fists, in the centre of their chests, with their elbows down, dropping their heads and closing their eyes in unison. They stayed in that position for a few seconds.

"Close," said Ken, and each man brought his left leg to his right and dropped his hands to the side.

"Let's start with basics," commanded Ken, and they all dropped into a fighting stance, with their left legs forwards and their hands clenched into fists, covering their faces, while their elbows were tucked into their ribs. For the next twenty minutes, they practiced punching, open-handed strikes, kicks, elbows, and knees. They then practiced the prearranged fight dances known as katas.

"Wanna do some sparring?" asked Steph.

"Thought you'd never ask," replied Mike as he jogged over to his bag and pulled out a pair of gloves and foot pads.

They were all approximately the same height, around five feet eight inches tall, but Ken was slimmer than the others. Steph and Mike pumped iron together in the department's gym in the mornings before work and were as wide as they were tall. Mike's handlebar moustache also gave him that "don't mess with me" look that only added to his musculature.

Steph and Mike stepped into the centre of the room and both assumed a fighting stance. Ken stepped between them. He scanned them both from head to toe.

"Ready?" he said.

"Yep," they both replied in unison.

"Begin," he commanded and swiped his right hand down between them, before jumping out of the way.

Steph launched his left back fist into Mike's face, knocking Mike off-balance so he fell back. He followed up with a right reverse punch into Mike's ribs. Mike collapsed onto one knee and clutched his chest with both arms. Steph began to advance, but Ken stood in front of him and pushed him back. Mike stood and steadied himself. Ken jumped back, and Steph once again advanced towards Mike. This time Mike launched a hook kick with his left leg, catching Steph on the left cheek with his heel. Steph spun rapidly to his right and landed face-first on the floor. Ken got between them and watched as Steph slowly got to his feet. He shook his head and rubbed his glove against his face, before resuming his stance. Back and forth they went, trading blows, kicks to the head, punches to the face. The mirrors were covered in condensation and the two of them sweated profusely as they circled one another, ducked under punches, and blocked kicks with both their arms and shins.

At last, Mike stepped forwards with his right foot and spun his body around, whipping his left leg towards Steph's head. At the same time, Steph launched a right roundhouse kick at Mike's head and both kicks landed on their targets at the same time. Both Mike and Steph were launched to opposite sides of the room and landed helplessly on the floor.

The room fell silent. Ken walked towards the centre of the room. Both men got to their feet and faced each other. Scowling, they stood at attention and bowed. They walked to the centre of the mat, and Ken stepped aside. They tapped gloves, then broke out into laughter as they embraced.

"Good work, brother." Steph slapped Mike on the shoulder.

"You too, brother," said Mike as he rubbed his head.

After showering and changing, the three of them descended

into the bar and sat around a table. Ken disappeared into the kitchen, and within a couple of minutes, he came back carrying a tray with three bowls of Irish stew and a loaf of fresh soda bread next to a block of butter.

"Nicole," said Ken to the bartender, "get us three pints of the black stuff." Ken sat down and glanced over to the far end of the bar. "That's him," he said quietly.

"That's who?" asked Steph.

"That's the guy who hangs around Norton and Gazzano. Actually, no, that's the guy who Norton and Gazzano hang around. His name's Derek," said Ken quietly out of the corner of his mouth.

"Then let's meet him," said Steph.

"Okay then," said Ken, "here goes nothin'."

Ken got up from the table and walked over to Joe, who was reading *The Orange County Register* at the bar.

"Hey, Derek," he said jovially, "I don't think the guys over here have met a real Irishman before, wanna join us?"

"Aye, don't mind if I do," said Joe as he folded his paper and placed it on the bar.

"Nicole, get Derek a bowl of stew and a pint of Guinness, and bring it to the table, will you?" he asked the bartender.

"Sure thing, boss," she said as she walked into the kitchen.

Mike and Steph rose from their seats and warmly shook Joe by the hand.

"Are you here on business or pleasure?" asked Steph.

"Pleasurable business," said Joe in reply. "What do you guys do?"

"I'm the Chief of Police. Mike here works for the department also," replied Steph without missing a beat.

"Oh, I feel safer already," said Joe, with obvious sarcasm.

"You've clearly got friends in high places, Ken."

"I'd like to think all my friends occupy those places." Ken smiled at Joe. Nicole brought Joe's bowl of stew and pint of Guinness.

"Wait there a second, love," said Joe to Nicole. He then raised the glass and downed the whole pint of Guinness. He licked his lips and wiped his mouth on his sleeve. "Bring me another one, will ya?" He handed her the empty glass. Nicole walked back to the bar, and Joe picked up his spoon and sampled the stew. He smacked his lips and looked up, as if pondering a problem. "That's more than satisfactory, Ken," he said as he winked and motioned his head towards the bowl of stew. "Just like Mother used to make, before she was butchered by the British Army," he said as he glanced at each man at the table for a reaction. They all stared at him, emotionless.

"God, you guys are cold," said Joe.

"We're just eager to hear more," said Mike.

Joe looked at his watch. "I've gotta be going, gentlemen." Nicole came back to the table with a fresh pint of Guinness. Standing up, Joe took it from her and gulped it down. He burped and wiped his mouth with his sleeve. Nicole rolled her eyes and sighed before returning to the bar. "We should do this again sometime," he said. He lazily saluted the table and walked out of the bar.

"He's a strange one," said Mike.

"Yep," said Ken.

"You say he has some kind of friendship with Norton and Gazzano?" said Steph as he looked at Ken.

"Yes. They have regular meetings. Everything seems hush-hush. They're usually whispering, and I think our friend

Derek is using the phone booth outside as an office," said Ken.

"Look," said Ken, as he motioned towards the front door.

"Holy shit," said Mike, "it's them."

Norton and Gazzano scanned the room and headed to the bar. Steph and Mike raised their glasses to catch their attention, and it worked. Gazzano tapped Norton on the shoulder and pointed at the trio's table.

"Come over here," yelled Mike.

"What're you guys doing in here?" asked Steph.

"We're just doing our rounds, Chief," smiled Matt.

"Proactive policing, I like it," said Mike as he thumped the table with his fist.

"Just doing our job, Sergeant," said Matt.

"Well, we have this place covered," said Steph, looking directly into Matt's eyes.

"Good to hear it. You guys have a good night," said Matt, and he and Gazzano walked off into the night.

"That was quite a coincidence," said Ken, before gulping down the last of his Guinness.

"I don't believe in coincidences," replied Steph as he pushed his empty glass towards Ken.

"Looks like we're having another round," said Mike, before biting off the end of a Dominican Romeo and lighting it.

Ken collected the empty glasses, walked behind the bar, and began pouring three fresh glasses of Guinness.

The door opened and in walked Laura. She was wearing a sleeveless turquoise long dress with a thick lavender belt cinched tight around her waist, accentuating her figure. A woollen shawl, wrapped around her shoulders and through the creases of her arms, matched her belt. Her hair was combed back into a single plait, which ran in a straight line perfectly down her spine.

"Good evening, Miss Bogart," said Ken, just loud enough to grab the attention of Steph and Mike.

"Good evening, Mr. Sullivan. You remembered my name, I'm flattered," said Laura.

"All part of the service, but you remembered mine, too," said Ken, trying not to appear too excited over her appearance.

"It helps that your name's on the side of the building," said Laura through a wry smile.

"Nicole, get Miss Bogart here a glass of house white wine on the house," chuckled Ken. He placed the three pints of Guinness on a tray and took it to the table. "That's her," he whispered when he reached the table.

"The Brit?" asked Steph.

"Yes, Jane Bogart," said Ken.

"You've gotta introduce us," said Mike as he sat with his gaze fixed on Laura.

"Hands off, you're married. You've gotta introduce *me*," said Steph as he punched Mike on the shoulder. "She could be my future ex-wife."

"Seriously?" asked Ken as he looked back and forth between his two friends.

"Do it," ordered Steph.

"Okay, here goes," said Ken, as he left the table and approached the bar.

"Miss Bogart, would you like to join us at our table back there?"

"Which table? It's hard to see through that cloud of cigar smoke," replied Laura with a wink.

"I'll make him put it out, if you say you will," said Ken.

"I'd love to," replied Laura, following Ken to the table.

The two men stood as she approached. They introduced themselves and waited for her to sit.

"Miss Bogart's on vacation here for a while," said Ken to break the ice.

"That's right, but please call me Jane," replied Laura.

"Do you have anyone to show you around?" asked Steph.

"Are you offering?" asked Jane matter-of-factly.

"Well, I suppose I could. I mean, it's probably easier for you if you have someone who knows the area," replied Steph, flustered.

"What's there to see?" asked Laura as she leaned in towards Steph.

Steph rubbed his chin and looked up, in an internal panic, trying to think of suggestions. "Well there's Knott's Berry Farm, Disneyland, whale-watching in Newport. I could even give you a tour of the department." He struggled through every word. Of course he was doing his job by investigating this woman, but that didn't mean her beauty and confidence didn't make him nervous as hell.

"Department?" asked Laura in confusion.

"Oh, Steph here's the city's Chief of Police," said Ken.

"That's interesting. How about all of the above?" said Laura. She found his schoolboy nervousness cute and alluring, and spending time with the Chief of Police could end up with some surprising benefits.

"Uh, seriously? Yes, okay, all of the above," stuttered Steph, confused and delighted that she'd taken him up on his offer.

"You were in the Special Forces," she said.

Steph looked at his friends and then back to Laura. "Yes, how do you know?"

"Your watch," replied Laura as she reached across the table and gently tapped on his gold Rolex Mariner. Steph looked down at his watch. The face displayed the cross-arrowed crest of U.S. Army Special Forces with the motto *de oppresso liber* under it.

"Very observant, I'm impressed," he said.

"I try. When can I expect to begin employing your services as a tour guide?" asked Laura nonchalantly.

"How about tomorrow afternoon?" answered Steph without hesitation.

"Okay, shall we say one o'clock, lunchtime?"

"Sure," he said.

Laura took a black Parker pen from her clutch and wrote her phone number and address on a napkin, before placing it in Steph's hand and curling his fingers over it. She took a sip from her wine glass and placed the half-full glass back on the table. "Goodnight, gentlemen," she said as she stood.

"Leaving so early?" asked Ken.

"I have a lunch date tomorrow, and I need plenty of time to prepare." Laura made her way out the front door.

"She's hot as hell," said Mike.

"Yes, she is," replied Steph, with a large grin. He took a sip of Guinness, grabbed his bag, and left the bar.

"Kinda felt like we weren't even there during that little chat," said Mike.

Ken nodded.

Eight

Thursday, January 16, 1986

"WHAT THE FUCK ARE YOU WEARING?" ASKED MIKE.

"You might want to start knocking before bursting into my office," replied Steph, as he anxiously smoothed out his Tommy Bahama Hawaiian shirt with his hands. "What's wrong with what I'm wearing? I'm wearing the same thing as you."

"There's nothing wrong with it," said Mike with a shrug, "I'm just used to seeing you in that three-piece suit. Does this have something to do with that chick, Jane?"

"I'm picking her up at her place at one. I thought slacks and a Hawaiian shirt would be casual, but not *too* casual, if you know what I mean."

"I wouldn't be too worried. The chick probably just needs someone to marry her for a green card, or something. You could probably arrive in a tutu, and she wouldn't give a shit," said Mike.

"I'm gonna bring her here for a tour of the department later today, at about three. I need you to do me a favour," said Steph as he slid his .38 Special into his ankle holster and pulled his pant leg over it.

"Shoot," said Mike.

"I want you to make sure that Norton and Gazzano are here when she arrives. Tell them the evidence room needs organizing or something, anything; just make sure they're here."

"Will do."

Steph reached into his pocket and pulled out a small can of mint breath freshener and blasted two squirts into his mouth. "Wish me luck," he said as he walked out of the door, leaving Mike in his office.

He arrived in Huntington Harbor at twelve fifty-five, plucked the small bouquet of flowers he'd bought from 7-Eleven off the passenger seat, and checked his hair in the rear-view mirror. He got out of the car, brushed down his pants and shirt with his free hand, and walked towards the door. He paused for a few seconds, took a deep breath, and knocked lightly three times.

She answered the door seconds later. Her pristine, white shirt and pink sweater draped over her shoulders gave her a classy, preppy appearance, but her tight blue jeans accentuated her legs. The whole thing together oozed sex appeal.

He nervously held out the bouquet, almost punching her in the chest with it.

"Oh, how sweet," she said. She took the flowers, kissed him on the cheek, and placed the bouquet on the side table next to the door, before closing it.

"What do you want to do?" he asked.

"Tell you what, take me to one of your favourite places," she suggested, as she curled her arm under his and walked him out of the drive towards his car.

He opened the passenger door and waited until she was settled before closing it.

"Okay," he said, "I'm gonna take you to the place I go when I need to clear my head, but I warn you, it's not very exciting."

She nodded and took in the scenery. They drove through Sunset Beach, and Laura looked back at the vast array of Harley Davidsons as they sped past Mother's Bar. They turned left as they entered Seal Beach and parked in an empty lot by the beachfront.

Steph opened the door for her and held her hand as she stepped out of the car. He popped open the trunk and retrieved a wicker picnic basket and a plaid, woollen blanket. He slung the blanket over his shoulder and slammed the boot closed.

"It's just a short walk," he said. He took her by the hand and guided her along the beach path, towards lifeguard tower seven.

The beach was deserted. To their left was tower seven, to their right, a wall of rocks. They were concealed from any onlookers. There before them was the roaring Pacific Ocean. The only thing they could hear was the sound of the waves crashing onto the sand, a mere twenty feet away.

Steph dropped the heavy blanket and smoothed it down. He then placed the basket on a corner of the blanket and motioned for Laura to sit. He opened the hamper. "On the menu today, we have cheddar and blue cheese with crackers, cucumber sandwiches, and tea," he said, feigning the nearest thing to a British accent he could muster.

"How sweet," she laughed and held up a sandwich, "you've even taken the crusts off of the sandwiches and cut them into triangles."

"Cup of tea?" offered Steph as he held up a glass bottle of brown liquid.

"Of course."

He poured the liquid into a glass and handed it to her. She took a sip and winced. "It's cold," she said.

"It's tea, isn't it supposed to be cold?" he asked.

"No, it's meant to be piping hot, with a splash of cream," she answered, "but it's not bad at all, so I'll take it." She smiled before taking another sip.

"If you don't like it, you can try this instead." Steph retrieved a bottle of Moët from the basket.

Steph handed her two glass flutes, popped the cork from the bottle, and poured until the foam gushed over the lips of both glasses and onto Laura's knuckles. He placed the bottle upright in the basket and took one of the flutes from Laura. They clinked glasses and stared at each other as they took their first sip.

"This is lovely," she said, looking out into the ocean.

"*You're* lovely," replied Steph.

"I have a gift," said Laura.

"What's that?"

"I'm usually a good judge of character, and I can tell you're a good man."

"Thanks. I try. What are you doing here, Jane?"

"I'm working through a few things. My father died recently. He was my only real relative, apart from a few distant cousins. I'm here to just decompress for a while, I suppose."

"I'm sorry, Jane. Was it sudden?" Steph asked softly.

"Yes, very," Laura replied. "He was strong. He had many more years left in him."

"What happened, was it an accident or something?"

She paused. "I'd rather not talk about it right now."

Steph reached back and grabbed the bottle of Moët. He poured her another glass, and she smiled. "Are you trying to get me drunk?" she asked.

"No, just relaxed," he answered.

She downed the champagne, laid her head on his lap, and curled into a fetal position. She felt safe and relaxed around him. He was educated, intelligent, competent, and strong. She sensed that his strength went much deeper than his muscular frame. He was shorter than her by a good two inches, but when they were together, she could feel him tower over her. She wanted to trust him. She had to trust *someone*, but she also wanted to wait a bit before letting her guard down.

She thought about how he compared to Clive. Clive was a shell of a man. A trust fund child, fickle, and spiritually weak. He used his physical strength and wealth to dominate others. He was an opportunist, a braggart, whose life had been mapped out for him by his father. Steph, on the other hand, was self-made, accomplished, and had seen and experienced horrors beyond the imagination. He had used those experiences to grow his strength of character, to be empathetic and kind, to serve the needs of others before himself.

She liked him, but if they became close, she'd have to tell him everything. She'd have to tell him about her noble past, her traumatic childhood, her propensity for violence. Not to mention explaining her commitments as the Countess of Britewood—and her real name, to start.

He lightly stroked her hair. The sea breeze had become

cold, so he took off his lightweight Members Only wind-breaker and spread it over her, tucking it between her neck and shoulder. Within a few minutes, she was fast asleep.

"Jane," he said softly. "It's two forty-five. Let me give you a tour of the department."

"How long did I sleep?" she asked.

"You've been out for about an hour."

It felt strange for her to sleep in front of a relative stranger. She was usually guarded, even around her closest associates, but with Steph, she felt comfortable enough to relax, to sleep.

They stood. She put on her sweater, and Steph wrapped his jacket around her shoulders. She knew he was cold because of the goose bumps on his arms, but she loved that her comfort was more important to him than his own. She watched him gather the food, plates, and cutlery and fill the basket, before once again slinging the blanket over his shoulder and guiding her back to the car. They drove back along the Pacific Coast Highway and turned left onto Seal Beach Boulevard, arriving at the department in a matter of minutes. He parked in his designated space and opened the door for her as they entered the building.

Murphy stood as they entered. "Good afternoon, Chief. Ma'am," he said.

"Murphy, this is Jane. I'm gonna show her around," said Steph. "This is my office. It's a little small, but it serves its purpose."

"It's charming." She sat on the guest chair next to his desk.

"Let's go see the rest of the building," he said.

They walked into the pool, and instantly Steph saw a plume of grey smoke billowing from Singer's cubicle.

"Damn it, Mike, how many times do I have to tell you?"

Mike ignored Steph, put out his cigar, and stood up. "Good to see you again," he said as he held out his hand to Laura.

"The pleasure's all mine," said Laura, as she shook his hand firmly.

"Did you do that thing for me?" Steph asked.

"Yep, just as you requested," said Mike. "Now leave me, and let me enjoy my cigar in peace."

Steph scowled in his direction, and Laura laughed. "Come on," he said, "let me show you the evidence room." They walked towards the rear of the building. He took a key from his pocket and opened a door to the right.

"Hey, guys," said Steph as he approached Norton and Gazzano, who were busy sorting through boxes of old evidence.

They stood open-mouthed, in disbelief, when they saw Laura. "Chief. Ma'am," said Norton.

"Jane, this is Officer Matt Norton and Officer Juan Gazzano, two of Seal Beach's finest," said Steph, watching for a reaction from the officers.

"I believe we've met," said Laura, as she shook Norton's hand. *Norton, that's too close to "Horton" for me not to dislike him,* she thought, as she locked eyes with him.

"Yes, ma'am," said Norton as he forced a smile.

"And where are you from?" asked Laura, moving to Gazzano.

"Colombia," he said without a smile or handshake.

"This is where we keep the evidence from all the crimes in Seal Beach over the past thirty years. When we moved from City Hall last year, we had to bring all this stuff with us. Now I'm going to categorize it by date and get rid of anything over five years old," said Steph. "Who knows, we may even have an auction and give the proceeds to my buddy Roy Benavidez."

"What does he do?" asked Laura.

"He's a former Special Forces buddy of mine. He runs a home for troubled kids in New Mexico," replied Steph.

Laura turned and stared at Steph. *Does he know about Grangeview? Why would he mention a home for kids?*

"Let's move along and leave these guys to their work," said Steph. He slapped Norton on the back. Norton and Gazzano watched them until they left the room.

Steph took her to the holding cells next.

"This is where we keep the drunkards, so you better watch out." He winked at her.

"It's clean enough," she said. "Do you supply room service?"

"If you're lucky, you'll get McDonald's or even pizza," he answered with a grin.

"It might be worth my while to get three sheets to the wind one night," she said.

They walked through the dispatch office and the motor pool and chatted with a few of the civilian staff before going back into the main building, where Norton and Gazzano stood whispering to each other.

Steph and Laura approached Mike in his cubicle. "We're out of here," said Steph.

"Where 'ya goin'?" asked Mike.

"You want some dinner?" Steph asked Laura. "I know a swanky place."

"How could a girl resist such an offer?" replied Laura.

"You guys stay safe," said Mike as they left the building.

Steph drove the car into the parking lot next to the Harbor House. "We've arrived."

"This is your idea of a swanky restaurant?" she asked.

"Don't knock it till you've tried it," he answered. He opened the restaurant door for her, and the bell over the door rang.

"Just seat yourself, Chief," said the waitress, preparing a malt behind the counter.

"I'll grab my usual table," said Steph, as he led Laura to the furthest booth on the left, right beside the dessert fridge.

She sat in the corner of the booth and looked around the room. It was a quaint, old building, with movie posters and memorabilia covering the walls. The walls, floor, and ceiling were all made of stained wood and the booths were finished with fake red leather. The whole thing reminded her of an old train carriage. She picked up a menu and thumbed through the heavily laminated book. "Liver and onions," she said, surprised. "They serve that here?"

"Yep," said Steph.

"There's too much choice, just order for me," said Laura as she tucked the menu back behind the condiments.

"Will do," said Steph. "You know this place was opened two years before the start of the war in 1939?"

"Actually, it opened the year the war began. The war began in Europe in 1939."

Steph held up his hands. "You're right," he said, "I forgot for a second that you were from across the pond."

The waitress came to the table. "Coffee?" she asked.

"I'll have coffee, but she'll have hot tea," said Steph as he looked at Laura.

"Do I know you?" asked the waitress, staring at Laura.

"I don't think so," said Laura.

"You're from England. I love your accent," said the waitress. "My mom's from Manchester. I'm sure I've seen you before."

"What's your name?" asked Laura. "Mine's Jane."

"Good to meet you, Jane. I'm Susan," said the waitress.

"Do you go back to England often?" asked Laura.

"No, but my aunty sends me magazines from there every month. Look." Susan put her hand into her apron and pulled out a copy of the December issue of *British Vogue* and held it in front of Laura's face.

Laura stared for a few seconds. She'd been featured on the cover of the October issue and just prayed that the girl didn't go looking through her old copies.

"What are we having for dinner, Steph?" she asked, hoping to divert Susan's attention.

"New York steak, rare, with eggs over easy, hash browns, and wheat toast," said Steph.

"For both of you?" asked Susan as she wrote down the order.

"Yep," said Steph.

"Pleased to meet you," said Susan. "You're beautiful, by the way." And she left the table to put in their orders.

"Looks like you've made a new friend," said Steph.

"So it would appear," said Laura.

Laura looked over at Susan. *Damn it, I'll have to stay away from her,* she thought. *She might just break my cover.*

They ate their meal and laughed as they chatted. For a while, Laura forgot about her mission and lived in the moment, revelling in Steph's attention. *Is this how normal people live?*

she thought as she listened to him. *Maybe I could continue to live like this?* She looked straight into his deep, brown eyes.

"You wanna see my place?" said Steph, just before he took the last bite of his key lime cheesecake.

"Okay, but this is our first date, Steph," she said in a serious tone.

"I'm shocked that you would even consider that I'd take advantage," said Steph, feigning indignation.

Steph dropped two twenty-dollar bills onto the table, stood, and took Laura by the hand to help her out of the booth.

"How far is your house?" asked Laura.

"Not far at all," said Steph as they left the building and walked away from his car.

"Your car's back there," said Laura pointing back towards the lot.

"I know, but this is my house," he said as he walked past Turk's Bar and pointed up.

"You're kidding," said Laura, gazing up.

"It used to be a water tower," said Steph, "but over the last three months, I've been converting it into a house."

He took out a key and unlocked the door to the elevator, which was hidden between the riveted, iron beams holding the structure up. In seconds they were out on a balcony that circled the whole living space. From the patio door, she went straight into the living room.

"This is wonderful," she said as she sat on a burgundy leather couch.

The tower was a circular structure, with windows covering the entirety of the building. Everywhere you looked, there was a magnificent view.

"How far up are we?" she asked.

"Forty feet," said Steph, "which means we can see out, but no one can see in."

He sat beside her and touched her knee, moving towards her. They kissed, first lightly, then deeper. Everything about him felt right. But now was not the time to fall into a romance. She reminded herself that she had accepted this date to make a connection for her mission should she need one. Going any further with him could be a catastrophic distraction. She pulled away and looked him in the eyes. "Thank you for all of your hospitality today. You really made me feel welcome."

"The pleasure was all mine." He rubbed his hand gently across her cheek. "Should I take you home?"

"Probably," she bit her lip in frustration. She wanted to stay so much more than she wanted to leave. "What time is it?"

"It's nine forty-five," he answered. "Come on, let me take you home."

He walked her to her front door and leaned in to kiss her. She pulled him close and ran her fingers down his spine.

"Are we going to do this again?" he asked as he released his grip.

"I like you, Steph, but I'll need some time to sort my life out."

"I understand," he said. "If you need me, call." He handed her a business card.

He left her at the door and walked back to his car. She watched him as he drove away, before she entered the house and locked the door.

She felt a sudden, sharp throbbing on the back of her head, and everything went black. While she was regaining awareness, she sensed her left hand being tied to the post of her headboard. She instantly began to struggle and noticed a figure wearing what appeared to be a gas mask, pulling her right arm towards the opposite post. She felt strange and noticed the faint mist that had filled the room. She pulled her right hand back and reached behind the headboard. The figure punched her in the face and mounted her, jumping onto her hips. Her mind began to wander. She felt faint and sleepy, as if in a dream. He grabbed her around the neck and began to squeeze. The edges of her vision began to go black and the blackness filled her entire field of view. She went limp. A vision of Jenkins came into her mind's eye. He was in a white gi.

The vision got more and more vivid. She grabbed her assailant by the wrists, trapped his right leg with her left foot, and shot her hips up high, circling left, until she was on top of her attacker. She stripped the mask from his face and elbowed him in the jaw repeatedly, until he reached up and grabbed her face. He pushed her off the bed, and she hit the floor with a thud. He followed her and kicked her in the chest, head, and abdomen. She rolled into a ball as he continued to kick her. He reached down and grabbed her by the hair and threw her onto the bed. He smiled, wiping blood from his lip and looked at it on his fingers.

"You fucking bitch," he said as he walked closer again.

That voice, that accent—it's Gazzano, she thought as she strained to see his face through the mist.

She reached behind the headboard and grabbed the handgun. He rushed her and grabbed it, twisting it to point at her. With a shriek, she pulled away, turned it at him and pulled the trigger. Instantaneously, brain matter and blood splashed violently across her bathroom door as Gazzano's body dropped to the floor.

Laura ran to the bedroom windows and opened them, coughing as she did so. She raced around the house opening all the windows and then into the kitchen to turn off the air conditioner. The house was freezing cold. Maybe whatever the mist was emitting was from the vents. She ran to her bathroom, stood on the toilet, and reached for the vent. The screws to hold it in place had been removed. She pried it off the wall with her fingernails. She felt around inside until her fingers touched something solid. She grabbed the object and carefully pulled it out. It was a small brown cardboard cube covered with white powder. Five of its sides were riddled with holes. The sixth side was taped shut.

She searched the house, and in every vent she found a similar box. Using a scarf to cover her mouth and nose, she cleaned each vent thoroughly, ensuring that every speck of powder was gone. Next, she took all the boxes to the kitchen and wrapped them in Saran Wrap, put them all in a black trash bag, and took the bag to the garage. She searched the shelves for anything she could use. They were filled with clutter from former tenants. She grabbed a roll of trash bags, a three-pack of duct tape, a pair of old gardening gloves, and a rusty old handsaw.

She moved to her bedroom. Blood and brains dripped from the door leading to the bathroom. She opened the door and dragged the body onto the bathroom tile. She rolled a towel and placed it in the doorway, creating a barrier against any more bodily fluids seeping onto the bedroom carpet.

The gardening gloves were awkward but necessary. The scarf around her face was still secure, so she went to work. She began with the head. She sawed into the neck. The blade was dull and rusted, so it jammed multiple times, once against the trachea and numerous times against the spine. Eventually, she stood behind the body with one foot on a shoulder, and she grabbed him by the hair and pulled and twisted until the head broke free in her hands. She dropped it into a trash bag and wrapped it over and over in duct tape.

She repeated the process with each of the limbs, until all that was left was the torso, which she packaged the same way.

Laura carefully carried each body part down the stairs one package at a time, through the kitchen and into the garage. Finally, she stuffed them into the boot of her car. She slammed it shut and then searched the cupboards in the garage for cleaning supplies. She found a box of old rags, some paper towels, and a large bottle of bleach.

She inspected the bedroom walls for any sign of blood. Fortunately, the blood and brain matter covered only the door. The glossy paint made it easy enough to clean. The tile in the bathroom was next. The red mess wiped away with a little bleach and elbow grease, but it took a toothbrush to get the grout as white as it had been before.

The carpet at the entrance to the bathroom en suite was a different matter entirely. A large rectangle, about two feet across, was soaked in a thick, dark red, gloopy mess. Laura poured water and bleach over it and cleaned it vigorously with a scrubbing brush. By the time she finished, it was nothing more than a light pink patch.

She thought for a moment, then retrieved a small floral

rug from the living room. She placed it over the patch. It fit perfectly over the mess and actually blended quite well with the décor of her bedroom.

She walked into the bathroom and stripped off her clothes, stuffing them into a trash bag, along with the rags and paper towels she'd used during the clean-up. She tied it shut and turned on the shower. She stood under a torrent of water and relaxed for the first time since the kill. She was still shaken, but the hot water put her at ease.

As she was drying herself, she caught a glimpse of her face in the steamed mirror. She had a slight black eye and a fat lip. She pulled on her bathrobe and made her way to the kitchen. She grabbed a Ziploc bag from a drawer and a handful of ice from the freezer. She filled the bag and place it on her lip.

She walked into the living room and sat on the couch. She was exhausted and desperate for sleep. Tomorrow she'd have to dispose of the body somewhere, but for now, she was as safe as she could be. She climbed the stairs and slipped into bed, but not before placing the handgun under her pillow.

Nine

Friday, January 17, 1986

MIKE WAS ON THE PHONE AT HIS DESK WHEN STEPH
arrived.

"Gotta go, see you this afternoon," said Mike before he
hung up his phone receiver.

"Here," said Steph, handing Mike a Styrofoam coffee
cup, "follow me." Mike followed Steph into his office. "Close
the door and sit down." Mike did as he was told.

"Do you have anything on Norton and Gazzano yet?"
asked Steph.

"Kinda, yes," answered Mike.

"Well?"

"They weren't here for the briefing today."

"Neither of them?"

"Yes, the watch commander called them, but nobody
answered. They got the answering machine."

"That was at six, right?" asked Steph, checking his watch.
"It's ten now. If one of them doesn't arrive by midday, send
a unit to Norton's place."

"Will do," said Mike. "Need anything else?"

"Just keep me in the loop about those two."

"Thanks for the coffee," said Mike as he left the office.

Steph picked up the phone and called Laura. There was no answer. The answering machine picked up. "Good morning, Jane, this is Steph. I enjoyed last night and just wondered if you'd like to spend the weekend with me. Maybe we can go somewhere, like Catalina, or maybe we could take a ride up to Solvang. Anyway, just wanted to call. Hope to speak to you soon." He hoped this thing with Jane wouldn't just be a one-time date. He'd thought about her all night and couldn't sleep because of it. He thought about calling again. Maybe she was busy, or just couldn't get to the phone in time and missed the call by seconds.

Laura listened to Steph's voice on her answering machine. She desperately wanted to answer him. The chance of a weekend getaway was thrilling, but she had to stay disciplined and remember why she was here. Joe Byrne and the cop, Norton, were now her only two chances of her getting to the bottom of this. With Joe, she could kill two birds with one stone. He and his associate Danny Buckley were in some way connected to her father's murder. One of them could've pulled the trigger. If she could just capture one of them, she knew she could make him talk.

She walked to her dressing room and sat at her dresser. Her lip had shrunk to its usual size, and the purple colour under her eye could easily be disguised with concealer.

She left the house via the front door. She looked down to the end of the street and noticed the transit van parked next to a silver BMW 3 Series. She opened her garage and pulled out into the driveway. She got out of the car and closed the garage door, all the while staring in the direction of the van, which was in its usual spot. *They know I'm here, and I want them to know I know,* she thought as she climbed back into her vehicle. She drove into Seal Beach and parked directly outside Sullivan's Pub. The van followed close behind and parked across the street in Hennessy's parking lot.

As she strolled into the pub, she looked around the room. It was empty, apart from one man sitting at the far corner of the bar. He was familiar—he'd been there on her previous visits.

Ken stepped out from the kitchen when he heard the door open and close.

"Good morning, Jane," he said in his usual, cheery manner. "What can I get you?"

"Has Officer Norton been here today?" she asked, taking a seat at the bar.

"No," said Ken as he turned and looked momentarily at Joe, who was staring at Jane.

Laura turned slightly and faced Joe. "Good morning," she said.

Joe got up from his stool, walked towards Laura, and sat to her immediate left. "Good morning, and who might you be?" he asked.

"I'm Jane. Is that a Northern Irish accent I hear?" She stared directly at him.

"It is," he said with a smile. "Is that an upper-crust British accent?"

"It is." She smiled back at him.

"Isn't it a little dangerous for a wee thing like you to be over here all alone?" He moved in closer.

"Who said I was alone?" She moved towards him.

They sat nose to nose for a few seconds, until Joe stuck out his hand. "Derek Wiggins," he said. She ignored his hand and stared straight ahead.

Ken glanced back and forth at the two of them. "Is everything okay here?" he asked.

"No, Ken, it's not. Could you please leave us alone for a few minutes?" Laura requested.

"No," said Joe, looking at Ken. "Stay right there." He pulled a Beretta nine-millimetre handgun from his leather jacket and pointed it upward, as if ready to direct it at either of them.

"Put your hands on the bar," he ordered, and both Ken and Laura did as they were told.

He pulled Laura's handbag from the hook under the bar and emptied it on the floor. Makeup, gloves, a compact, and a Browning handgun fell and clattered onto the tile. He moved towards the door, locked it, and turned the sign from *open* to *closed*.

"Get out here," he said to Ken. Ken lifted the gate to the bar, stepped out, and stood next to Laura. "Over there!" He motioned to a table in the corner, which could not be seen from the window. "Sit down and keep your hands on the table where I can see them."

"What the hell's going on?" demanded Ken.

"My name's not Derek Wiggins, and this woman isn't Jane," he said, staring at Ken.

"This is fucking crazy," said Ken as he shook his head. "What the fuck does this have to do with me?" Panic was evident in his voice.

"Nothing, until I saw you with the chief and his detective buddy the other night. I heard some of your conversation and have come to the conclusion that they don't know anything about this."

"About what?" asked Ken.

"This is IRA bigwig Joe Byrne," said Laura, sarcastically. "He's gone from blowing up buildings in London to supplying children to high-profile paedophiles here in the good old USA. Not to mention the small business of killing my dad."

"Shut the fuck up!" screamed Joe, as he pushed the muzzle of the weapon into her forehead.

"Go on, Joe, kill me. This is the end of the line for you anyway, you may as well take us all with you," she calmly said as she smiled in his face.

"Holy shit," said Ken.

"I didn't kill your daddy. I don't even know who did," said Joe.

Laura laughed. "You should start telling the truth, Joe. Either you or your partner Danny Buckley killed my father. As for what you've done to the kids, I don't know how you can live with yourself."

The mention of children seemed to disturb Joe. His eye began to twitch.

"You're a predator, Joe, the worst of the worst. What kind of a monster does such things?"

Joe began to shake uncontrollably. He sat down, closed his eyes, and began to cry. "Dear God, what have I done?" he sobbed.

"You pathetic little shit," said Laura, in disgust.

"It's over for me, I know," he said. "Just let me tell you the truth, and I swear, I'll kill myself right afterwards, here at the table."

"Just do it now, you lying bastard," said Laura, leaning forward.

Joe put the muzzle of the gun into his mouth and placed his finger on the trigger.

"No!" shouted Ken. "Just talk to us. She might not want to hear it, but I do."

"Do it," said Laura, "kill yourself and save me the hassle of disposing of your body."

"Shut the fuck up," said Ken in anger. "Who in the fuck are you anyway?"

Joe began to laugh. It was a maniacal laugh, so strange that both Laura and Ken dropped their vitriolic tone and stared at him. "She's the Lady Laura Lacy, the daughter of Henry Lacy, Earl of Britewood."

"Not anymore, my father's dead, and you're to blame!" screamed Laura.

"The night your father was murdered," began Joe, "Danny called me. He told me your father had been found murdered and that Sir Giles Gessup had also been murdered. He thought he was next. Danny was a friend; we've been through a lot together. He told me he had to leave and never come back.

"He asked me if I could get some money and a weapon for him. I agreed and asked him to meet me in a safe house in Chapeltown. When he arrived, he broke down. He told me that he'd been working for the Secret Intelligence Service, MI6. He told me how he'd done it to protect our organization. He told me about Gessup arranging for kids to be kidnapped and taken to America to be abused and sometimes murdered by high-profile politicians and diplomats. He told me that these acts were filmed and used as leverage by British Intelligence and the corporation that helped them over here in the States. They'd brought him to California, using a false name on a diplomatic passport and filmed him doing terrible things to children, things that he couldn't help doing, and he didn't know why. He told me that the haze in the room made him do it. He wasn't making sense at that point, he was hysterical.

"He told me the name of his contact in MI6, Sebastian Davenport, and when he told me what I needed to know, I killed him with my bare hands. I couldn't help it. I punched him off his chair until he was on the ground, and I continued to punch him until his face was just a bloody hole in his head.

"I knew Davenport died with your dad, so I used various channels to contact the new director, Sir Geoffrey Marsden. I made up a bullshit story about Danny leaving and asking me to take his place, and they bought it. I thought I could stop them, but within a day of being here, I was taken to a place far away, up in the snow, and I did unspeakable things to a young girl. God, it comes back to me in flashes every night, and I can't understand why I did those things. But when Danny told me that the haze made him do it, he was right, because the haze made me do it."

Joe put the gun in his mouth and once again placed his finger on the trigger. Laura thought about the incident the night before. *The haze,* she thought, *the haze.*

She leapt across the table and knocked the gun from Joe's hand. He was lying on the floor with Laura on top of him. Ken jumped away from the table. Laura grabbed Joe by the lapels and faced him directly. "Is Officer Norton involved with this little caper?" she asked.

"Yes, and his partner, Juan Gazzano," replied Joe through tears.

Laura jumped to her feet and ran to the door. "Wait here," she ordered, and the door slammed shut behind her. The two men just stared at one another in shock. Joe on his back and Ken on his feet, both unable to move.

Laura returned with what looked like a soccer ball wrapped in black plastic. She tore the plastic open and held up Juan's head by the hair. "This little shit tried to murder me in my house last night. After I killed the bastard, I noticed there was a haze in every room."

Ken ran to the trashcan behind the bar and vomited into it. He groaned as he grabbed the sides of the can. Joe just continued to lie there in shock. Ken grabbed a trash bag and held it open in front of Laura. She nonchalantly dropped the head in the bag, and Ken tied it shut and held it with his arm extended and dropped it into the garbage.

Joe crawled to his knees and sat on his chair at the table. He bowed his head and wept. Laura pulled her chair up to sit across from him. She crossed her legs and began to drum her fingers on the table. Ken stood at the bar and steadied himself by holding onto the top of it as his knees slightly trembled.

Laura composed herself. "I believe you," she said without emotion. "I can't believe I'm saying this, but we're going to have to work together to defeat these bastards."

Joe rubbed his eyes. "Are you serious?" he asked.

"Unfortunately, yes," she replied.

"It would seem that I know too much now," said Ken. "Looks like you'll either have to accept my help or kill me."

"What now?" said Joe.

"Now we tell Steph and Mike," said Ken.

"What if they're involved?" asked Laura.

"They're not," replied Ken. "I've known those hard-chargin' motherfuckers for just over twenty years and can tell you that they're the good guys."

"I was hoping you'd say that," said Laura.

"My handlers are expecting me to kill you," Joe said to Laura.

"Best of luck with that, Joe." Laura smiled and patted him on the cheek.

"I'll call Steph," said Ken. "Joe, stay there, and don't do anything stupid. Jane, Laura, or whatever-the-fuck-your-name-is, when I'm done calling Steph, we'll take that piece of Juan out of the trash and put it in your trunk. Now, come with me."

Ken made his way behind the bar and walked into the small office at the rear of the building. Laura followed. He grabbed the phone receiver and dialled Steph. Laura pushed her head close to the receiver.

"Hello, Steph Angelo."

"It's me, Ken. We need to meet, like, now," said Ken, obviously flustered.

"Calm down, buddy. What's going on?" asked Steph.

"That woman, Jane . . . she's not Jane at all. She's Laura, I mean, she's Lady Laura, some British aristocrat or something. She's in trouble, I mean real trouble, and . . ."

"Ken, stop, you're not making sense," said Steph.

"Okay," said Ken, breathing deeply to calm himself, "let's just meet, but you've got to know a few things before you do."

"Go on," said Steph.

"Your officer, Juan Gazzano, tried to kill her last night and failed miserably."

"What the fuck?"

"Yes, he failed so miserably that his body is now in her trunk, and, just a few minutes ago, she brought his head into the bar to show us."

"Holy Christ!"

"No shit. And that guy Derek from Ireland is not Derek at all. His name's Joe, and he's some IRA mobster, who's apparently been sent to kill the broad."

"Is he there?"

"Yes, they're both here in the bar."

"What the hell?"

"It's okay. He had no intention of killing her. Just meet us at Harbor House in twenty minutes, and bring Mike."

Ken put down the receiver and looked at Laura. "Did you really need that conversation to be so candid?" Laura asked.

"It's best to just put it all out there. Steph's a good guy. He'll do the right thing. Trust me."

The bald man didn't take his eyes away from his *People* magazine as Matt Norton walked past the receptionist and through the stainless-steel doors. Ron Beck sat behind his desk wearing a salmon-coloured Pringle's polo shirt and blue, plaid pants.

"Where the fuck have you been? Where's that fucking Spic partner of yours, and is *she* either on board or dead?" demanded Ron.

"Sir, I tried to tell Juan not to approach her by himself, but . . ." stammered Matt.

"Where the fuck is he?"

"I don't know, sir."

"I know where he is. He's probably in a shallow grave," said a voice coming from the far corner of the room. Geoffrey walked towards the desk. "I told both of you not to approach her alone, ever." He pulled a chair to the side of Ron's desk and sat down.

"He told me he was just going to talk to her and use his stuff," said Matt nervously.

"Why didn't you go with him?" asked Geoffrey, so calmly that his voice was almost hypnotic.

"I was on a date with a chick from Orange Coast College. I told him to wait, but he wanted to . . ."

"You went on a date," Geoffrey said through a forced smile. "I think your use to us is coming to an end, Matt."

"No, sir, I can still be useful," said Matt in a panic. "What do I need to do to make this right?"

"We can now be certain that Lady Laura has no intention of joining us in this operation, and she's placed her own feelings ahead of Great Britain. I want her dead, Matt. And if you're unwilling to kill her, our friend outside will be happy to do so, immediately after killing you. Am I understood?"

Matt nodded. The fear was evident in his posture.

"Our friend, Joe, was given a job or two yesterday and doesn't seem to have done it yet. Now he's gone missing. You don't want what's going to happen to him to happen to you, Matt. Now, leave us and get the job done," said Ron as he flicked his hand towards the door.

Matt left the room.

"You guys told me that this shit would go smoothly and that you'd learned from your mistakes on the island of

Jersey. I should've quit this shit when that one-eyed fool Davenport got himself killed," said Ron as he looked directly at Geoffrey.

"You've got leverage on many in the highest echelons of the state and Federal government. You've made hundreds of millions of dollars from those people issuing your licences, granting planning permission, and excusing your tax debts. Those assets come with a price, Ron. You're as expendable as our friend Matt. There's nowhere for you to turn. We own you now. Remember this, my friend," said Geoffrey.

He walked out of the office and slammed the door shut, leaving Ron alone with his mouth agape.

Laura, Ken, and Joe pulled into the car park of Harbor House. They exited the car, and Laura walked clockwise around the building clutching her gun inside her handbag. Ken walked counter-clockwise, keeping close to the building and ducking beneath the windows. Joe kept watch from the rear seat of the car, scanning the environment for unwelcome visitors.

When they were certain the coast was clear, they entered through the front door. There was no one to greet them, and Steph's usual table by the dessert fridge was taken by a group of high school girls. They continued to the back of the restaurant. The room was filled with large, circular tables, surrounded by plastic patio chairs. The tables were occupied by a variety of groups, none of which appeared to be a threat. Steph and Mike were sitting at the closest table to the rear fire exit.

"We're over here," said Mike, waving at them.

"Thank Christ," said Ken. "Maybe we can start making sense of this shit."

Laura sat next to Steph and squeezed his hand under the table. "How're you doing, *Laura*?" he said as they locked eyes.

Steph lifted a magazine off his lap and threw it on the table. It was the October issue of *British Vogue*, with her portrait on the cover accompanied by the bold headline, "The Elegant Style of the Lady Laura."

"I'm sorry, Steph," she said. "I had to maintain my cover for as long as possible." She squeezed his hand, pulled him close, and whispered in his ear, "It's okay if you want to back out now. I'd understand."

Steph squeezed her hand affectionately, turned to her, and winked. "I was ready for a change," he said, "be careful what you ask for . . ."

Susan approached the table and curtsied. "I knew it was you, Lady Laura; right after you left, I checked my magazines. It was the blond hair that threw me off," she said. "Can I get you any drinks to start with?"

"No need to curtsy, Susan, we're in America now," said Laura with a smile. "Steph will have coffee, and Joe and I will have hot tea, please. Oh, and here's your magazine," said Laura as she handed it back.

Steph and Mike listened as Laura and Joe told them everything they'd discussed earlier.

"Ron Beck's a powerful man," said Steph. "He owns the Newport Company. That makes him the biggest land-owner in Southern California."

"Sir Geoffrey's no pushover, either," said Laura. "He

served as a senior officer in the Special Air Service and had been an Operations Officer in MI6 for over twenty years, before being promoted to C."

"This is serious shit," said Ken. "Why can't we just turn this over to the FBI? A foreign power's working on U.S. soil, raping and killing kids, all while conducting an operation to bribe high-ranking politicians, and an American corporation's aiding and abetting them for financial gain and leverage. Surely they'd listen."

"We don't know who else is involved in this, Ken," said Steph. "Two of my officers are involved, and before today, we were clueless. Who knows who they've got on the payroll? If we tell anyone else, we could be signing our death warrants."

At that moment, everyone seated around the table who hadn't already figured it out, realized they were in danger— not only them, but their families, friends, and acquaintances.

Mike was usually upbeat, but when he broke the silence, his voice was dull and sombre. He stared into the corner of the room, as if in a trance. His affect was so strange and yet soft that everyone at the table listened.

"During my first tour of Nam with the Corps," he began, "my unit was assigned to the Agency, in Da Nang, as a security detail. One of the spooks was an expert in making people talk and do things that no one in their right mind would do. He was always well-dressed in a white shirt and beige slacks. But, more than anything, I remember the Panama hat he used to wear. He was always smiling. It was demonic. He seemed to really enjoy his work. The Army Corps of engineers set up this tent for him, a big tent, like in the circus. We were told to never go in there, and none of us wanted to. We'd seen and experienced some horrific shit over there, but when we heard the screams, moans, and laughter—yes, this cackling, horrible laughter, like the devil or some shit—even we were scared.

"Anyway, one day, we're playin' Texas Hold 'Em to pass the time, but we had nothin' to bet with, so the bets became dares, and the dares start gettin' more and more stupid. One guy loses a hand and has to play Russian Roulette, with one round in a revolver, that kind of thing. Then I lose a round. The guys look at each other and then one of 'em tells me to go in the tent. I laugh and tell him to go fuck himself. I even offered to do the Russian Roulette thing, but they all insisted."

Mike's face was expressionless. His voice became quiet, almost a whisper. "Anyway, I didn't want 'em to think I was some kind a pussy, so I went into that tent. Man, just thinkin' about it now gives me the creeps. I opened the canvass door, and the first thing that hit me was the mist, this fine haze fillin' the tent. No one even noticed I was there. There were all these men wearin' gas masks, six or seven of them, watchin' . . . just watchin.' I pulled my gas mask from my belt, blew into the filters to clear it, and put it on.

"I noticed him, because he was wearin' that hat. There was a prisoner tied to a chair who was bein' interrogated, just talkin' calmly as some dude asked him questions, but the other guy still gives me nightmares. The prisoners stood there naked. Hat Guy's talking to one of them in English through a translator. Hat Guy's voice is muffled, and so is the translator's, because of the gas masks, but I could still hear what he was saying. He hands the prisoner this blade, like a razor, and tells him to slice off his own nipple. He does it without question. He just looks down and slices his nipple off, like he was peeling an apple or some shit. Hat

Guy then asks him to cut off his own scalp. He does that too! No question, or emotion, or any hint of pain. He just grabs his own hair at the front with one hand and cuts into his own fuckin' scalp. He's pullin' and slicin' and cuttin,' and he keeps goin' until his scalp is clean off his head. The sound it made as it tore was terrifyin.'

"Anyway, I'm standin' there petrified. I couldn't even move; I was so scared. The last thing he told him to do, before I left, was to cut off his own dick. Within just a few seconds, he was holdin' it in his hand, just emotionless.

"I turned around and walked as calmly as I could out of the tent. When I got back to the guys, I just sat there. To this day, I've never told anyone else about that, but now it's time. You know why?"

"Why?" asked Steph.

"Well, when I was talking to one of the Agency guys, I asked him what that mist was. He told me that it was called Burundanga."

"What the hell's that?"

"They call it 'The Devil's Breath' in English. It contains a drug called scopolamine. When it's inhaled, the drug can be used to make people compliant. Under the right circumstances, it can make people do terrible things. It's found in Bogotá. That's why they were using Hat Guy. He was from Colombia, and he'd been using the shit for years with the criminal underground, to make people do despicable things."

"Juan Gazzano," murmured Steph.

"Exactly," said Mike.

"He could hardly speak English, and the guy I replaced as Chief, Pat Rooney, hired him. Then Rooney, out of the blue, kills himself. You see," said Steph as he looked around the table, "we can't trust anyone who's not at this table."

"Joe," said Ken, "you're not to blame for anything you did while under the influence of that Colombian shit, whatever it's called."

Joe nodded, and Ken put his hand on his shoulder. "You came here to put all this right, so this is your chance."

"So, what now?" asked Joe.

"Now we move to a place that's not so public," said Laura. "We devise a plan, save as many of those kids as we can, and destroy these evil fuckers."

"There's still the matter of the body in the trunk," Ken interjected.

"The Pacific Ocean's a huge place," said Steph with a smile.

"I have all we need at my place," said Laura, "but someone's been following me in a white transit van. When we left the bar on the way here, it was nowhere in sight, but mark my words, it'll be outside the house when we get there."

"Let's pay 'em a visit," said Mike.

"What do you mean?" asked Laura.

"We'll approach the van, badge 'em, and tell 'em we had a report of a suspicious van in the neighbourhood."

"Can you do that?" asked Laura.

"We got a dead cop, a cop working for a sex-trafficking ring, an IRA terrorist, and a killer aristocrat. Right now, I think we've pretty much crossed the line of doing anything," Mike replied.

"Let's get out of here," ordered Steph, and everyone stood and made their way to the door.

"I have your drinks here," said Susan.

"Here." Steph threw a twenty-dollar bill onto the table. "Gotta run."

As they arrived at Laura's house, she pointed to the van. "Mike, come with me," Steph said as he sprung from the car. Mike followed as they sprinted towards the van with their weapons drawn.

Laura pulled into the driveway and watched the spectacle from her rear-view mirror, as Ken and Joe twisted their necks to see the action.

"Get the fuck out of the van," said Steph to the driver as Mike pulled at the handle of the rear sliding door.

The rear door opened, and Mike was instantly dragged inside. Two men in ski masks ran to the front of the vehicle, disarmed Steph, dragged him to the side of the van, and yanked him inside, slamming the door. The van screeched away from the curb and out of sight.

Ken exited the car and ran in the direction of the van, followed closely by Laura and Joe, until they realized their foot pursuit was useless.

They'd spent hours driving around the neighbourhood, trying to find the slightest hint of where the van could've gone. It was dark. By the time they had returned to Laura's house, they were exhausted. Laura pulled into the garage. Joe leapt from the rear door as the car was still moving and pulled down the garage door, as the rear fending entered.

"Don't turn on the lights, and stay away from the windows," said Joe.

"We can't stay here," said Ken as he flopped onto the couch, "They'll come back for us?"

"I've seen the van at the pub, and if it's Marsden's crew, they know where Joe lives," said Laura.

"What about Steph's pad?" said Joe.

"No," said Laura, shaking her head, "he lives in the water tower. If they find us there, we've got no way of getting out. Anyway, they have him, and when he talks, if he's not already dead, they'll know where he lives, and it'll be the next place they look after our homes."

"Steph won't talk," said Ken.

"Everyone talks when the right buttons are pushed," said Laura without hesitation.

"She's right," said Joe, "her kind have been making my kind talk for centuries."

Laura rolled her eyes. "There's something odd about the van thing," she said.

"What do you mean?" said Ken.

"They've been watching me since I got here. They follow me everywhere, and it's only when they're approached by Steph and Mike that they make a move. I mean, why didn't they just move on us all, while they had the chance? If you were sent to kill me, Joe, and if they're with Marsden, then why wouldn't they have killed me by now?"

"What if you have something they need?" said Ken.

"Then they could've tortured whatever it is out of her, like her people did to mine," said Joe with a knowing smile.

"Will you please shut up?" Laura retorted. "Your lamentations are so distracting."

"Okay, we'll stay here," said Ken, "but we'll need weapons. I've got my .38 special, you've got the Beretta, but Joe here's got nothing."

"Ah, gentlemen," said Laura, "I think it's time I showed you my shed. Follow me."

Laura turned the key and pushed on the door. She flipped a switch and a single one-hundred-watt bulb lit up from a cord fixture. She ushered the guys in and closed the door behind them.

"Holy fuck," said Joe as he looked around the room, "this isn't a shed, it's a fucking armoury."

"Where did you get all this?" asked Ken as his eyes widened in disbelief.

"It's all originally part of Her Majesty's arsenal," said Laura as she pulled an HK MP5 from the wall and performed a function check.

"I'll take this," said Joe as he took a Beretta off the wall and stripped the magazine from the magazine well, "Where's the ammo?"

Laura pulled out the ammo cases from under the workstation.

"We've got enough here to take down Cuba," said Ken.

"Here, hold this open," said Laura as she handed Joe a large, black trash bag. She filled it with weapons. Knives, rifles, handguns, even frag grenades were thrown in. Next, she handed a box of assorted magazines to Ken. "Let's get these to the house and then start moving the ammo," she ordered, and the men followed her lead.

Over the next few hours, they sorted out their kit, filled magazines with ammo, and fitted slings to their rifles.

She watched their handling skills. Ken seemed a bit out of practice, but he still knew his way around the equipment, and the more he did, the more it seemed to come back to him. Joe looked like a seasoned professional.

"Where did you learn soldiering, Joe?" she asked nonchalantly.

"Libya, at the expense of Gaddafi," said Joe, without looking up from his weapon.

"No one is to go anywhere without their weapon, not even the toilet," said Laura.

"Aye, Captain," said Ken, as he threw up an exaggerated, British-style salute.

"We need to know where they took you, the place in the snow," ordered Laura to Joe.

"They had my head covered the whole drive up there."

"How long did the journey take?" asked Ken.

"About an hour and forty-five minutes," said Joe.

"Where did you start from?" asked Ken.

"The In-N-Out burger in Westminster. I know that we went straight onto the freeway."

"That's the 405 North," said Ken. "Were there any stops on the way?"

"We stopped once, about two miles into the journey, and then two or three times before we began ascending."

Laura ran into the garage and came back with her Thomas Guide.

"You stopped once, about two miles in. Did you go left, right, or straight after the stop?" asked Ken.

"Straight," said Joe without hesitation.

"Let me just check the guide." Laura flipped frantically through the book.

"No need," said Ken. "If they stopped at a light two miles into their journey on the 405 North from Westminster Boulevard and then went straight, it has to be the light at the entrance of the 22 East. What then, Joe? Any turns, stops, anything?"

"No," said Joe, searching his head for answers. "I know that we moved into the fast lane and just stayed there for about an hour."

"If you stayed in the fast lane, then odds are you just carried on to the 55 Freeway and then the 215. Laura, give me the book," said Ken as he snatched the guide from Laura's hand and then flicked through the pages.

"Do you remember anything else about the journey?" asked Ken without taking his eyes off the guide.

"After about an hour on the freeway, we stopped for just a few minutes, turned left, then stopped two or three times again, after only a few minutes before we began to climb. My mind was foggy, but I tried to pay attention and count as many stops as I could."

Ken placed the guide on the coffee table as all three of them gathered around it. "How long was the drive from the bottom of the climb to your destination?"

"About twenty minutes, but I can't be sure. I can tell you that it was a winding road and we were driving like a bat out of hell, because I kept banging my head on the car roof."

"Got it," said Ken, looking up at Joe. "Look, if you guys followed the 215 to the 210, then exited the freeway at Waterman, you'd have to turn left and potentially stop at four lights before ascending the mountain at Highway 22." Ken dragged his finger along the lines on the map. Laura and Joe looked at each other and nodded.

"What do you think?" asked Laura.

"Sounds good," replied Joe.

"Will you be able to recognize the place when we get there?" asked Ken.

"How could I ever forget?" Tears welled up in Joe's eyes.

"We're gonna make this right, Joe," said Ken as he stood and grabbed him by the shoulders. "We're gonna make them pay for this, for everything. Then we're gonna find Steph and Mike. One way or another, Joe, we're gonna make this right."

"Enough of the theatrics," said Laura. "We need a plan, but to start with, one of us will need to watch the street from the window of the bedroom upstairs. It's the only direction they can attack from, given the fact that we have the harbour to the rear. We'll do two-hour shifts in rotation. Joe, take the first shift."

"I can't believe I'm taking orders from a British aristocrat," said Joe as he shook his head and wandered into the hallway and up the staircase.

"First thing's first," said Laura. "How are we going to explain your absence at the pub?"

"I've been known to go missing for days. The staff will take care of business. They'll probably enjoy the fact that I'm not there looking over their shoulders."

"Good, we've got to make things appear as normal as possible."

"We're good on that front," said Ken.

"Shall we start with Beck?" asked Laura.

"He's heavily guarded and probably knows you're onto him. I say we just take this hellhole in the mountain down. After all, the kids up there are being tortured, and the longer we leave it, the longer they suffer. Besides, if we go after Beck, they'll probably close the place down and relocate the whole operation. Right now, we've got a good idea of where they are. I say we just head up there and take the place down," Ken declared.

"Well, you would say that—you're a marine," said Laura with a grin. "If we're going to do this, we need to do some reconnaissance on the place. The only way we can do that is to actually find it."

"I agree. We can stay around Lake Spearhead. There are plenty of hotels and quaint resorts. We might have to go undercover as a married couple, though. You might just have to choose between me and Joe, so who's it gonna be?"

"Funny," replied Laura. "Joe and I are allies on this little operation, but make no mistake, we are not friends. I'm still not even sure if he's lying about not having a hand in my father's death."

"So I'm it, then. You know we'll have to share a bedroom, to make the whole thing look more believable?"

"Why isn't a man like you married anyway?" asked Laura.

"She passed away three years ago. Brain tumour."

"I'm sorry, Ken," said Laura as she reached over and touched his knee.

"That's all right," said Ken, trying to force a smile. "She was in so much pain. The end was quite a relief. What about you?" he asked. "I thought all British blue bloods married, just to have kids to carry on the family traditions."

"There are, many things about me, many anomalies that I have to resolve before I get serious with anyone. Anyway, I may have to bite the bullet and marry my father's successor, whomever that may be, so as not to lose Britewood."

"We don't know if he's even alive right now but Steph's a good guy, and smart. You could do a lot worse."

"And he could do better," said Laura. "Come on, we need to get supplies: ski jackets, binoculars, boots, that kind of thing, before we head up the mountain."

"Okay," said Ken. "Let's load up the car and sleep here for the night. Tomorrow morning, we'll stop off at Big Five Sporting Goods, on the corner of Golden West and Bolsa, to pick up supplies. The freeway's right next to it."

Ken drove, with Laura riding shotgun and Joe in the back. They all prayed they wouldn't get caught at a routine traffic stop. After all, it'd be hard to explain away the hardware they were carrying in the trunk.

After over an hour on the freeway, they exited on Waterman and stopped at a Chevron to fill the tank. Ken took the Thomas Guide in and approached the teller, who was busy filing her nails and seemed oblivious to his presence.

"Excuse me," said Ken.

"Yep," said the teller, as her eyes remained fixed on her nails. Madonna's "Like a Virgin" blasted from her portable radio.

"Can I get fifteen bucks on three and some directions?" asked Ken, as he smiled sarcastically.

"What d'ya want to know?" she asked as she rolled her eyes and placed the file on the counter.

"I'm looking for a place up here, around this area," he said as he circled a spot with his finger on the map.

"My mom lives up there. What are you looking for?"

"Some kind of a resort, or conference centre. Some place where people stay, kind of a swanky place."

"Well, between the turnoff to Crestline and Arrowhead,

there are a few places. There's a couple of church retreats. That used to be one of them, but it changed owners a few years ago. It's supposed to be really nice, but none of the locals are allowed anywhere near the place. It used to be called Pinegrove, but the name's changed."

Laura saw Ken throw some money on the counter and run out of the door and into the car, slamming the car door in excitement.

"Look at this," he said as he pointed to a page in the guide and explained what the girl had just told him. "When the new guys bought it, they changed its name. You know what it's called now?"

"I wait with bated breath. Just tell me," said Laura in frustration.

"Britewood."

"You're kidding," said Joe from the back seat.

"Those fucking bastards!" screamed Laura as she hammered her fists on the dashboard. "I'll kill them. I'll kill their families and everyone associated with them."

Both men sat back and stared in horror.

Laura composed herself and combed back her hair with her hands. "Just drive, Ken," she said. "Just get us to a suitable hotel. I'm going to need some time to process this."

They drove up the winding road. The farther they went, the more detached from civilization they became. The vegetation became thicker. Evergreens and oak trees lined the road, and as they ascended, the stunning mountains came into view.

Laura's thoughts overwhelmed her. *Did Father name this vile place, and if so, was he involved? Did he devise this demonic enterprise? Did he himself take pleasure in the bodies of innocents?* The thoughts played over in her head, like a depressing mantra.

They passed the turn towards Crestline, turned left onto Lake Martin Drive and an immediate right onto Highway 229. The road became narrower and the brush thickened. A slight dusting of snow covered the treetops. The whole thing reminded her of the Swiss Alps.

"That's it. That's the place!" said Joe, his voice a mixture of excitement and horror. He dropped down into the back seat to hide himself from unwanted attention. As they drove by, Laura made a note of the features of the buildings and the signs, which read "Britewood" and "Trespassers Will Be Prosecuted."

"Keep driving," said Laura, as she pointed to a page in the guide. "Let's get to Arrowhead, find a place to stay, and come up with a plan to take these bastards down."

They had no problem finding a suitable accommodation. They opted for Montpellier, a small resort made up of chalets, similar to the Alpine cabins she'd often stayed in during her trips to the Swiss Alps. Ken checked them in and paid cash for a triple occupancy cabin nestled away at the back of the resort. It was perfect for their operational needs.

Laura stood at the entrance to the cabin and watched from its porch, while the men emptied the trunk.

"We need one of us on watch at all times," said Laura.

"I'll take first watch," said Ken. He closed the curtains, grabbed a chair from a writing desk, and sat by the window, making use of a slight crack in the curtains to watch for any sign of an assault.

Laura stripped down to her underwear. Joe stared at her body and didn't even hide the fact that he was watching. She grabbed a set of navy blue overalls and began to pull them on over her legs. "What's the matter, Joe, never seen a woman's body before?"

"Yes, but never one as impressive as that. You must have a lot of time on your hands to maintain those legs," he replied. "And what's with all the scars?"

"I suppose I'm accident-prone," she said.

"Women like you don't have those kinds of accidents. All the tactical knowledge, the scars, the attitude, and the body . . . if I had to take a guess, I'd say that your daddy's regiment had been using you in some capacity, but then again, what does a thick Paddy like me know?"

Laura didn't respond, she just threw a pair of overalls at Joe. He stripped to his underwear and pulled them on. "Well, look at this, we're even wearing the same uniform. I think you and I have done more for Anglo-Irish relations in the past ten minutes than the British government and Sinn Fein have in twenty years," he said as he winked at her.

Laura rolled her eyes and took three gas masks from a cloth bag. "Test this," she said, as she threw one at him.

"Yes, ma'am," he said, before pulling his mask over his head, blowing the excess air out of it, putting his hand over the external filter and attempting to suck air through it. He pulled it off of his head and threw it on the couch. "This one's good," he said.

"Can you remember anything about the building?" asked Laura.

"There's one central building, like a hotel. It has a downstairs lobby and one set of stairs to the guest rooms.

That's all I remember about the structure. There are probably some other buildings on the property, but I know one thing: it's obviously fortified and during that drive-by today, I noticed Closed Circuit Television cameras around the perimeter. If they have CCTV, they have a command post where those cameras are being monitored. They also had men on the roof—sentries—and they were armed. They've probably got men patrolling the grounds. With the limited intel we have, this is going to be a difficult operation to pull off."

"Yes, I can see that," said Laura. "I was going to suggest that we split up and assault the place from different directions, but I think we should stay together, find a door to breech. If all goes to plan, then we'll have to exfiltrate with the children. How are we going to do that with my Audi?"

"I think I have the answer," said Ken. "Someone take my position; I'll be back in a couple minutes." Joe took the position by the window, and Ken made his way out the door.

Minutes later, Ken came back and threw a set of keys at Laura.

"What're these for?" she asked.

"Remember that old yellow school bus that was in the reception driveway when we arrived?" asked Ken.

"Great job," said Laura.

"It belongs to the resort, but I greased the wheels with the receptionist, and she gave it to me for the evening for fifty bucks. I'll back it into the driveway right outside when it gets dark. It'll be less conspicuous that way. I also got this from reception." He unfolded a map of the area on the large living room coffee table and smoothed it out.

"Britewood's right there," said Laura. "There's a large turnout, there, about a mile and a half from Britewood. That's where we'll park the bus. The hill across from it is Federal land. Joe and I can climb up the hill to get an aerial view. It's not ideal, but it'll give us some intel about the layout of the property. We'll need you to stay with the bus."

"Will do," said Ken. "What weapons are we taking?"

"I suggest we each take an MP5 and a Beretta. That way we only have to deal with nine-millimetre rounds. We should each choose a blade for when things get up close and personal. I'm going with my trusty kukri. Oh, and I'm going to take this." She pulled a crossbow from a black, drawstring sack. "This'll take care of any sentries as we approach. Now, we'll have to spend a couple of hours loading magazines."

As the hours of preparation passed, things began to take shape. Laura and Joe had filled their webbing with magazines, and fragmentation grenades hung from their chests like dull Christmas ornaments. "Ken," said Laura, "I'll take over watch, while you get the bus and then get dressed."

Just a short time later, they all stood ready in the living room of their quaint Alpine cabin, their weapons slung and resting on their chests. Laura inspected her troops, tugging at their rigger's belts and webbing to ensure a correct and secure fit. She then handed each of them a heavy parka with a fur-lined hood. "We'll wear these on the way out. They'll hide our tactical gear. We'll discard them when we begin the operation. All right, chaps," she said, "if anyone wants to back out, now would be a good time to speak up."

"Never. I haven't had this much fun in years," said Ken, as he slammed a magazine into the well of his MP5.

"I'm with you, fella," said Joe.

"Okay, we'll eat now. We'll wait until just after eight, when the traffic dies down, then we'll drive to the turnout."

Ten

THEY REACHED THE TURNOUT AT PRECISELY EIGHT-fifteen. It was cold, but the Santa Ana winds made it all the more frigid. Laura and Joe disembarked, ran across the street, and scaled the hill in the darkness.

Ken sat in the driver's seat of the resort bus. He turned on the hazard lights and waited. Yes, he was scared, but the sensation made him feel alive. He hadn't felt this good since his combat tour of Korea almost thirty years earlier.

Fifteen minutes passed, when he saw blue and red lights flash in his rear-view mirror. A San Bernardino Sheriff's unit pulled up behind him.

Fuck, thought Ken in a panic, when the familiar beige uniform and Stetson hat approached. "What the fuck does he want?" he said out loud. Ken opened the door and cordially greeted the deputy.

"Good evening, deputy."

"Good evening, sir. I saw you had your hazard lights on and thought you might need some help."

"No, sir, the wind was blowing me all over the road, so I thought I'd rest here awhile and hope it dies down soon."

"Weather report says the wind ain't going no place this evening, sir. Doesn't this vehicle belong to the folks up there at Montpellier?"

"Yes, sir, I'm staying up there and asked if I could borrow it for a few days. Candace on the front desk up there said I could take it as long as I fill it up afterwards."

"Okay, sir, sounds good. I'll be on my way. You have a good night."

"Thanks, deputy. You too."

Ken watched as the deputy walked back to his patrol car and drove off into the night.

There was a bang at the back door. It startled Ken. It was Joe with Laura right behind him. "What the fuck took you so long?" said Ken.

"Joe here has a problem with hills," said Laura. "It took him almost ten minutes to get up the bloody thing. He was so exhausted at the top that he had to lie down to recover."

"I should give up the smokes," said Joe as his face turned pink.

"Anyway," said Laura, "there's a central building and what looks like a servants' quarters at the back. There's a rear door near the dumpsters. That's most likely a kitchen entrance. There're people in there. It's probably best if we scale the south wall and go in straight through the front door. Joe here knows the layout from there, so we can just stack on the front door, breach it, and move through the house clearing each room one at a time."

"This obviously isn't your first rodeo," said Ken.

"Hopefully it won't be our last," said Joe.

"I'll scale the wall first and try to take out any sentries with the crossbow, but we should start by removing the cameras. We'll disable just two, the one on the west wall and the one on the front of the building. Taking them all out will alert them to an attack. If we take out two, they'll probably just put it down to the wind, and hopefully they'll just send someone out to do repairs," said Laura.

"That might just work," said Joe.

Laura took the map out of a cargo pocket and pointed to it. "This is Spring Road. It's a dirt road about a half-mile from Britewood. It's unlit, and from the top of the hill it looks unused. Not a single vehicle used it while we were up there. We can park the bus by the side of it, close to the brush."

"Will we be able to walk the kids that far?" asked Ken. "We don't know how many there are, or what state they'll be in."

"True," said Laura, "but this is the best location we have. If all goes to plan, we'll be able to take down all these bastards. Then the exfil won't be a problem. We could even park the thing in their front drive afterwards."

"Okay, let's get going," said Ken as he turned off the hazards and shifted the bus into drive. They approached Spring Road and bumped along the uneven dirt path.

"Park right there, next to that tree," Laura pointed.

Without a word, they all pulled off their jackets and helped each other put on their assault packs, pulling the cords tight to avoid any unnecessary movement. They each then performed a function check of their weapons and finally pulled their ski masks down over their faces.

"No torches, and verbal communication at a minimum," directed Laura.

"Torches," exclaimed Ken, "you mean fire?"

"Flashlights," said Joe. "She means flashlights."

They walked north, moving slowly through the trees. The wind muffled the sounds they made as they walked and covered their smell, so that any trained dogs wouldn't detect them.

At last, they reached the south wall. It was a large, closed wooden fence, twenty feet high, with concertina wire circling the top of it.

"Stay as close to the wall as possible. Can you see the camera?" she whispered as she pointed to the top of the fence. She then slid the Beretta out of her drop holster and affixed the suppressor she had just taken out of her pocket. She aimed for a few seconds, then pulled the trigger.

"Well, that takes care of that, but how the fuck are we gonna make it over that wall?" whispered Ken.

Laura reached into her webbing and took out two small objects. She placed one on each foot. She then took out two more objects and placed them over the palms of each hand. They were *tegaki*—spiked, steel hand and foot claws, which were used by medieval warriors in Japan to block swords and scale wooden walls. She walked away from the wall, turned to face it, and sprinted back towards it. She jumped into the air and slammed her hands hard against the wall. Like a cat, she scampered up. At the top, she maintained three points of contact with the wall, and with her right hand, she plucked a pair of wire cutters from her webbing. She quickly cut away about three feet of wire from the top of the wall. She then pulled herself up and straddled the top of the wall. She scanned the dimly lit grounds. She aimed the Beretta at the camera pointing towards the front of the building and pulled the trigger. It must've made a noise on impact, but the whoosh of the wind took care of that.

There was one guard sitting on a bench smoking a cigarette and one on the roof. She unslung the crossbow, pulled an arrow from the quiver on her back next to her assault pack, and aimed at the guard on the bench. The arrow hit her target—straight through the guard's eye. He didn't move or make a sound. She pulled out another arrow and aimed again, this time at the guard on the roof. The arrow penetrated straight through his neck. He didn't cry out, but his body landed with a thud on the footpath below.

She surveyed the wall. It was an easy climb for her, but she knew the men would have trouble. She backed away a few steps and then ran forward. With a single bound, she caught the top of the wall with her hands and pulled herself up. She sat on top of the wall, took off her assault pack, and pulled out a wire ladder, fixing it to the top of the wall and dropping it to the men. Then she disappeared out of sight as she jumped onto the grounds, rolling forwards and coming to her feet as she fell.

She waited as the guys huffed and puffed their way up the ladder and over the wall. Joe went first, and as Ken reached the top, the two of them swayed and struggled as they pulled up the ladder and reattached it to the north side of the wall to make their descent.

Joe was out of breath. "Give me a few seconds," he gasped.

"We don't have time for this, Joe," whispered Laura as she pulled him from his knees to his feet. "They'll already be alerted to the downed cameras."

"Okay, okay," said Joe, "I'm ready. Let's do this."

They ran single-file towards the building with Laura at

the front, and when they reached it, they squatted under the first window as low and close to the wall as they possibly could without touching it. Joe, at the back of the formation, was now facing the rear.

"When we reach the door," uttered Laura, "I'll check the lock. If it's open, we'll immediately enter. If not, you'll have to move from the rear, Joe. Kick the door open just above the lock, then fall back to your position. When we enter, we move fast. Get out of the doorway as quickly as possible. Got it?"

"Yes, ma'am," said Joe.

Laura held her left hand high, as she gave the command, "One, two, three, go, go, go!"

They quickly walked towards the front door. Laura aimed her weapon straight ahead, Ken's weapon faced outward, and Joe's weapon pointed behind them. When they reached the door, Laura silently twisted the doorknob. It didn't move. She softly whistled. Joe ran from the rear, and with a thrust of his right foot, violently kicked the door just under the lock. The door crashed open, with splinters of wood flying through the air.

Laura moved in first, scanning the room with her weapon, as she quickly side-stepped down the wall to her right. She rested in the first corner. Ken moved in second in a similar way and rested in the second corner. A gunman came running down the stairs. As Joe entered, he shot the guy twice in the chest, but continued to run towards Laura, as she moved to the next corner. Two more gunmen followed down the stairs. Laura caught them both from the flank. "Room clear!" shouted Laura, and her team stacked up once again, this time on the kitchen door.

They moved through the kitchen with ease. The staff had bolted through the back door as the first shots were fired. She secured the door and jammed a broomstick under the lock to stop anyone else from entering.

They heard steps running from the second floor and the hiss of voices. They moved to the stairs. This was the tricky part. Laura lay on her back, with her weapon held against her face, pointing in the direction of travel and pushed herself up each step. When she reached the top, she crouched next to the corner of the wall and waited as the men followed.

They walked down the corridor and stacked on the first door.

"I think we need our gas masks," said Joe.

They all stripped their masks from their belts and put them on, each in succession, with someone always maintaining watch.

Laura turned the knob and the door opened. She crashed violently through the door and moved to the right corner, scanning as she walked. Joe followed, as Ken remained crouched in the corridor.

There was a naked young boy, no more than eight years old, shivering with terror on top of the bed. Someone was in the bathroom. Laura entered to find a fat, naked, middle-aged man trying desperately to push himself out the window. She unsheathed her kukri and stabbed him once through the back. The blade made a crunching sound as it tore through his ribcage. He let out a gasp and fell headfirst onto the concrete down below.

Joe came in behind her. "Laura, for fuck's sake, he could've been a victim, too," he said as he pulled her away from the window.

"Do you see any mist in the room, Joe?" she asked coldly.

"Fair enough," said Joe.

Laura ran to the bedroom and gently took the boy's arm. She tugged him into the bathroom and placed him into the bath. "Lie down here," she said softly. "Don't move until I come back for you." She covered him with a towel.

Laura tried the door of the next room and a shot came bursting through the door as she attempted to turn the knob. Instinctively, she returned fire through the door, with the selector switch of her weapon turned to three-round bursts. She depressed the trigger four times, dropped to her knee, and changed her magazine. She crouched by the side of the door while Joe came from the rear and kicked it hard. The door flew from its hinges and tumbled into the room. Ken moved in first and scanned the room. When Joe entered, he rushed towards the bathroom and after a brief scan, he called, "Clear!"

Laura looked through the haze and saw the gunman lying dead on the floor.

They moved through the next four rooms and encountered more scared children. Laura placed them all in the baths of their rooms and instructed them to stay still.

They entered the fifth room. They peered through the haze as they cleared the bedroom. There was activity in the bathroom. Laura entered first and stopped dead still in the doorway.

"Stay out!" she screamed to Joe. She entered the bathroom and closed the door behind her. A young girl, not more than six years old, stood before her. Laura could see by the tips of her long hair that she was blonde, and her beautiful green eyes shone like emeralds. Her hair and face were covered in thick, dark, red blood and what appeared to be bodily matter. The thick, gloopy liquid dropped from her chin to her chest and from her fingers to the floor, as she chewed monotonously with her mouth wide open.

Laura looked down on the floor and saw the remains of a slender man lying motionless, his throat now just a deep black hole gushing with blood.

The girl stared up at Laura and began to giggle. The giggle metastasized into a demonic laugh, as the girl lunged towards her. Laura pushed hard on the girl's right shoulder, spinning her around and putting her to sleep with a rear, naked choke. Laura placed her gently in the bath and softly massaged her neck, until she began to move. She then covered her with a towel and left the bathroom, closing the door and securing it with the back of a chair under the door handle.

"I want her," said Laura as she stared into Joe's eyes. "She will be my daughter." A chill ran through Joe. All he could do was nod in agreement.

A shot came ringing from outside, then another. Ken came flying into the room. Joe crouched down just inside the door and rested the muzzle of his weapon on the frame. Laura stood over him, and together they opened fire. Gun smoke filled the air, and thuds resonated down the corridor. Laura peered through the smoke and noticed two men lying flat on the floor apparently dead. She aimed down and fired twice, once at each of their heads. They twitched as the shots landed.

They ran towards the stairwell. Laura glanced over the railing, and a shot narrowly missed her head. "Fuck this," she said as she pulled a fragmentation grenade from her webbing. She pulled the pin and threw it down. Immediately after the blast, she ran down the stairs, followed by her team. The place was silent apart from the sound of plaster intermittently falling from the ceiling. "We need to get these kids out of here." She walked towards the front door.

"I'll get the bus," said Ken as they slowly left the grounds, confident that their mission was a success.

In an instant, the darkness gave way to blinding light. Laura raised her hand to her eyes and strained to see three black-clad figures standing before her. She attempted to raise her weapon, but a sharp pain surged from her neck. She reached up and pulled out a large dart. "Fuck!" she screamed as she fell to her knees. She turned her head to see her team lying flat beside her. She struggled to get to her feet, but blackness filled her field of view, and she slouched into unconsciousness.

She awoke to see the haze in the room. She was in one of the guest rooms of The Britewood Resort. She tried to move her arms, but they were zip-tied to the posts of the bed. She was still in her overalls. She concentrated on each part of her body, starting with her toes, until she reached the top of her head. She was unhurt. She heard a noise coming from the bathroom, the flushing of a toilet, then water running. *At least whoever's in there has washed his hands,* she thought in a desperate attempt to find humour in the situation.

The bathroom door opened. A short, fat man, wearing similar overalls to hers and a gas mask walked out.

"Relax, you won't be harmed. I just have to ask you a few questions," said the man. His voice was changed by a similar robotic-sounding voice-changing device she'd used when she'd questioned Roy Gallagher. "Who are you working for?" he asked calmly.

"I work for me," she said. She tried as hard as she could to remain quiet, but the haze was taking effect and was rendering her powerless.

"What motivates you?" he asked.

"Justice, a justice that our laws can't provide."

"How many times have you sought this kind of justice?"

"Many times. I can't remember the exact amount of times, maybe hundreds."

"What is the cause of your need to seek justice?"

"I was tortured as a child. I want to mitigate the suffering of innocents and make the guilty suffer. That's my God-given purpose."

"Could you ever be persuaded to work under the leadership of a government agency in pursuit of your kind of justice?"

"Not without having complete trust in the leadership."

"Who do you trust?"

"My staff at Britewood, My Commanding Officer, Inspector Billy Smythe, Steph Angelo, Ken Sullivan, and, oh yes, my family attorney, Mosley."

The man moved closer and sat on the bed. Laura pulled her legs up to her chest and tried in vain to move her body away from him. He lifted the gas mask to his forehead and then pulled the voice changer down under his chin.

"Mosley," she said, "what's going on?" Her eyes opened wide with shock as she began to cry.

"Don't worry darling, everything will be okay" said Mosley as he smiled down at her. "Mr. Angelo," he shouted. The door opened, and Steph walked in wearing the same navy blue overalls. Mosley left them alone in the room. Steph pulled out a tactical folding knife from a cargo pocket and cut the zip ties away from her wrists. Laura hugged him tightly, sobbing. "Can someone please tell me what's going on here?"

"You're safe, I promise. Everything will be explained." He gently wrapped his arms around her and carried her down the stairs and out of the building.

An eighteen-wheel Peterbilt truck waited outside in the driveway of the resort. The trailer attached was not so much a trailer, but a mobile building. A few men in suits and trench coats chatted outside, one of them seemingly ordering the others.

The driver's side door of the truck opened up, and a familiar figure jumped out.

"Jesus Gonzalez," said Laura as she pushed away from Steph's arms and landed onto her feet. "What are you doing here?"

"I'm with the FBI, ma'am, and I'm a friend of Mr. Mosley's. I kinda let him take the lead on this one."

Laura climbed into the trailer. Two long rows of hospital beds with the children safely inside them flanked the interior of the trailer. Laura looked at each child, desperately trying to find her blood-soaked beauty. A blonde child lay motionless, her head turned away. Laura gently tapped her on the shoulder and the child turned to face her.

Laura smiled and the child smiled back. "Mummy?" said the child in an English accent as she reached up and put her arms around Laura's neck, pulling her close.

"Yes, child, I'll be your mummy." Laura embraced the

girl and rocked her back and forth. "What's your name?"

"I don't know. I don't think I have one," said the girl.

"From now on," whispered Laura, "you'll be called Aurora, after the Sleeping Beauty, and when you are awake, you'll be just like me: strong, powerful, and oh-so-beautiful."

Laura picked up Aurora. Aurora wrapped her legs around Laura's waist, her arms still clutching her neck.

They walked towards the back of the trailer, and Laura opened a door. Mike and Ken sat on a couch drinking bottles of Coors Lite, and there on a chair behind a desk sat Billy Smythe.

"What the hell are you doing here, Billy?" she gasped.

"Mosley and I have been here all along. Jesus gave us two agents as escorts while we were here, so we sat and watched you from the transit van that you tried chasing when we kidnapped your friends Steph and Mike."

"What's the purpose of all this?" she said.

"Did you think I'd send you here alone? Mosely and I have been with you almost every step of the way. We thought we'd observe you and how well you'd do under extreme pressure. You've obviously passed this selection process with flying colours."

Laura shook her head. "That explains Mosely's little question-and-answer session. He scared me half to death. What am I being selected for, by the way?"

"I'll leave that for Mosely to tell you. By the way who's this little thing?" He glanced towards the girl and back to Laura.

"This is Aurora. I'll take care of her until we find her parents."

The guys all looked at each other. "Seriously?"

"Yes, Billy, I'm going to take her home. I have a feeling we're kindred spirits."

Mosley walked in and slumped into an armchair. "I think this all went rather well."

Laura knelt down and looked into Aurora's eyes. "Wait outside, child," she said as she opened the door for her and let her out.

The moment the child was out of ear shot, she turned her gaze to Mosley. "What the fuck is going on here? How is my family solicitor on a covert operation, in a foreign country, with my SAS superior and the FBI?"

"Ken and Mike, will you please allow me to speak with Laura and Billy in private for a few moments?" asked Mosley.

"Sure," said Ken as he tapped Mike on the knee, and the two of them left the room.

Mosley waited for the door to close. He plucked a Havana cigar from the breast pocket of his overalls, bit the end off, and spat it into the trash can beside him. He dug into his front pocket and eventually found a lighter. He puffed on the cigar for a few seconds, and smoke billowed around his head. He looked up, gathering his thoughts.

"My dear Laura, very few things in your life have been truly what they seemed. I am indeed your family attorney, but your family—actually, your father—was my only client, and now that courtesy has been passed to you. I work predominantly for the British government. Sometimes for the Home Office and sometimes the Foreign Office."

"I really don't understand," said Laura.

"Then let me explain," continued Mosley. "I'm a problem-solver. Sometimes I clean up the mistakes of other departments. I watch the watchers. I'm an overseer."

"But which department do you actually work for?" Laura was frustrated.

"You could say that I *am* a department of the government. I report directly to the executive branch."

"Her Majesty?" asked Laura, through a somewhat condescending laugh.

"Indeed," said Mosley, "and of course, some of her closest allies and confidants. That's why your father and I worked very closely. The problem with this little operation was that The Director of Secret Intelligence, that one-eyed madman Davenport never told your father exactly what was going on. It was only when Davenport told your father about this sordid mess that he relayed the details to me. Let me tell you, Laura, your father was devastated. I'd never heard him cry before, but this truly crushed him.

"You were at the Dorchester with your friends when he broke the news to me, but he also told me about your, let's just say, your compulsions and personal enterprises in seeking justice. He made it clear, at that point, that should anything untowards happen to him, you would make an ideal heir.

"You see, my dear Laura, as Her Majesty's cousin, your father was probably the most loyal and faithful servant of Her Majesty, and she knew it. That trust she had in him will obviously be passed on to you, should you choose to replace him."

"You tied me up and subjected me to that gas, The Devil's Breath," stammered Laura.

"Ah, yes, Burundanga. I do apologize, but I had to be sure of your intentions and your suitability for the tasks that may present themselves under my leadership. Your words under the influence of scopolamine proved to me that you are indeed the perfect candidate."

"What about Marsden and Beck?"

"Beck was found hanging in his Newport Beach office this morning. It looks like suicide, but we'll leave that business to Jesus. I'm sure his real estate empire profited immensely from the blackmail of the powerful people involved in this affair. As for Marsden, at the moment, we have no idea where he is. He was Davenport's immediate subordinate in MI6, so they were obviously in this together, and from the look of things, they made an incredible amount of money and gained leverage on some very powerful people. Marsden was promoted to the position of Director of Secret Intelligence when Davenport died, and technically he's still C. No one knows about this sordid affair in White-hall, thank God; so as far as most people are concerned, it's business as usual. It looks like I'll have to take care of him in my own way."

"Do you have any idea who killed Daddy?" she asked.

"At this moment, no, but we still haven't ruled out Joe Byrne, so he's been taken into custody, pending the results of the investigation."

"Okay, but I won't rest until we find the truth, Mr. Mosley," said Laura.

"And what of my job offer, my dear?" Mosley asked casually.

"I have other things to think about before committing. I don't even know who my father's heir will be. When things settle and I know my place in this world, I'll give you an answer."

"Then let me help you with that, my dear Laura," said Mosley as he reached into the leather attaché case beside him and brought out a manila envelope. He looked inside and took out a maroon, leather-bound book, embossed with the letter G and the Roman numeral three in gold leaf.

"This is the original patent for the First Earl of Britewood, Edwin DeLacy, commissioned by the Regent himself, who later became King George IV of the House of Hanover. As you know, the title cannot be passed to a woman, but this one actually states, in the body of the document, that this title may pass to any legitimate heir—either male or female. We don't know why it's written that way, but it may have something to do with the love Edwin had for his only child, Victoria."

Laura was exasperated. "Please, Mosley, just get to the point."

"The point is, my dear, that after exhaustive research and advice from the most prestigious of counsel, including Her Majesty herself, due to the wording of this document, at the time of your father's passing, you became Laura, Countess of Britewood, along with the entirety of your father's estate."

She walked to the couch and collapsed onto it. She sat with her head in her hands.

"Why didn't you just tell me this earlier," she said.

"Because I had to be sure my dear. This is highly unusual, in fact, it's never happened before in our nation's history. Are you okay, my dear?"

Laura looked up and grinned. "Okay, Mr. Mosley? I'm ecstatic!"

"And what of my job offer?" asked Mosley.

"I'll consider it," said Laura.

"Good," said Mosley. "Take your time, but know this:

Great Britain will be all the more secure with us at the helm."

"Does anyone else know about my ascension to countess?" Laura asked.

"Her Majesty and her secretary. Other than that, not a soul," replied Mosley.

"Then let's keep it that way for the time being—until I return to Britewood, anyway." The trailer began to move. "Where are we going?"

"Our job here is done, Laura," said Mosley.

She bolted through the door and into the makeshift hospital and peered out the window. In the distance, through the dark night and thick foliage, she saw the resort, the despicable den of despair, in flames.

Mosley followed close behind her. He put his hand on her shoulder. "All evidence of this place and all proof of Britain's association with it has been destroyed," he said.

Laura turned to him and nodded. She looked around the room. She saw the children being cared for and her closest friends Billy, Ken, Mike, and, of course, Steph chatting, drinking beer, and laughing.

Steph got up and walked towards her. "What now?" he asked.

"What do you mean?" she smiled.

"What will happen with *us*?"

"What do you want to happen?"

"I'd like you to stay around for a while. At least until the middle of February," he said flirtatiously.

"Why then?"

"There's something important I want to take you to on the eleventh."

"What's that?"

Steph reached into his pocket and took out a small, white envelope. "I've got two VIP tickets for KISS in Torrance. It's their Asylum tour. It's gonna be epic."

"Am I supposed to know who they are?" asked Laura.

"They're American royalty. I thought you'd at least know that," said Steph as he pulled her into his arms.

"Then I'd be honoured to go with you, on one condition."

"Name it," said Steph.

"That you first come with me to England and help me sort out a few things."

"Consider it done. Lucky for me I have quite a bit of flexibility at work, one of my subordinates can step in while I'm gone. You are my priority, Laura." said Steph. He kissed her.

"Get a room," yelled Mike, and he threw an empty beer can, which bounced off Steph's head.

Jesus parked the truck near a huge, unmarked warehouse by the port in Long Beach. Ambulances waited for the children, and a few cars with Federal licence plates stood by to take people home.

"Where are you staying?" Laura asked Mosley.

"Billy and I are staying at the Five Crowns in Newport Beach. It's right on Pacific Coast Highway and has the best steak and kidney pies in America. Take a few days to unwind. When you're ready, I'll make arrangements to get us all home," he said.

"Aurora," said Laura. "Remember, she's mine."

"It's all taken care of. She'll be taken to the Hoag Hospital on Superior in Newport Beach for treatment. You can visit her anytime. The medical staff have you listed as her next of kin," said Mosley as he and Billy walked to the nearest limousine and disappeared into the back seat.

"Look over there," said Steph. "Is that your car in the parking lot?"

"Yes, it is," she said, "and look, the key's in the door." Steph opened the passenger door for her, and the moment she sat down, she fell asleep.

He drove her back to the house and gently woke her when they reached the driveway. They walked in through the door, and, as it closed behind them, Laura grabbed Steph by the waist and pulled him into her embrace. They moved towards the stairs and tugged at each other's clothes, pulling each item off, and they ascended the staircase, smashed through the bedroom door, and fell on the bed.

Afterwards, she lay there, on her back, smiling. He watched her with the aid of the moonlight streaming through the window, a mixture of horror and love evident in his face.

She turned towards him and kissed him softly on the forehead. "Goodnight, my love," she said as she drifted off to sleep.

"Goodnight, Laura," he said, and he watched her in wonder.

Eleven

Sunday, January 19, 1986

LAURA WOKE UP, AND STEPH WAS GONE. SHE GRABBED her robe and pulled it on, before sleepily making her way down the stairs and into the kitchen. There was a note on the centre island.

> Laura,
>
> I had to go to work. I made coffee. Think of me when you drink it.
>
> Let's meet at Harbor House for lunch at 1 p.m.
>
> Steph

She poured herself a mug of coffee and sipped it. She beamed as she held the note close to her chest. Just yesterday, she thought she had nothing. Britewood and Steph both seemed lost, and the odds were stacked against her and her team. Now she knew that she was the rightful heir to

Britewood, Steph would be hers, and she had a daughter, a daughter whom she knew had what it took to be trained in her oh-so-dark arts.

She glanced at the clock in the kitchen. It was eight-thirty. She gulped down her coffee and quickly showered and changed. She got into her car and drove out towards the ocean, turning left at the corner of Pacific Coast Highway and Warner. She travelled along the PCH until she got to Superior and made a left. Within a quarter mile, she turned into the parking structure of Hoag Hospital.

She walked through the automatic sliding doors and approached the reception desk, where a small, middle-aged woman greeted her. "Good morning. How can I help you?"

"I'm here to see Aurora," replied Laura.

"Can I have a last name please?" asked the woman as she looked down at the patient list.

"Try Lacy," said Laura, and the woman gave her a suspicious glance, before resuming her search on the list.

"What is your relationship with the patient?" asked the woman, without taking her eyes off the list.

"I'm her mother, sort of."

"Sort of?" The woman peered at Laura over her glasses.

"I'm her mother," said Laura, frustration growing in her voice.

"She's in Paediatrics. Room thirty-eight, on the third floor."

"Thanks," said Laura and she ran towards the lift and quickly pushed the button when she reached it. When the elevator opened, Laura approached the nurses' station, where a young nurse was standing, holding a patient's chart on a clipboard and making notes on it. "I'm here to see Aurora."

"Are you Laura?" asked the nurse, in a soft, caring manner.

"Yes," said Laura.

"I'm Eileen, the on-duty nurse. Follow me." As they walked along the corridor, Eileen continued. "She's had a rough time. We had to sedate her last night, but she woke up a few hours ago and ate breakfast. She has some injuries, mostly internal, but none are too serious. She should be ready to go home in a few days." They arrived at the room. Beside the door, a man in jeans, a blue-and-white plaid shirt, and a black rain jacket sat on a plastic dining chair. As he stood to greet them, he seemed to get taller and taller, until he reached his full height of six feet seven inches tall. His shaggy, mid-length hair and beard gave him a tough appearance, but his voice was soothing. "Ma'am," he said, "I'm Special Agent Doug Satterfield. I've been assigned as the security detail for Aurora."

"Pleased to meet you, Agent Satterfield, I'm Laura. I can see Aurora's definitely in safe hands." Laura extended her right hand, and the special agent shook it firmly.

"If you need any assistance, just press the red button next to the bed," said Eileen.

Laura closed the door behind her. Aurora looked up, tears in her eyes. "You came for me. You were telling the truth."

Laura hugged her tightly and kissed her on the forehead. "You're safe now. I'm here," she said as she swayed the child from side to side.

For the next two hours, Aurora and Laura played board games, sang, and chatted as they embraced on the bed. Laura told her about Britewood House, the grounds, and her beloved horses.

"I have to go now," Laura said, glancing at the clock.

"Don't leave me, Mummy," cried Aurora, tears welling in her eyes.

"I have to," said Laura, "and besides, you must never be so attached that you can't bear to be without me."

Aurora nodded and looked up at Laura with sadness in her eyes.

"I'll be back later," said Laura. "Get some rest."

Laura arrived at Harbor House a little after one o'clock. She walked through the front door and turned to see Steph waiting in his favourite booth, by the dessert fridge.

Susan saw her from the food hatch in the kitchen and rushed behind the front counter to greet her. "Good afternoon, m'lady," she curtsied.

"Good afternoon, Susan, and please stop with the curtsying and the m'lady nonsense."

"Okay," said Susan. "What can I get you?"

"I'll take a cup of tea and whatever food he's having."

"Liver and onions coming up," said Susan as she walked back into the kitchen.

Laura sat on the seat opposite Steph. "Did you see the kid?" he asked.

"Yes, I just got back from the hospital. She's not that physically damaged."

"Will she need a shrink?" said Steph.

"No, she'll just need me, or maybe us," she said, gazing into his eyes.

"Well, you've got me, but are you prepared to stay here? I could get you a job. I'd even hire you as a cop."

"I can't. I have responsibilities."

Just then, Susan approached and left the tea on the table. At the same time, the front door opened and a man wearing board shorts and a black, hooded Ocean Pacific sweatshirt walked in, with the hood over his head.

"Take a seat anywhere," said Susan, as she walked back into the kitchen and the man sat in the next booth behind Laura and Steph.

Steph stared at the back of the man's head for a few seconds. "What's wrong?" asked Laura, and she began to feel uneasy.

The man turned in his seat, grabbed Laura by the hair, and instantly held a Colt M1911 to her head. "I'm gonna fucking kill both of you," he said as he pushed the muzzle of the weapon hard against Laura's temple.

"No!" said Steph in a panic, noticing the hammer of the weapon cocked and locked. "Let's just talk about this, Matt."

"Oh, my God," said Laura, "tell me it's not Norton."

"Yes, bitch, it's me," he said as he pulled her around and stared directly in her face. "I'm a fucking dead man, I know it, but you're coming with me—both of you."

"Let's just talk, Matt. We can work something out. You're in no danger from Beck, he's dead, and that place in the mountains is gone. All the evidence has been burned. You can start again, Matt," said Steph, trying to remember the hostage negotiation skills he'd learned on that mandatory course at Quantico years earlier.

"Your fucking bullshit won't work. Now get up, and keep your hands where I can see them," said Matt in a frenzy.

A shot rang out, and Laura dropped onto the seat of the booth, blood and brains all over her face. Steph screamed and dove over the table to Laura. He covered her with his body and then looked up. Norton was slumped across the backrest of the booth, motionless, with blood and brains dripping from his head. Susan stood behind him with a .38 Special, raised and still pointed at Norton's body.

"Give me the gun," ordered Steph, as he slowly moved to her with his hands out.

"I didn't want to kill him," lamented Susan. Steph took the weapon and passed it to Laura, who sat at the booth in shock. He embraced Susan, who was trembling. "Am I going to jail, Chief?" she cried as she looked up at him, tears in her eyes.

"No, Susan," he whispered, "you're a hero. You saved our lives."

Within twenty minutes, everything was on lockdown. Detective Mike Singer was assigned to the case. There were three ambulances and two uniformed units from Seal Beach Police Department. Susan was taken to be treated for shock.

"I'll take it from here," said Mike as he put his arm around Steph's shoulders. "I'm gonna need a statement, as will the sheriff, but it looks like this is the end. We've taken them all out. Why don't you go upstairs and get some rest?"

"Thanks, Mike," said Steph. "You're a good friend."

Laura and Steph silently took the lift up to the water tower. They walked through the door of the observation deck into the living room and sat on the couch arm in arm.

"We haven't known each other long," he said, "but we've been through more than most couples go through in a lifetime."

"Are you prepared to live with me in England?" she asked.

"No, but I'm prepared to compromise. We can live here

throughout the winter and then go to England in the summer. I really don't want to be in England in the winter months. Cold-blooded creatures like me die in places like that."

"We can work it out, but I have responsibilities there."

"Like what? Listen, I did a little digging. One of my officers is a fan of your people and by that I mean, British royalty. He even drinks his coffee out of a Charles and whatever-her-name-is commemorative wedding mug. I asked him about your father. He didn't know much, but he did tell me that when an Earl dies only a man can inherit his title and his wealth. I knew at that point that when your father died, you lost your house and most of your father's wealth. We can start again here. We can start a new life together. I have a good career, assets, and a retirement coming up."

"Well, that's just it," replied Laura. "Things are not exactly what they seem."

"What are you talking about?" asked Steph.

"Well, according to the patent given to the first Earl of Britewood by the Prince Regent in the eighteenth century, the title can be passed to either a man or woman."

"This is all new to me. I thought only a man could inherit your father's title, land, and wealth. Does the patent specifically state that?" said Steph.

"Yes. It has something to do with the First Earl Edwin's love for his daughter, Victoria."

"What does that make you?" Steph was sitting on the edge of the couch.

"Well, that means that at the moment of Daddy's death, I became The Right Honourable Laura Lacy, Countess of Britewood."

CALIGULA, BOOK I: BEAUTY IS THE BEAST

"That's a bit of a mouthful," chuckled Steph. "Is it okay if I just call you Laura?"

"Yes, silly." She kissed him on the nose.

"Are you sure you want me involved in all this?" inquired Steph.

"More than anything. I've been waiting my whole life for someone like you, a self-made man who's strong and educated, who's experienced horrors, but still maintained his bearings. There have been other lovers in my life. Each had a facet that I longed for: some were physically strong, some were tall and good-looking, some were witty and educated, and some were just plain old sexy, but you have far more than one."

"Which facets do I have?" he asked.

"If you're fishing for compliments, you've come to the wrong place," she laughed as she softly smacked his face.

The doorbell rang. Steph walked to the door and hit the button on the intercom. "Who's there?" he said.

"It's Mosley and Smythe," came the answer.

"Come on up," said Steph as he raised his eyebrows at Laura.

When the door slid open, Mosley walked in with his cane. He plopped down onto the nearest armchair. Billy sat next to him at a writing desk. "We heard about the shooting on the evening news," said Mosley. "Are you all right?"

"Yes, we're fine," said Laura.

"Good, but in light of this event, we're here to ask if you want to move things ahead."

"What do you mean?" asked Laura.

"Well, according to the hospital, there's no further need for them to keep Aurora. She's physically fine, and although she has no difficulty speaking and socializing, she won't tell us anything about her life before being saved by us. She'll obviously need extensive psychological work.

"Our job is done here, and according to the powers that be at the Foreign Office, Marsden is supposedly in England. He's still the Director of the Secret Intelligence Service. After all, he's technically a free man. We've destroyed all evidence against him. He'll just go back to business and do whatever he can to destroy you and Billy. He could even go so far as to deal with Steph, Mike, and Ken in some way. He will definitely neutralise Joe Byrne, who's currently on remand until we find out who murdered your father."

"That bastard Marsden," said Laura. "Even though he served with Daddy in The Regiment, I didn't trust him. The moment I saw his dead, sunken eyes for the first time at Daddy's funeral he gave me the creeps."

She paused for a moment and her expression softened, "I know that Aurora's well enough to travel, but I don't want to push things unnecessarily. We need to at least pack, and there're all my things at the house that need shipping," said Laura.

"I can get Gonzalez to pack and ship everything you brought. We can collect Aurora right now. We'll be flying on a private jet provided by Her Majesty, so there'll be no need for passports," said Mosley as if he'd already planned the whole thing out.

"What about you, Steph?" asked Laura.

"I can take a leave of absence, especially after the events of the last few days. In fact, they'll expect me to take time off. Mike can fill in while I'm gone. I even have my passport in the safe," said Steph.

"Good, then it's settled." Mosley looked at his watch. "It's half-past three right now. Let's meet in the departure lounge at John Wayne Airport at nine this evening."

"And what about Aurora?" said Laura.

"I've already arranged an emergency diplomatic passport. At the moment, she's being prepared for you to collect her at the hospital. She'll be waiting for you when you arrive," said Mosley.

Laura approached him, bent forward, and kissed him on the forehead. "Thank you, Mr. Mosley," she said.

"Please, don't thank me, m'lady," said Mosley. "You'll have plenty of opportunities to pay me back."

When Billy and Mosley left, Steph grabbed Laura around the waist. "I'm gonna pack. Make yourself comfortable," he said as he went to his bedroom and closed the door. Laura was mesmerised by a beautiful teak writing bureau, which was pushed against the centre wall next to the television. She opened a drawer and found photos scattered inside. There were black-and-white photos of Steph as a child, being held by his mother, photos of family Christmas gatherings, and school photos. A small album rested in the centre of the drawer. She opened it and flipped through the pages. These were his memories of Vietnam. There were the standard unit photos. There were photos of the guys on patrol. Most were mundane. When she reached the final two pages, she noticed that some photos were hidden behind the pages. She opened the plastic covers and slowly pulled them out. She looked towards the bedroom door, fearful that Steph may find her delving into his secrets. The first photo was of Steph, in green fatigues, holding up a machine gun. In the second, he was wearing the same uniform, but this time, a necklace of ammunition was tied around his neck as he smiled. Laura quickly pushed the photos back into their respective compartments and slammed the drawer shut. She smiled. *Maybe we do have some things in common after all,* she thought.

"What was that noise?" asked Steph, as he open the bedroom door. He was carrying a suitcase and an army-issue duffle bag.

"Oh, silly me, I banged my knee on the cabinet," she said.

"Are you okay?" asked Steph.

"Better than ever," replied Laura, and she meant it.

They drove along the Pacific Coast Highway to Laura's house. Laura wrote a note asking Jesus to pack everything from the shed and the equipment she'd taken into the mountains and send it to her secured with diplomatic seals to Britewood House. She sat on the couch next to Steph.

"Aren't you going to pack?" he said.

"Almost everything in the house was already here when I arrived. I didn't know what the styles were over here, so I just sent my sizes and had a company set up my wardrobe, house, and car."

"Wow," said Steph, "I didn't know companies like that existed."

"I wonder if Susan at Harbor House wants them?" asked Laura.

"I'll have Mike bring her here when she's out of the hospital," said Steph. "That way she can choose what she wants. Are you ready?"

"Yes," said Laura.

"Come on, then, let's get out of here."

They arrived at the airport just before nine. They walked through to the British Airways departure lounge to find Mosley and Billy chatting over Styrofoam cups of tea. There was a cloud of cigar smoke around Mosley's head, as he sipped from the cup with one hand and puffed a cigar with the other.

"Just in time," said Mosley as he threw his cup into a nearby trash can. "Follow me," he said as he stood up and walked towards a door marked *Authorized Personnel Only.*

Billy followed and threw his cup in the same trash can and rushed to keep up with Mosley as he limped along briskly, with the help of his cane. Laura and Steph followed closely behind. Steph carried Aurora.

They walked through the door, passed two seated security officers who nodded at Mosley, and then they went down a long, white corridor, and through a door. They were on a runway and right before them was a sky blue Gulfstream IV with a mobile staircase.

"All aboard!" yelled Mosley as he limped up the stairs and entered the aircraft.

It was beautiful inside: white leather upholstery, surrounded by a mahogany veneer, and plenty of comfortable armchairs and sleeping quarters in the rear.

Aurora was fast asleep in Steph's arms. He walked towards the sleeping quarters at the rear of the plane and gently laid her down on the farthest bed. He kissed her on the forehead and covered her with a quilt, gently tucking the edge under her chin. He closed the door softly so as to not disturb her and joined the rest of the group.

"Champagne, anyone?" offered Mosley. He pulled a bottle of Bollinger from a silver ice bucket in a centre console and popped the cork. He pulled four champagne flutes from a cupboard and lined them up. As he poured, the foam filled the flutes and spilled onto the countertop. Mosley passed the flutes to his guests and held his glass aloft. "To the future," he said, "and a glorious one it shall be." Everyone raised their glasses and drank.

A man in a white shirt, with a captain's rank on his epaulets, came out of the cabin and pulled the door of the aircraft closed. "Are we ready to depart, sir?" he asked Mosley.

"Quite so," responded Mosley.

The captain returned to the cockpit, and the twin Rolls Royce jet turbines began to make a soft humming sound. Moments later, the humming became louder until the plane moved forwards slowly. Faster and faster it got, until it lifted off the runway and hurtled through the air. It ascended until at last it levelled out, and the engines quieted, no more than a soft and gentle purr.

"There's no going back now," said Steph. "You're stuck with me."

"I wouldn't have it any other way," said Laura. She walked towards the gigantic leather chair he was sitting on and sat across his lap, throwing her arms around his neck, as she settled into her seat, pulling her chest into his torso.

She looked across at Billy. He was asleep with his head against the headrest. She glanced at Mosley—he was snoring loudly, his lips quivering with every exhale.

"Come on," she whispered as she pulled Steph from his seat, "the beds are in the back."

"Laura, are you crazy?" he murmured. "We can't do that here, they'll hear us."

"Nonsense," said Laura as she grabbed him by the shirt and dragged him like a dog on a leash to the sleeping quarters. She slid the door open, tossed Steph onto a twin bed, and quietly closed the door behind her.

Twelve

Monday, January 20, 1986
Leeds Bradford International Airport

IT WAS DARK WHEN THEY GOT OFF THE PLANE. TWO uniformed police officers escorted them from the runway through arrivals and into the pick-up area. Billy and Mosley entered the back seat of a waiting limo.

Tony Wilcox stood waiting for Laura in a brand new, starched and pressed chauffeur's uniform. The rear door of the Silver Shadow was open. "Welcome back, m'lady!" he exclaimed as he tipped his hat and bowed slightly.

"Thank you, Wilcox," she replied.

"Sandy and Debbie have dinner prepared, m'lady. How's about we get you home?"

"That sounds wonderful, Wilcox," she replied. "By the way, this is my companion, Mr. Angelo. He'll be my guest for a few weeks. And, this," she beamed, "this is my daughter, Aurora."

"Well, then! Hello, Aurora." He knelt down to greet the girl. "And pleased to meet you, sir."

"Likewise." Steph shook Wilcox's hand.

Laura secured Aurora into the back seat. The girl sat patiently, in a warm, blue duffle coat. "Darling," she said, as she slid into the back seat next to her and squeezed her around the shoulders. "You're home now." Steph slid in beside Laura and held her, as she held Aurora, all the way back to Britewood.

Harris opened the gate as they arrived. He took off his tweed flat cap and held it close to his chest, with his head bowed as the gates slowly opened. "We're home," said Laura.

"I kinda figured that out," said Steph as he stared open-mouthed into the gardens.

"Wow!" said Aurora.

They drove through the grounds and onto the gravel drive. Liz, Sandy, and Debbie waited on the stairs of the great house and ran to the car.

Tony opened the door and Steph stepped out. Liz looked at him quizzically and then glanced at Laura. "It's okay, Liz," she said, "this is my companion, Steph. He'll be staying with us for a while." Liz was unable to control herself and hugged Laura tightly.

"Who's this?" asked Debbie, peering into the rear window.

"This is Aurora, she'll be staying with us also," said Laura. She walked around to the opposite side of the car and opened the door. She released the seatbelt and lifted the young girl out of her seat, holding her in her arms as Aurora wrapped her legs around her waist.

"I'll make up a room for her," said Sandy as they all walked slowly into the manor.

Steph was speechless. He'd never seen anything as grand as Britewood House. Laura saw his expression and gently dropped Aurora to her feet. "Debbie, take Aurora into the kitchen for warm milk and biscuits," she said.

"Yes, m'lady." Aurora reached up and took Debbie's hand.

"Come on," said Laura, "let me show you around."

They perused the servants' quarters first and then the majesty of the house itself. The grand ballroom, the drawing room, and the great gallery. Steph was awed by the portraits of all the former Lords of Britewood, captured in their formal regalia. He found the portraits of each Countess just as stunning. She pulled back the curtain of the study, took a large key from her purse, and unlocked the door. The smell of leather and dust overwhelmed Steph as the door swung open. That sweet smell of tradition and intellect.

"Is that your father?" he asked, pointing to the gigantic portrait behind the desk.

"No, that's my great-grandfather, King George V of the House of Saxe, Gotha, and Coburg and the creator of the House of Windsor.

"Wow," said Steph. He walked to the desk and saw the faded brown stains on the carpet. "Is this where it happened?" He dropped down on one knee to scrutinise the stains.

"Yes."

"There are three distinct stains here," he said looking at the floor.

"Yes, Davenport and Jenkins were found in front of the desk, killed by wounds to the head, approximately three feet from each other. Apparently, they were shot from just behind the door. Daddy was found behind the desk, shot in the chest at point-blank range."

"How strange," said Steph. "If the gunman wanted them dead and was so good a shot that he pulled off two head shots from the distance of the door to the desk, without the victims having a chance to react, why wouldn't he just kill your dad the same way? I mean, your dad was a renowned SAS officer. Why would the killer take the chance of confronting him, or give him an opportunity to pull a weapon from a desk drawer?"

"I asked Billy the same thing," said Laura.

"And what answer did he give you?"

"He didn't answer. He was just as perplexed as I was," Laura mused.

"Other than the actual killing, was anything missing or changed in here?" asked Steph in detective mode.

"Billy asked me the same question. The curtains were closed, which was unusual, and the gold-braided curtain ties, which held them back from the windows, were gone."

"Anything else?"

"Not really, other than the fact that the doors and windows were locked from the inside. Oh, and for some reason, that portrait up there on the bookshelf was lying face down. It was his favourite photo of my mother and me. He kept it there so he could see it from behind his desk."

Laura sat behind the desk and looked around the room. Steph took a seat on the guest chair and watched her as she searched her mind for anomalies. Her eyes widened. "Churchill," she said.

"What?" Steph moved to the edge of his seat.

"My father's bust of Churchill; it's gone. It was a small onyx bust, with a brass base. He used it as a paperweight."

Steph looked around the room. His eyes rested on the curtains. He briskly walked over and pulled them open. The hooks which had once held the ties were there. He looked across the floor and behind the beautiful Chippendale bureau next to the window.

He moved to the bookcase, grabbed the desk chair, stood on it, and reached up and took down the photo of the Lacy family. He scrutinized the photo: its front, back, and edges. He closed his eyes as he felt over the top of the bookshelf and ran his hand along the front edge of it. He stepped off the chair and moved to the end of the bookcase. He ran his hand behind it, then gently moved it a few inches away from the wall. He looked behind it, then turned to face Laura.

"What is it?" asked Laura.

Steph sat on the guest chair at the desk and reached over and took Laura's hands in his. "I think I might know who killed your father," he said.

"Who?" she asked. "Just tell me, Steph."

"Come with me," he said as he led her by the hand to the edge of the bookcase. He held it with both hands and pulled it away from the wall. The dust, built up over a hundred years, puffed its way out, and they waved it away from their faces.

Steph reached behind it and felt with his hand until it rested on a firm object. He gripped it, and out from the darkness came the bust of Churchill with a red ribbon around its neck, connected to a rolled piece of parchment, kept closed with red wax, sealed and stamped with Lord Henry's personal coat-of-arms. It was connected to a golden rope adorned with tassels.

"The curtain ties," said Laura as Steph continued to pull.

Finally, he dragged out a Browning nine-millimetre handgun, with the end of the golden rope tied to the pistol grip. He stood there with the Churchill bust in one hand

and the gun in the other, connected by the two golden ropes tied in the middle.

"What does this mean?" she gasped.

"When you told me that the room was locked from the inside, I had to consider that maybe one of the victims was actually the killer. I mean, if the room was locked from the inside, how could the killer possibly leave?"

"Go on," she said.

"Well, then there were the missing curtain ties. You told me that it was strange that the curtains were closed, so those ties must've always been a fixture in the room. Why would anyone take them away? The Churchill bust was the most important key to this, as far as I'm concerned."

"How so?"

"You referred to it as a paperweight. It's made of onyx and brass, so it had to be heavy. There was only one other piece to the puzzle."

"For God's sake, Steph, just tell me," she begged.

"Okay, calm down. Here goes. The photo on the shelf was your father's favourite photo. So why would he grab a chair, reach up, and drop it on its face? That makes no sense at all. It would make more sense if it were knocked over."

"Then what knocked it over?" asked Laura.

"The gun," said Steph, "watch me."

He cleared the weapon and locked the slide to the rear. He pushed the chair against the bookcase, stood on it, and reached up and then back to drop the bust behind the bookcase. The weight of the bust pulled on the rope. Holding the gun, he stepped off the chair, held the gun to his chest, and pretended to pull the trigger. He let go of the weapon and it flew into the air, knocked over the photo frame, and disappeared behind the bookcase, propelled by the weight of the bust.

"Your father killed Davenport and Jenkins, then used the curtain ropes and bust to create a weighted pulley, which he attached to his weapon, before shooting himself in the chest."

Laura sat on her desk chair and held her head in her hands. "Why would he do such a thing?" she despaired.

"I don't know, Laura, but maybe he can still tell you." He held out the rolled parchment. She took it from him. "I'll be outside." He walked out of the study.

She waited for the door to close behind him, cracked open the wax seal and unrolled the parchment. She smoothed it onto the desk and secured it at the top with the Churchill bust. She trembled when she recognized her father's handwriting.

Thursday, December 12, 1985

My Dearest Little Boots,

Hopefully, you will be reading this epistle from your rightful seat at Her Majesty Queen Victoria's Resolute desk, and with the help of our trusted friend Arthur Mosley's legal wranglings, you will now have ascended to the position of Countess of Britewood.

As Queen Victoria turned a blind eye to the Whitechapel murders and the culpability of those closest to her, I have turned a blind eye to your various, nefarious escapades. I have also learned that your addiction to violence is worse than I ever thought. I convinced myself that it was the incident in your youth which led to your compulsions, but this is by no means the truth. In reality, our family has been genetically predisposed to violence and cruelty, but fortunately, that violence and the threat thereof has resulted in order, an order so powerful that it controlled the masses so prevalently, that it led to the empire on which the sun never set.

My life has been dedicated to the preservation of order and justice, but the halls of power are rife with those who are hungry for dominance, so hungry they will destroy their very souls and the souls of others to attain it.

In the last few days, I've been informed that my second-most trusted companion, David Jenkins, has betrayed us and that the Director of Secret Intelligence, Sebastian Davenport, has been using me in an operation—an operation of which I had no knowledge. It involves the propagation of the ultimate evil, an evil we hadn't seen since the Grangeview affair.

It is now my responsibility to make things right, and in doing so, I hope to somehow obtain your forgiveness, the forgiveness of God, and an end to my overwhelming sorrow.

You are probably asking yourself why I did things this way. Well, to simply sound the alarm and turn in Davenport would not have changed things in the long run. Someone would merely replace him, and the evil would continue, but in a different form.

I know that if the deaths of Davenport, Jenkins, and me resemble murders, rather than a murder/suicide, your loyalty to me, along with your keen sense of justice, will result in a personal quest for the truth. West Yorkshire Police Constabulary has neither the resources nor the will to solve my little mystery, and they, too, are susceptible to corruption. This way, you can proclaim yourself detective, judge, jury, and executioner.

Mosley and Smythe are honourable men. They will help you in your quest. Hopefully, you'll use their assistance and their counsel. Together, you can right the wrongs of the past and create a better, more just society for the people.

I'm taking a chance in the belief that you alone will find this letter. If you find it immediately after my death, you must investigate Davenport and do what is best for the children involved in this matter. If you find it sometime in the distant future, I am sure that your actions will have resulted in an honourable end to the present situation and the start of something new and better.

Your ascension is still in its infancy. You will soon be exposed to a plan I have hatched, along with trusted friends, designed to aid you to lead this world into a revolution, the result of which will be order from chaos, and justice for all.

You are my only hope for a future of peace in this world. I urge you to stay strong, do what is right, and quench your thirst with only the blood of those who are truly evil. It is now time for you to embrace your fate.

Memento Mori,

Henry

She rolled up the parchment, locked it in a drawer, and

picked up the phone. She dialled a number and waited for an answer. "Mosley," she said.

"Yes, my dear, how can I help you?"

"Where is Joe Byrne at this moment?"

"He's in Armley Prison on remand."

"You must have him released immediately."

"But we're still investigating your father's murder."

"I know who the culprit was, and I have the evidence, but I can't tell you on the phone, and only you, me, and Steph can know the circumstances."

"Well Laura, I suppose we can find evidence to suggest this whole thing was the work of Danny Buckley. I mean, it makes no difference to him now."

"Thank you, Mosley," said Laura, as she hung up the phone.

She found Steph in the drawing room sitting on one of the large, oversized couches. "Everything good?" There was concern in his voice.

"Everything is just how it's supposed to be. Looks like my new career will start soon." She settled onto his lap.

"And what, exactly will your career entail?" asked Steph with a slight sense of trepidation.

"Justice," she answered without missing a beat. "I'm sure Mr. Mosley will have plenty for me to do."

Steph nodded. "I'd like to have some time alone with you," he said.

"But we're already alone," she replied.

"I mean alone: no servants, gardeners, or cooks—just you Aurora and me."

Laura smiled. "Okay, do you want me to give the staff a couple days off, so we can live in the big, old house like ordinary folks?" He nodded again. "Okay, I'll arrange a paid holiday for the Wilcox family and Liz, but I don't think Harris has anyone else. He never comes near the house anyway. He's far too busy with the grounds. Can he just stay doing what he's doing?"

"Of course," said Steph, "it's your house, I'm just making suggestions."

Laura knelt down in front of the fireplace. She reached into the basket next to the hearth and pulled out some firewood, stripping the bark and laid it in the grate as tinder. She lit a match and used it to ignite the bark in three places, before gently placing the wood in a triangle around the flames. She completed it by dropping twigs and scraps from the bottom of the basket on top of it as kindling. She lit a match and dropped it into the kindling, blowing the small embers until they grew into a small fire. She looked into the flames and prodded the fire with a poker, before turning off the lights and returning to the couch on Steph's lap.

She wrapped her arms around him and sunk her head into his chest. "This thing isn't over yet," she said. "There are so many questions left to answer and monsters who still want us dead."

"I'm here," said Steph.

"I know, but we have to prepare for a storm. I can feel it getting close."

"It might be wise to request a police security detail."

"The police can't be trusted while Marsden's still out there. Billy's arranging for some of the lads from the regiment to protect us. I trust them with my life. It'll take them a few days to put a security detail together, so for the moment we'll need to keep our heads on a swivel."

"Things'll work out. They always do," said Steph as he gently ran his fingers through her hair.

"Yes darling, I know," she replied, turning her head and smiling up at his face.

She turned away from him, once again resting her head on his chest and the smile disappeared from her face. She knew that the world was a dangerous place and even after the loose ends of her mission were neatly tied up, more monsters would rise to threaten the world and the only defence that her small corner of the world had to offer was her and her small band of allies.

Lady Britewood will return in

Caligula Book 2: Shiny Things

ABOUT THE AUTHOR

Domnic "D. James" McGee was born in Leeds, West Yorkshire. A sickly child, he was raised in a council estate to a single mother. At school, he was a poor student and failed dismally.

He developed a passion for martial arts, so in his teens, he moved to Ireland where he trained full-time while working in menial jobs to survive.

A chance encounter then gave him the opportunity to work as an Executive Protection Agent for some of the most influential figures in European society.

He came to the US in 2001 to further his studies of martial arts. He decided to stay and earned his citizenship by serving in an Army infantry unit and later with a reserve Military Police unit.

He currently lives in Huntington Beach, where he works as an Executive Protection Agent, trains, and writes as much as he can.

Made in the USA
Middletown, DE
07 March 2022

62204935R00158